Praise
Li

"Kritzer shows off her worldbuilding chops in this impressive mystery set in a near future world in which a group of 'libertarian separatists' have built an archipelago of man-made islands in the Pacific Ocean near the California coast. Each of the six islands is an independent country, with differing approaches to which laws—if any—apply to their citizens. For example, on the least-restrictive, Lib, 'it's legal to kill people,' but the hope is that murder will be deterred by the prospect of an equally permissible revenge killing. Kritzer makes this world plausible through the eyes of her endearing protagonist, 16-year-old Beck Garrison, who earns money tracking down hard-to-find goods for clients across the islands. Her latest job—a request for size eight sandals—leads her to Debbie Miller, an indentured laborer on the island of Amsterdam, who agrees to hand over the footgear only if Beck locates Debbie's missing sister, Lynn, who hasn't been heard from for weeks. Beck's resourcefulness and audacity garner a clue to Lynn's whereabouts—but chasing this trail also uncovers a sinister plot, places Beck's life in danger, and reveals secrets about her life and the world that Beck's powerful father, Paul, has been keeping from her. The political critique is sharp and the mystery is gripping. Admirers of Chris McKinney's Water City trilogy will be riveted."
    — *Publishers Weekly*, starred review

"Kritzer's got a sharp knife and she slips it in so smoothly that you barely notice that you're bleeding. The best sf uses the future to make a point about the present, and Kritzer's got today's enshittified, profit-worshipping, sociopathic present's number."
    — Cory Doctorow, author of the *Little Brother* series
        and *The Lost Cause*

"Everything Naomi Kritzer writes is amazing. Smash that preorder button."
    — Elizabeth Bear, author of *Ancestral Night*

"I loved *Liberty's Daughter*. This book offers a different kind of dystopia and a different kind of rebellion against it: a libertarian seastead that has managed to survive forty years while walking smack into all the expected bears, and a kid fighting those bears with all the strength of freedom and agency that the place has accidentally given her. Beck is delightfully skilled in all the things that discomfit adults, sheltered without turning away from unpleasant truths, and stubbornly determined to solve problems wherever she finds them. She's a Heinlein juvenile protagonist grown clear-eyed about his 'utopias,' and updated to critique his modern descendants: good company for a disturbing, nuanced, and wind-tossed future."

— Ruthanna Emrys, author of *A Half-Built Garden*

"*Liberty's Daughter* is a fast-paced, forthright, funny voyage through libertarian seasteads and teenage heroism. Beck Garrison's tendency to wade into trouble to pull others out makes her the perfect mix of thought-provoking and action-packed. Naomi Kritzer always brings both heart and brains to her tales, and *Liberty's Daughter* is no exception."

— Marissa Lingen, Novel Gazing Redux

"I have been waiting most of a literal decade for this."

— John Chu, author of *Beyond the El*

"I love Kritzer's work, and I always will."

— Kelly Barnhill, Newbery Medalist

LIBERTY'S
DAUGHTER

ALSO BY NAOMI KRITZER

LIBERTY'S DAUGHTER

NAOMI KRITZER

FAIRWOOD PRESS
Bonney Lake, WA

LIBERTY'S DAUGHTER
A Fairwood Press Book
November 2023
Copyright © 2023 Naomi Kritzer
All Rights Reserved

First Edition

Fairwood Press
21528 104th Street Court East
Bonney Lake, WA 98391
www.fairwoodpress.com

Portions of the chapters of *Liberty's Daughter* have been previously published and com-
piled into this novel, and appeared as the following: "Liberty's Daughter: A Seastead
Story," *The Magazine of Fantasy and Science Fiction*, May/June 2012 | "High Stakes:
A Seastead Story," *The Magazine of Fantasy and Science Fiction*, November/December
2012 | "Solidarity: A Seastead Story," *The Magazine of Fantasy and Science Fiction*,
March/April 2013 | "Containment Zone: A Seastead Story," *The Magazine of Fantasy
and Science Fiction*, May/June 2014 | "Jubilee: A Seastead Story," *The Magazine of
Fantasy and Science Fiction*, January 2015 | "The Silicon Curtain: A Seastead Story,"
The Magazine of Fantasy and Science Fiction, July/August 2015

Cover art © Leon Tukker
Cover and book design by Patrick Swenson

ISBN: 978-1-958880-16-6
First Fairwood Press Edition: November 2023

To Francis, Kiera, and Ed Burke

PART ONE
MISSING

CHAPTER ONE

"SHOW ME THE SANDALS FIRST," I SAID.

Debbie held out the pair of size eight sparkly high-heeled strappy sandals. I had been knocking on doors all afternoon, hunting for sandals like this for some lady over on Rosa.

"My sister's name is Lynn Miller," Debbie said. "She's been missing for three weeks."

I had a bad feeling about this. My job is finding things, but normally that just means finding willing sellers for interested buyers. That's why I was looking for the sandals. Finding a *person* was a whole different kettle of shark bait. But the seastead wasn't that big, so unless she'd fallen over the side and drowned . . . I pulled out my gadget to take notes. "Okay," I said, and keyed in the name. "What else can you tell me?"

"We're both guest workers," Debbie said, which I'd guessed from the overcrowded quarters where they lived. It always smelled like feet down here. "Bonded labor," she added, which was very nearly redundant. "Our bond-holder is Dennis Gibbon, the guy who owns Gibbon's Dining Hall. He has me working elsewhere as a cleaner; Lynn washes dishes at the dining hall. Washed, I mean. She's not there anymore."

My father and I had a subscription to Gibbon's; maybe this would be easier than I'd thought. I nodded, waiting for her to go on.

"Three weeks ago, Lynn got sick and had to miss work. She doesn't get paid if she doesn't work, so then two weeks ago she missed a payment to Gibbon. She went to talk to him—actually, what she wanted was to borrow money to see a doctor. She never came back."

"Did you ask Gibbon what happened to her?"

"He wouldn't talk to me."

"Do you have a picture of her?"

She did, in the form of a U.S. Passport. I captured an image of the photo with my gadget. "What's going to satisfy you?" I asked. "I mean, if I come back and say, 'I saw her and she's fine, give me the sandals,' I don't imagine that'll do it."

"You could bring me a note from her. I'd recognize her hand-writing."

"Okay," I said. I put my gadget in my pocket. "I'll see what I can do."

I live on Min, short for New Minerva, which is a seastead in the Pacific Ocean, 220 nautical miles west from Los Angeles, California. The seastead is basically a chain of man-made islands, anchored into place, with some bonus retired cruise ships and ocean freighters chained up to the platforms. Min is only one part: there's also Lib, Rosa, Pete, Sal, and Amsterdarn, and each one is its own country with its own set of rules (except for Lib, which doesn't have any rules at all; that's sort of the point).

The seasteads were built by people who wanted more free-dom and less government (a *lot* less government, in the case of Lib) than they thought they'd ever be able to get in any existing country. And since all the land that existed was already claimed by *someone*, they built their own. That was forty-nine years ago. My father and I came to live on Min when I was four, after my mother died. I'm sixteen now.

I'd wanted to get a job, but it was hard to find one. Mostly, the people who were hiring wanted real grown-ups with PhDs. For the scut work, stuff like mopping floors and washing dishes, they wanted to hire guest workers, because they're cheap and reliable.

Guest workers are non-citizens; to become a citizen, you have to buy a stake, and that's not cheap. Most of the people who come here without the cash to buy a stake don't have the money to get here, so they take out a bonded loan and work to pay it off.

I finally found a job at Miscellenry, which is this general store run by a guy named Jamie. Jamie hired me to find stuff. Here's a weird thing about the seastead: people have a lot of money (stakeholders do, anyway—guest workers, not so much) but there's still a lot of stuff they can't just go buy easily. I mean, you *can* go to California to shop, but it's a long boat ride or an expensive flight, and entering the U.S. can be a huge hassle because they don't recognize seastead citizenship as a thing. You can order stuff, but shipping things to the seastead takes forever and costs a ton.

But there are about 80,000 people who live on the seastead permanently, like me and my dad, and sometimes we need stuff. We get a lot of tourists—Amsterdarn does, anyway—and they bring stuff to sell or trade, but let's say you need something really specific, like a size six black bathing suit. There's only a few stores and they might not have one in stock. But there's probably *someone* on the seastead who's got one, who'll sell it for the right price, or trade it for the right thing. And that was my job: finding that stuff, and then getting the person who owned it what they wanted in exchange.

I found the size six black bikini and I found a case of White Musk scented shampoo and I found a particular brand of baby binky. Not to mention a bottle of fancy single-malt scotch (that was actually pretty easy; tourists bring fancy booze because the guide books say it's easy to sell or trade here) and a pair of sapphire drop-style earrings *and* a nice presentation box for them. Sparkly strappy high-heeled sandals in size eight had been my downfall but now I'd found those, too. All I had to do now was find Lynn and get a note saying she was okay.

I started at Gibbon's Dining Hall. Most steader apartments don't have full kitchens. For meals, you buy a subscription to a cafeteria. There are super fancy ones that have a dozen vats going at once so you can eat anything from beef to emu to lobster, and there are really basic ones with a single vat that grows beef that smells fishy because they never clean it. Gibbon's is nice enough but not top end. He serves fresh vegetables but nothing fancy, and there's a choice of three meats most nights. He doesn't have windows. Dad has a window in his office at home, so he says he doesn't see a reason to pay for a view to go with his food. Especially since half the time, he sends out for food and takes a working meal in his office anyway.

Dad wasn't at dinner tonight. I read a book while I ate my steak and fries and steamed baby carrots (see? fresh vegetables, but nothing fancy). When I was done, I left my tray to be cleared and walked back to the kitchens. A swinging door separated the work areas from the eating areas: beyond, it was noisy and hot. I could see the kitchen, crowded with workers plating food and washing dishes, on my left. At the end of the hall was a door marked "Office."

"Miss, this area is staff only," someone said from the kitchen.

"I want to talk to Mr. Gibbon," I said, pushing my hair back behind my ear. I was sweating in the heat. "I'll only be a minute. Is he available?"

"Uh . . ."

I walked up to the office door and knocked on it. There was a grumbling sound from inside and the door was yanked open. "What?" Mr. Gibbon loomed in the doorway, scowling down at me through his bushy moustache. The office behind him was small and messy. Someone was sitting in the visitor's chair; I could see their knees.

"Mr. Gibbon?"

"Yeah?" He looked down at me and his scowl was slowly replaced by the sort of blankly courteous, slightly wary expression that people usually wore when they were talking to my father. "Is there a problem?"

Back before I got this job, I would have been a lot more nervous, but working as a Finder I'd kind of gotten used to bugging people. "I'm looking for Lynn Miller. She's a guest worker who worked here until two weeks ago."

"I have no idea who you're talking about."

"You are her bond-holder," I said. "Or you were at the time."

"I can't possibly keep track of every one of my bond-workers."

"Can you check your records?"

He gave me an exasperated look. "They're organized by number, not name. Do you have her ID number? I didn't think so. Look, we're very busy back here. Was the food good tonight? Go on out and dessert will be along in just a minute." He shuffled me toward the swinging door and added, "You really shouldn't come back here. It's not safe for customers. Call my secretary if you want to make an appointment to see me."

Well, *that* was a brush-off if I'd ever heard one. I sat down, wondering why he'd been so incredibly unhelpful. Was he hiding something, or did he honestly not recognize her name? I could totally believe that he kept records by number. Bonded guest workers had a thin plastic bracelet with a number on it. If I went back, maybe Debbie would be able to tell me what Lynn's number was. Of course, if her bond *had* been sold, it would've been changed . . .

Anyway, if I was supposed to "make an appointment" I had a bad feeling he'd be busy for the next year and a half.

"Dessert, miss?"

The server set a slice of chocolate cake in front of me and hurried away. It wasn't until I'd almost finished eating that I noticed the slip of paper under the plate.

Meet me at St. Peter's in an hour if you want to know what happened to Lynn.

St. Peter's was the Catholic church. It was over on Rosa, and was pretty small—not many people here are particularly religious. But there are more families on Rosa, and there are a couple of churches.

It was a Wednesday, the day the new episode of Stead Life usually dropped, and my father and I always watched it together. I checked the time. An hour would make me late enough getting home that my father would notice, but he probably wouldn't care if it was for my job. I sent him a quick text in case he wondered: *still trying to track down some sandals, don't start the show without me.* I read my book for a while as Gibbon's slowly emptied out, and then I walked over to Rosa.

The church had a statue out by the door, a life-sized plaster statue of a man holding a fishing net in one hand and a key in the other. A plaque at the bottom said *St. Peter the Fisherman* on it. I could tell it was plaster because there was a large chip out of the draping brown robes St. Peter was wearing. The door to the church was closed but had a hand-written sign taped to it saying *please come in, all are welcome.*

I stood around awkwardly in the corridor for a minute or two, then decided I'd be less conspicuous if I went inside to wait. People went into churches to pray, right? No one could tell from *looking* that I was an atheist (and anyway, I'm sixteen—lots of teenagers experiment with religiosity). I was relieved that they weren't holding a church service inside, although there were lots of people. Some looked like they were praying—people were kneeling, their eyes closed, whispering to themselves, I couldn't think what else they might be doing—but others were just sitting quietly. A couple of people had found better-lit spots and were reading. I sat down and waited.

"In an hour" was 8:15 p.m. but no one came at 8:15. No one came at 8:20. I started to wonder at 8:25 if I'd misunderstood where I was supposed to meet him—had he meant for me to wait outside? I started to stand up, but a man dressed in damp white clothes and heavy black work shoes was dropping into a half-kneel and crossing himself, and then sliding in next to me. He was thickly built, with dark hair and large hands that were covered in little knife scars. Chef's hands.

"You're Beck Garrison, aren't you?" he whispered. "Someone in the kitchen said you're Paul Garrison's daughter."

"Yes," I said, wondering if this would make him clam up. My father makes people nervous.

Instead, he turned his head to give me a long, appraising look. "Lynn's bond was sold to someone named Janus," he said.

"Is that a first name or a last one?"

"I don't know. What I can tell you is, Lynn was sick. She came in to talk to Mr. Gibbon, and they went into his office. They left together and she hasn't been back—not to the kitchen, not to her old spot in the locker rooms." The locker rooms were the dorms where people rented a space just big enough to sleep in; that's where I'd met Debbie. "You know her sister's been looking, right?"

"Yeah, she said she'd—" I bit back the information about the sandals, suddenly a little embarrassed by it. "We're bartering. What she wanted from me was to find out whether her sister is okay. Do you know anything else about Janus?"

The man—I still didn't know *his* name, I realized—bit his lip and looked down. "There have been a few other disappearances in the last month. Janus's name comes up every time."

Well, the others weren't my problem. Just Lynn.

"What's your name?" I asked.

"I'd rather you didn't know it. Mr. Gibbon holds *my* bond, too."

*

My father was still working when I got home, but he looked up as soon as I came in. "Did you find what you needed?" he asked.

"Getting closer," I said, and shrugged. I wondered if he knew who Janus was, but asking him that question would start a cascade of other questions that I thought would end in, "you really should be minding your own business, Beck," and I decided not to ask. "You didn't start watching *Stead Life* without me, did you?"

"Wouldn't think of it." He stood up and stretched, then came out to the living room, closing his office behind him. We sat side by side on the couch and turned on the wall TV. *Stead Life* is weekly reality show filmed on the seastead. All the mainland subscribers watch it for the exotic outré seastead lifestyle. All the seasteaders watch it so we can gossip after we see our friends on the show.

Tonight's show was about dating on the seastead. There was a clip of a woman saying "the odds are good, but the goods are *odd*," because there are more men than women who live here. Then the show followed her around as she went on a date with a guy—not someone I knew. They started by going for drinks at a bar on one of Min's outside decks, which could have been very nice but it was chilly when they arrived and shortly after it started raining. They walked over to Rosa for a bar there, instead. The date went really badly, and not because of the weather—the guy just wanted to talk about himself, and he wasn't interesting enough to justify it. When they were done, *Stead Life* interviewed them both separately. The woman said that she wanted a man who laughed at *her* jokes some of the time. The man said that women on the Stead were all entitled because there were too many men and not enough women and he was going to give up on dating.

I did catch a glimpse of Thor, one of the boys in my Humanities tutoring group, as they walked down the hallway. He looked up at the camera open-mouthed and then caught himself and walked away quickly.

The imbalanced numbers weren't a factor for the teenagers with dating. The fact that there just weren't all that many kids here was a much bigger issue. I'd never seen my father go on a date, and I glanced at him now, wondering if there was a reason for that. He was reading something off his tablet. He was too old for the woman on *Stead Life*, probably, but he was good about laughing at other people's jokes. He laughed at my jokes, anyway. Usually.

I went back to wondering about Janus.

I had no idea who Janus was, but the seastead is pretty tightly knit. I was pretty sure that if I asked around, he'd turn up.

The seastead doesn't have public schools (obviously) or even any *schools* per se at all. Little kids usually get schooled by their parents, although since my mother wasn't around, my father paid Shara's mom to tutor me along with Shara. That worked out fine until we got to be about eleven and math got complicated enough that her mother didn't feel confident teaching us anymore.

For older kids, most people hire tutors. I had math and science tutoring in the morning with Mrs. Leonard, who rented space to hold classes and taught fifteen kids at once. Then a lunch break; I could walk back to Gibbon's, if I wanted, or buy something at one of the little sandwich shops on Rosa. In the afternoons, I had Humanities tutoring with Mrs. Rodriguez, who taught Literature, History, and Econ out of her apartment. There were six of us in her high school group.

When Shara and I first graduated from home schooling to tutoring, we had lunch together every day. But then Maureen moved to the stead. For about six months, when Shara and I were thirteen and Maureen was fourteen, they made a point of *not* inviting me with them when they went to lunch. Then Shara's mom found out and after that I was always invited, but I'd never felt exactly welcome.

That morning, I took notes and drank coffee and tried, unsuccessfully, to pay attention. My mind kept wandering to the sparkly sandals and the mystery of what had happened to Lynn. When we broke for lunch, Shara dutifully invited me to join her and Maureen, but I shrugged her off and went down to Miscellenry to get Jamie's new list for me and start looking for stuff.

I grabbed a sandwich to go from a shop while looking for the items on the list: a coffee grinder, potting soil, and a pair of brown shoelaces for men's dress shoes (or really, a single unbroken shoelace would do). As I made my way around from one apartment to the next, I asked about Janus. I found the coffee grinder with no problems (I tried a newcomer; that's exactly the sort of thing people bring to the stead, then decide within six months they don't need). The shoelaces (a pair, still in their package) were similarly easy. I got a good lead on the potting soil just as I realized I was going to be late for afternoon tutoring. No one knew Janus.

I ran up the stairs two at a time and was only barely late. Mrs. Rodriguez had a permanent sign on her door saying *Experienced Humanities and Social Sciences Tutor, all ages, now accepting students*. There were six of us in the high school group: Shara and Maureen, John and Andy and Thor, and me. Thor was new to the seastead, kind of. His family had moved last year and bought their stake right away. Rumors said his father paid in *actual gold*, which is always one of the options but still, you don't see that very often.

Mrs. Rodriguez had a really nice apartment—couches for everyone and a lovely big window. It always smelled faintly of coffee, even when she wasn't brewing any. Coffee, and clean sheets. She kept a spider plant hanging in her window; it trailed little tendrils all the way down to the floor.

Maureen and Shara exchanged amused looks as I came in late and out of breath. I ignored them. Thor scooted over on the couch to make room for me, and I sat down, pulling out my gadget. "Saw you on *Stead Life* last night," I said, and he blushed.

Mrs. Rodriguez was teaching Econ today. She talked about

Adam Smith's invisible hand and the noble experiment of the sea-stead founding fathers. "Thor, you've lived somewhere with taxes. Why don't you talk about that?" she said.

He blushed and stammered a little, because she'd put him on the spot, and pushed a loose hair back out of his face. Thor had longish dark hair, curly, that was constantly in his eyes. "I didn't have to pay them, my parents did," he said.

"Did you pay taxes when you went shopping?" she asked.

"Oh—yeah! Sales taxes." He grinned, showing his dimple. "Back on shore—well, in the U.S. anyway, I don't know about other places—we had to pay money to the government *every time we bought something.* They also took money out of my parents' pay and at the end of the year they had to fill out this huge form that said whether they'd taken out enough. If the government decided that they *hadn't* taken enough they'd make my parents send in *even more* and if they didn't, they could go to jail. Or they'd take our house." He frowned at the memory. "Anyway, that's part of why we moved here."

"I've paid sales taxes," Shara said. "We go to shore every year and do some shopping, and yeah, you think you're going to have to pay one thing and WHAM, it's like . . . way more." She flipped her ponytail over her shoulder and let out an exaggerated sigh.

"We won't be going back," Thor said. "At least, my dad won't. Because right before we left, the government came with a HUGE bill and said, 'Well actually there was some sort of mistake and you owe a lot more than we thought,' and my father told them to shove it up their—um, he told them where to shove it. And we came here."

"Aw, there's more to shore than the U.S. of A.," Andy said. "We never go to San Fran, but we visit the Caymans every year, and the shopping's almost as good."

Thor shrugged. "We'll see if they change their mind. Right now my parents say we'll *never leave ever.*"

John stirred. "Like Beck's father," he said. "She hasn't been to shore since she was four."

Shara and Maureen looked at each other; they probably thought they were being discreet, but Shara giggled, and Maureen looked disdainful behind her long blonde eyelashes, and I felt my cheeks burn despite my best efforts to keep a neutral face. Thor, on the other hand, glanced at me with sudden interest. "They'll take you to the Caymans," I blurted. "Sooner or later." My father was eccentric. I was the *only* teenager on the stead who was stuck here all the time, I was pretty sure.

We talked Econ until the coffee break, when Mrs. Rodriguez made us a pot of coffee and everyone pulled out literature homework. "Hey," I said as I added sugar to my coffee. "Does anyone know a guy named Janus?"

"Is that a first name or a last name?" Thor asked.

"I don't know."

Mrs. Rodriguez looked over from her kitchenette, where she was getting a carton of creamer out of the fridge. "Why are you looking for him?"

"I'm trying to find a woman named Lynn. He's her bond-holder."

"He probably isn't, actually," Mrs. Rodriguez said. "He's sort of a bond wholesaler. Buys bonds from people who don't need or want a particular bond-worker anymore, and resells to whoever. He doesn't usually keep people very long."

"Why are you such an expert?" Sarah asked.

Mrs. Rodriguez shrugged. "He eats at my dining hall. We've shared a table once or twice."

What did I tell you? In a place this cut off from everywhere else, sooner or later you'll run into someone who knows the person you're looking for.

I didn't ask Mrs. Rodriguez where she ate, because I already knew. She mentioned twice that she ate at Primrose, which was on the top deck of one of Rosa's former cruise ships, and had one of the nicest views on the stead. She had a husband who worked as a bioengineer on Sal, and *she* believed it was worth paying for scenery with her food.

If I was going to infiltrate Primrose, I needed to try to guess whether Janus usually ate dinner early or late. Or if he ate dinner in his office most of the time anyway, like my dad, and I'd have a better bet finding him at lunchtime. I finally decided to hope he was a late eater, because that way I could grab dinner at my own dining hall before my father was likely to turn up, and then scoot up to Primrose. He had let me get a job, but he didn't entirely approve of it, and I had a vague feeling he would not approve at all of this particular task. Usually I just pestered people at home about cologne and coffee beans. This time, I was bothering important businessmen at work.

I wondered if my father knew Janus.

They don't check IDs at the door of Gibbon's because the staff pretty much know everyone who eats there. There was a maitre d' at the door of Primrose, though, and I wouldn't be able to just slip in. She certainly wasn't going to let me in to stalk Janus, either, so honesty was out. Instead, I smiled broadly and introduced myself and said that although my father really liked Gibbon's, I was getting tired of eating in a cave and wanted to try to talk him into upgrading. "I think it'll work better if I sample your food, though," I said. "If I can tell him what a meal's like. But even if you could just let me in to soak up the atmosphere . . . ?"

She gave me an anticipatory smile. "You're Paul Garrison's daughter, aren't you? We be delighted to invite you in for a complimentary dinner." She waved me inside.

Primrose is *a lot* fancier than Gibbon's. It's not just the windows (and they have an entire *wall* of windows). There are white tablecloths on all the tables, and they have wine to drink instead of just beer, and people really were eating lobster. There were more women here than in Gibbon's—probably nearly a third of the people eating at Primrose were female. There are a lot more men than women on the seastead, but there are places where women cluster a bit, and this was apparently one.

I couldn't go off into a corner and read since I needed to try to figure out who Janus was, so I pulled out a chair next to a table and beamed at the dozen or so strangers. "Is this seat taken?" Assured that it wasn't, I repeated my line about how I wanted to try to talk my father into upgrading and asked everyone what their favorite dish was at Primrose. It was easy to segue from that into introductions, but no one there was Janus. Well, it had been a long shot.

The woman sitting next to me was older than me, and friendly. "I've heard all the *really interesting* people on the stead eat at Primrose," I whispered. "Is it true the stars from *Stead Life* eat here?" My table neighbor craned her neck and said she didn't see them, but yes, Primrose was where the *Stead Life* hosts ate their meals.

"So who here have I heard of?"

She pointed out a dozen or so people, including an elected official (we have a few of those, on Min), one of the chief surgeons from the hospital, and an old guy who was one of the handful of remaining founders (he came over to help start the seastead when he was nineteen, which is why he's still around, forty-nine years later).

"My teacher eats here, too," I said. "Mrs. Rodriguez. Do you know her?" I listed a few other people who I thought might plausibly eat in Primrose (some did, some didn't) and then tried for Janus.

"You mean Rick Janus?" Oh: a last name. Good to know. "Yeah, see him over there?"

"In the green?" I said, looking where she was pointing.

"Yeah, he's just sitting down."

I suppressed a gleeful grin (or at least, I thought I did), threw out another name or two for camouflage, and finished my dinner. *Target acquired.*

I decided not to approach him at dinner because it would be too easy for him to have me thrown out, so I waited until he was done, then followed him out. "Mr. Janus?" I said as soon as we were out in the hall.

He turned around, looking surprised. "Yes? Do I know you from somewhere?" He was a little older than my father, with slate-gray hair and very bushy gray eyebrows.

"I don't think so. My name is Rebecca Garrison, I work as a Finder for Jamie at Miscellenry."

"Oh . . . ?" He wasn't walking away, yet.

"I'm looking for a woman named Lynn Miller. You bought her bond, probably about two weeks ago?"

His eyes narrowed and he leaned back against the wall, folding his arms. "What about her?"

"I've been asked to find her and check on whether she's okay."

"I sold her bond."

"Can you please tell me who you sold it to? Because I've been asked to get a note from her, just confirming that she's okay."

"I'm not going to tell you her new bond-holder," he said. "I don't discuss my deals; it's bad business." He stared at me and waited.

"She was sick—"

"She's been treated."

"That's good," I said, feeling desperate. "I just need a *note*—"

"Can't give you one." He waited a moment longer, then raised his gray eyebrows, said, "Nice to meet you, Rebecca," and walked away.

It took me a long time to walk home from Primrose, partly because it was on Rosa, but also because on my way back I had to go out of my way to avoid Embassy Row. The U.S. maintains an office they call American Institute, because if they had an *embassy* that would be saying they thought Minerva counted as a country.

My father is offended by the fact that they don't recognize our sovereignty so he doesn't let me go anywhere *near* the Institute. (We do have a couple of actual embassies, but one of them is from Rosa, which is kind of silly because they are *right there* and it's not as if we have to show a passport to cross the bridge that connects Rosa to Min.)

The main room light was off when I came in, but my father's office door was open and light spilled out from there. "Beck?"

I put down my bag on the table by the couch and went over to his office door, hesitating in the doorway. I wasn't allowed to go in when he wasn't there, and it left me feeling sort of weird about going in at all. "Yes?"

"I've been hearing rumors," he said. "You were pestering Mr. Gibbon, back in the kitchens."

I wondered what he knew, and who'd told him. "Only for a minute," I said. "I left right away."

"You were rude," he said. "He put up with it because you're my child, and he doesn't want to lose me as a customer. I told him to send you packing, next time." He looked up from his desk, his eyes cold. My father has blue eyes that are almost the exact same color as mine. I gazed over his shoulder, at the window behind him, even though I couldn't see anything this time of night but my own reflection.

"Yessir," I said.

"If your job becomes a problem," he said, "you'll have to quit."

"Yessir," I said again.

"Good." He looked down. "I'm glad you understand."

I took that as a dismissal and went to my own room. I put on an old episode of *Stead Life* with the volume turned down low while I did my homework for Mrs. Rodriguez. After a while, I shoved my gadget aside and set my picture of my mother on my lap.

I barely remembered her. She died in a car wreck. When I turned eleven, my father told me she'd been drinking when it happened. In my picture, she was laughing, holding me in her lap as we both sat on a big porch swing. I could see myself, a little, in the picture of my mother: she had freckles, like me. Her smile looked like mine. I couldn't see what color her eyes were.

I wondered what she'd think of Min. If she'd have schooled me herself when I was little, instead of sending me to Shara's mother, and if Shara would have seen me as more of a friend, in that case, and less of an annoying hanger-on to be shed when she met someone more interesting. If she'd insist on eating at Primrose, even if it cost extra.

When would my trip to Primrose get back to my father? Maybe I could convince him that I really had just been trying to sample the food, and my conversation with Janus was total coincidence. I'd bumped into him while leaving and said, "Excuse me," and you know how rumors are . . .

I really didn't want to quit my job. Having a job, a real job that brought in real money and not Min scrip, felt more important every time I got paid.

The most frustrating thing was that I *still* hadn't found Lynn.

When I woke up to pee at 4 a.m., I thought of a way out of my dead end.

"I'm feeling sick," I told my father when I saw him at breakfast. "It hurts to pee. Kind of a lot."

"Who've you been sleeping with?" he asked.

"*Dad.* Don't be ridiculous. I think I have a UTI, not some sort of weird STD."

"It'll be antibiotics either way, I suppose," he said. "You know where the clinic is. I don't need to take you in, do I?"

"No, I can go by myself," I said. "Do you want me to call Mrs. Leonard? She may want to talk to you."

"I'll call your teacher. Go on to the doc."

I walked to the health center. The one we use is over on Rosa. I had to go around stupid Embassy Row again, and I checked in with the stead ID that didn't so much say that I was Beck Garrison as that I was Paul Garrison's daughter, because the money for my treatment would come out of his account. I got checked in, was told that my temperature was normal although my pulse was a little fast, and then the nurse said the doctor would come see me shortly.

"Don't make her hurry," I said, and gave the nurse my best most pathetic look. "I'm missing a calculus test. If I miss the whole thing she'll let me make it up. If I only miss half, she'll make me try to do it with half the time."

The nurse sighed sympathetically and closed the door.

The tablet she left behind was locked, of course, but I'd watched her type in her password to look up my record and I got it right on the second try. I hit the button to search records and typed in LYNN MILLER.

Her record opened. Footsteps were coming and I almost hit the LOCK key but they went on by. It had never been less than ten minutes between the nurse leaving and the doctor arriving, so hopefully today would not be a nasty surprise. I didn't care about Lynn's diagnosis; I just wanted to know who'd paid for it.

Butterfield. Davis Butterfield. That was John's father, John in my math class that I was missing. I actually *knew* this person. This next part might actually be *easy*.

The bill was really high. What the hell *had* been wrong with her? I pulled up the details and saw that five people were treated, not just one, all with the same condition. On the same day, even. That was weird. Every single one had kidney failure requiring regenerative therapy.

There was a brusque knock and the door swung open before I could lock the screen and put the tablet down. I did manage to clear the screen so no one would know what I'd been looking at, but I jumped at least a foot and I'm sure I looked extremely guilty, standing there with the tablet in my hand.

"You're not supposed to touch that," the doctor said irritably.

"Sorry," I said. "I just wanted to see how it felt in my hand. I'm hoping for a new gadget soon."

She picked it up and gave me a suspicious glare, then started asking me about my symptoms. "Have you been slumming?" she asked.

"What? It's *not* an STD, I told my father—"

She waved her hand impatiently. "I'm not accusing you of sleeping around," she said. "I'm wondering where you've been eating."

"I ate at Primrose last night. Usually I eat at Gibbon's."

"What else have you eaten or drunk in the last week?"

I listed everything I could think of: cereal at home, coffee at Mrs. Rodriguez's, the sandwich I'd had for lunch the other day . . .

The doctor ordered blood and urine tests. The lab technician came in and drew what looked like about a pint of blood from my arm, and then they sent me off to the lavatory to pee in a cup. "Nothing turned up," the doctor said when she came back, "but we'll do a twenty-four-hour culture to be sure. In the meantime, drink extra water but carry it with you from home. You need to be careful with what you eat and drink—Gibbon's is fine, and Primrose, but if it's somewhere you see folks from the locker rooms eating, you can do better."

She hadn't asked me any more questions about why I was looking at her gadget. I felt a flush of relief, and then wondered if she was going to tell my father I'd been snooping when she called with my lab results. Probably not; it would look as bad for her as for me if I'd actually managed to do anything more than admire the shiny screen.

Morning was almost over, but I headed for my math class anyway. Hopefully I'd get brownie points for coming for the last five minutes when I could have skipped, *and* I might have a chance to ask John what sort of business his father owned. As it turned out, Mrs. Leonard was more irritated by the interruption than impressed by my dedication, but I did manage to attach myself to John when we all went out to lunch. (At a sandwich shop, a nice upscale one that the doctor would undoubtedly have approved of.) I told him a funny story about hunting down a fancy hand-wound pocket watch and then noted that I'd been wondering if any of my classmates' parents were hiring for something steadier.

"Oh, you wouldn't want to work for my dad," John said. "He owns a skin farm on Lib."

"Ew," I said.

"Yeah," John said, and finished his sandwich. "Who want to work *there?*"

One of the things people come to the seastead for is cosmetic surgery. They don't come here because it's cheaper (although it is) but because there are things we can do that are illegal in other countries, or at least not approved, because they're so experimental. Skin transplants are one of the big new things.

When you get old, your skin loses elasticity. You get wrinkles and liver spots, your risk of skin cancer goes up . . . your skin really starts to *wear out*. And that's where skin farming comes in. You can send a sample of genetic material to John's father, and he'll give it to his technicians, and they'll grow it until they've got this entire blanket of fresh, young skin. And then the surgeons can transplant it onto you, and when you heal you really do look *a lot* younger, and not creepy the way people who get face-lifts sometimes look.

The technician jobs sort of suck, though.

The skin can't just be grown in a vat (though it uses the same technology); it has to be grown on screens, and it's a lot of work. The skin techs have to spread the cells on a screen, and they have to paint it with growth matrix, and then later they have to paint it with acid, and they go back and forth between the growth matrix and the acid to get it to grow right. If you spill the acid on yourself, you can get burns. If you spill the growth matrix on yourself, you can get cancer.

And since it's a crappy job, but not a *complicated* job, they use bonded labor for it.

When tutoring was done for the day, I decided to go see Debbie again, and tell her what I'd found out. I wasn't sure I'd be able to get a note, and I didn't think Lynn would write, "Doing fine, wish you were here!" even if she could. The thing is, normally bond-workers can at least go back to their bunks at the end of the day. The fact that they weren't letting Lynn go home wasn't a good sign.

Debbie lived in the locker rooms. The locker rooms were a set of dorms that rented each person a space just big enough to sleep in; the bunks had a door that you could pull down and lock, like a locker, so that you had some secure storage for your stuff, and you could lock yourself inside, too, if you were nervous about your roommates. They were used mostly by bond-workers, because they were the cheapest housing on the stead. Debbie's held twelve women, three bunks on each wall, and Debbie answered the door when I knocked.

"I don't have a note," I said, "but I can tell you where she is."

Debbie's eyes went wide and she stood up, looking hopeful. "Where?" she said.

"Her new bond-holder is Davis Butterfield," I said. "At least, he's the one who paid for her medical treatment—she had to have a kidney regeneration. He has a skin farm on Lib. I assume that's where she is now."

The hope drained out of Debbie's face like someone had pulled a stopper out of a tub. "Oh," she said, her voice an inaudible whisper. "*Oh. Are you sure?*"

"Well—Mr. Gibbon sold her bond to some guy named Rick Janus. And Janus wouldn't tell me who he sold it to, but he did tell me she'd gotten medical treatment, and I broke into one of the tablets at the clinic to look up her record and it said Davis Butterfield had covered the costs of her treatment. And I doubt he'd have done that just to be nice, so . . ."

Debbie shook her head. "You're right," she said. Numbly, she reached back into her bunk, and handed me the sandals.

"I didn't bring a note . . ."

"What I asked you for wasn't fair," Debbie said. "I wanted you to tell me she was all right. But she's not all right. You did find out what happened to her, though, so . . . the sandals are yours." She blinked back tears.

"Are you going to try negotiating with Mr. Butterfield?"

Debbie shook her head. "No point. I don't have any money. I sure as hell don't have enough to buy out her bond *and* the cost of a kidney regeneration." She stared at the floor. "I wish he'd at least let her out in the evenings to come here, so I could see her. But the U.S. said last year that they consider certain contracts void because the work is so hazardous, so . . ." She broke off abruptly, and looked up at me warily, her mouth clamped shut.

But I knew where she'd been going. The U.S. considered those contracts void; therefore, they'd help you get out of them. If Butterfield let her out, even for a few hours, she could run away. She could escape back to the U.S. and leave him with uncollectable debt.

I took the sandals, muttered something apologetic, and fled.

I delivered the sandals to the woman who wanted them and took my payment. Which wasn't enough to pay for anyone's surgery, or to buy out anyone's bond, of course. It was pocket money, no more than that.

I'd finished the job. I'd found Lynn. My obligation was done. I looked at the latest list from Jamie: extra-plush tri-layer TP, a two-inch-diameter black button with four holes, and another pair of sandals, but this person was a lot less fussy, so long as they were size 9.

I headed back down to the locker rooms; someone would have the button, and people there were always glad to see me since I paid in hard currency for stuff they could spare. I'd just avoid Debbie's dorm, because the thought of seeing her again made me feel uncomfortable. I wished her answer had been different.

I passed one of the cheap, nasty dining halls and smelled dinner cooking. People were lined up outside, waiting for it to open. If I'd needed something more complicated than a black button I'd probably have stopped to ask people about it, but instead I kept going.

I was turning down one of the hallways with a low ceiling when someone grabbed me from behind.

"Don't go snooping around places that don't concern you," a male voice hissed in my ear. "Even being Paul Garrison's daughter will only protect you up to a point."

He hit me, hard, in the back. It hurt, a *lot*, and I screamed and he dropped me to the deck. "Stick to finding potting soil and Swiss Army knives," he said, and walked away.

CHAPTER TWO

I PICKED MYSELF UP AND RUBBED THE SORE SPOT ON MY back, struggling to catch my breath. My legs were shaking, and I had to lean against the wall of the corridor. What the *hell*? I was *done* with the snooping. Well, he was right about one thing: being Paul Garrison's daughter wasn't going to protect me here, because I wasn't about to go to my father and tell him about this.

But no one would go to the trouble of trying to intimidate me unless I was actually about to find something out that was *really a secret*. What was so important about Lynn? Anyway, I'd *found out* where she was, and there wasn't anything I could do about it.

Or was there?

Maybe the final piece of the puzzle was something I could get by talking to Lynn.

My back throbbed in time with my pounding heart. The thought of this next step made me feel queasy and shaky. Some-one who could punch me in the back could have shot me in the back just as easily. Of course, if you murder Paul Garrison's daughter, people will come asking questions. But depending on what I found out, killing me might be the lesser risk.

And if Lynn knew something—if she had that final piece—

The adrenaline was wearing off, leaving me even shakier than the pain had. I found a sandwich shop and bought myself a soda, sitting down to drink it. Maybe I could go back to Debbie and tell *her* about this. But the thought of facing Debbie again, after the news I'd given her, made me quail.

As Paul Garrison's daughter, I have certain privileges, as long as my father doesn't choose to revoke them, anyway. There are places I'm not technically *allowed* to go, but no one's actually going to stop me from going to them. If I did this right, I'd be perfectly safe. Until later, anyway, when my father found out, and would be furious, but . . .

I tipped up the bottle to drink the last of my soda, feeling my heart speeding up with fear and excitement.

I was going to have only one chance to do this.

I turned away from home and headed for Rosa. Then I kept going—through Rosa, through Pete, and all the way to Lib.

Most of the stead nations were founded by people who wanted more freedom. No one here has to pay taxes (though there are all sorts of fees). There are a few more things that are illegal on Rosa, like it's illegal to sell addictive substances to minors without a note from their parents. That's why it's supposed to be the best stead to raise a family. On Lib, though, nothing's illegal *at all*.

Stead Life did a whole series of shows about Lib, because it's the stead that mainlanders find most confusing. To answer the question everyone asks first: yes, this means it's legal to kill people, but it also means it's legal to kill *you*, so if you're planning to kill someone you'd better hope they don't have any friends. This means it's legal to steal, but see above about how it's legal to kill you. But in fact people mostly don't go around randomly killing and stealing. *Stead Life* told viewers that it was mostly a stead full of people who like to mind their own business.

If you get in trouble on Lib, though, you want to have a subscription to a security group. If you don't have a subscription, you can do a last-minute hire, but that costs a *lot*. My father and I don't live on Lib, but he keeps a subscription to the ADs, the Alpha Dogs, who are the biggest and toughest security group. So if I got in trouble on Lib, I could call the ADs to help me out. If I disappeared and there was some reason to think that *I* was being held in a skin farm and forced to work with growth matrix, the ADs would come looking for me, and although no one *has* to let the ADs in to look around (because they're not the police; there *aren't* any police) they are very capable of making you sorry if you don't.

I'm not actually supposed to go to Lib without permission.

I was going to be in huge, huge trouble.

But "trouble" for me meant grounded for life. Not bonded in a skin farm until I earned out my contract or died of cancer.

The first place I went after I crossed into Lib was the AD's office. I told the receptionist who I was and she buzzed me in and looked up my picture. "Can I see my security contract?" I asked.

"Of course, Miss Garrison." She handed it over. I read through the different services they provided and my heart started beating faster.

"OK," I said, wishing my voice wasn't all shaky. "I'd like an escort, please."

The receptionist pressed a buzzer and one of the ADs came out to the office. He was tall, muscular, and carrying a gun: exactly what you wanted if you were going to be wandering around Lib, sticking your nose where it didn't belong. Actually, ideally you'd want ten guys like this, but my contract said I could have one. Whatever. Being Paul Garrison's daughter was worth at least a half-dozen all on its own. "I'm going to the Butterfield Skin Factory," I said. "Are they contracted with you?"

"Nope," the bodyguard said. "They use the Tigers."

"Great," I said, because the Tigers were not as tough as the ADs, and this meant no conflict of interest. (There's a process they go through when two of their clients are in conflict, but I wasn't sure it would work out to my advantage, considering.) "Let's go."

We walked through the corridors. Lib is probably the creakiest and least pleasant of the steads. Min is a mix of man-made islands and old cruise ships; Rosa is mostly cruise ships. Lib is an old Russian cargo ship. (Pete, which is the stead that was founded by Russians, is *not* on a Russian cargo ship, because they knew better.) There are not a lot of windows.

It was a good thing my bodyguard knew where the skin farm was because there wasn't a sign. "You're sure this is it?" I said. He nodded. "Okay. I want to go in."

He hesitated, and looked me over.

"Are you my bodyguard, or my minder? I want to go in."

He shrugged and pressed the buzzer. "I'm here from the ADs," he said into the intercom. "We like to come in. Don't make this difficult."

The door buzzed and clicked open. "I hope you don't want a lot of time," he said. "Your contract doesn't provide for backup, so if I need it, there's going to be a serious extra charge."

Which my father would take out of my hide. I stepped in: there was a long straight hallway of shut doors. "LYNN MILLER!" I shouted. "I'M LOOKING FOR LYNN MILLER."

Doors opened and heads poked out to look at me—pale, sickly, nervous women in blue lab scrubs and latex gloves. "Lynn is in lab three," someone called to me, nervously.

A security guard came out—I could tell he was security because of his uniform, and his gun. The AD stepped forward. "Are you managerial level?" he asked conversationally. The security guard shook his head. "Then you're not paid well enough to have to deal with me. Go call the Tigers."

The security guard swallowed hard and retreated into his office.

"Come on," I said to my escort. The doors were labeled with numbers, so lab three was easy to find. The door was locked; my bodyguard kicked it down.

I'd noticed the smell as soon as I came in the front door, but here by the skin, the stench was incredible, stomach-turning. The skin itself was red and almost pulsing, in layers of screens; the techs crouched over it, prodding it with things that looked like long-handled tiny spoons. "Is Lynn Miller here?" I asked.

One of the women straightened up. "I'm Lynn Miller," she said.

She was *chained* to the workbench. "Can you get her loose?" I said to my bodyguard.

He gave me a *look*. "I'm hired to protect *you*. *She* is not on my contract."

"Yeah?" I walked over and grabbed her arm. "Lynn, will you give me the honor of your company? *Say yes*."

". . . Yes?"

"Lynn is my *date* and my contract specifies that you will provide protection services for me *and my date* at all times. And I want you to get us out of here."

My bodyguard heaved a sigh. "Okay," he said. "But if you insist, your father's going to have to get a full report. Are you *sure* about this?"

My stomach lurched. But I was going to have to explain all this sooner or later; I might as well get in huge trouble for *actually rescuing someone*. And I wasn't going to have another chance.

"Do it," I said.

He yanked a tool out of his pocket that snapped Lynn's shackles open in two seconds. "Can we go now?" he asked.

"The sooner the better," I said.

"Where are you taking me?" Lynn said, stripping off her gloves.

"You're an American, right?" I said.

"Yeah."

"We've got a super-romantic date on Min, then." At the American Institute, which I wasn't going to say out loud in front of someone who was going to report back to my father.

The Tigers hadn't arrived yet, so we just walked out. The bodyguard urged us to pick up the pace, which we did, or at least as much as Lynn could; she was still recovering from her surgery and winced with every step. The AD escorted us to the edge of Lib, then washed his hands of us.

"Who are you?" Lynn asked.

"My name is Beck, and your sister, um, hired me. To look for you."

Lynn looked me over skeptically.

"You disappeared," I said. "She wanted to know where you were, and if you were okay. Which you weren't."

"Surely she didn't have the money to pay for you rescuing me like that."

"No," I said. "By the way, do you know some deep, dark secret that's not supposed to get out? Because someone assaulted me earlier today to tell me to mind my own business. That's why I decided to come find you."

Lynn eyed me with renewed suspicion. "No," she said. "If I knew some deep, dark secret I'd be down at the bottom of the deep, dark ocean right about now. I wouldn't have been in a skin farm."

"So what happened to you, exactly?"

"I got sick—really sick. I hit up Gibbon for a loan, and he said he'd sell my bond to someone who'd arrange treatment for me. I had to sign a consent, because of the laws on Min. Janus took me to the clinic, and they said I needed kidney regeneration. That's horribly expensive, but without it . . . Anyway, Janus told me the only place that would pay for that sort of treatment was a skin farm. I still wanted to refuse, but there's a loophole when someone has a terminal condition and can't pay for their treatment. Their contract can be sold without their consent to anyone willing to foot the bill. So that's how I wound up in the skin farm."

There was something here I wasn't seeing.

"Where are we going?" she asked.

"The American Institute," I said.

"Do you think they'll let me use a phone?" she asked.

"Probably," I said, assuming she'd want to call her sister to come meet her.

I felt nervous going down Embassy Row. It basically looked like any other corridor full of shops, but really well-kept with very clean windows, and each had a flag displayed in the big window in front instead of merchandise. We passed Mexico and France before we got to the American one. A bell tinkled as we went in, like in a store. There was a young man sitting at a desk, with a nametag that said, "Tyrone LeBlanc, Director." He was Black, which was unusual on the stead; most of the locals were white, Asian, or Hispanic. Mr. LeBlanc looked at Lynn, and at me, and then said, "May I help you?"

"This is Lynn Miller," I said. "She's bonded to a skin farm and wants to—"

"—Make a phone call," she said. "If you don't mind. I don't have my passport with me."

"Did you register with us when you arrived?" he asked.

"Not exactly."

"Well—you can definitely use a phone," he said, and handed one to her before turning to me. "Forgive me if I'm mistaken, but are you Rebecca Garrison?" he asked.

"Yes," I said.

"Don't go anywhere, I have something for you." He stepped into the back and returned with a sealed paper envelope, with *Rebecca Garrison* written on the front.

My stomach lurched. It was *just* like my father to do something like this—just in case I ever disobeyed him. Well, I didn't have to read it now. I stuffed it into my pocket, mumbling, "Thanks."

Near me, Lynn had gotten through to someone. "I'm calling to renegotiate my contract," she said, her voice triumphant.

*

The U.S. government will provide transportation to citizens in danger under certain circumstances, and that was one of the reasons I'd snatched Lynn. They don't recognize the validity of bond contracts generally and they consider a U.S. citizen being held to work in a skin farm to essentially have been kidnapped and imprisoned under dangerous circumstances. I'd figured Lynn would take the first boat back to California, but instead she was spelling out a set of conditions under which she'd let John Butterfield resell her bond to someone else. "We're not talking about profit," she said furiously, pacing back and forth in front of the desk. "We're talking about *how much* of a loss you're going to take."

"What happened to her?" Mr. LeBlanc asked me.

"She had kidney failure," I said, and explained the sequence of events.

"Huh," he said. "Kidney failure, really? Same thing happened with an escaped bond-worker last month, too."

"What causes kidney failure, anyway?"

"Oh, lots of things. Untreated diabetes, certain illnesses, drug overdoses . . . Kidneys filter out toxins, so an overdose of anything toxic." He pursed his lips. "You're not big on food and water inspectors here, you know. I'm surprised it doesn't happen more often."

"Lynn?"

She pressed the mute button on the phone. "Yes?"

"Which canteen do you subscribe to?"

"Clark's. It's near the locker rooms."

Could that be the secret? That Clark's was poisoning people? But thousands of bond-workers ate there; if it were poisoning people, the clinic would be overflowing with dying bond-workers.

No; if Lynn had been poisoned, she'd surely been singled out.

"Don't renegotiate your contract," I said. "Go back to California."

She shook her head and returned to her conversation. I looked mutely at Mr. LeBlanc. He shrugged. "Fugitive bond-workers stay here more often than you'd think. In Lynn's case, maybe there's a warrant out for her arrest, and she's taking advantage of the laws here to avoid extradition."

Lynn glared at him and muted the phone again. "Drug charges," she said. "Possession and manufacture of substances that are *entirely legal* on every island in the seastead. I'd bet dollars to scrip Mr. American Representative here has been known to possess an illegal substance from time to time."

He shrugged.

"But even though she's up on criminal charges back in the States, you'd still take her home, for free?"

"Well, not exactly for free," he said. "We send her a bill later. She wouldn't get sold into debt-slavery if she didn't pay, though, we just garnish her paychecks."

"Lynn," I said. "I think the secret they're protecting is that you were poisoned on purpose. Four other bond-workers were treated for kidney failure the same day as you, and all had their contracts bought by the same guy who bought yours. Other workers have disappeared from Gibbon's dining hall, haven't they? They've gotten sick, and never come back. I think Gibbon's doing it. I think Gibbon, Janus, and Butterfield are conspiring to use the 'terminal condition' loophole to make sure Butterfield gets a steady stream of bond-workers."

Lynn turned back to the phone. "Also," she said, "I don't want to be sold back to Gibbon."

Gibbon, Janus, and Butterfield.

Min does have police, after a fashion; we're not like Lib. But we don't have a *lot* of police. Basically, they break up fist fights. If something gets stolen, you'd usually hire someone privately to try to retrieve it for you. There was a murder on the stead a few years ago and here's what happened: everyone knew who did it, so the police went and arrested him and there was a lot of talk about trial procedures. While people were arguing about how exactly a murder trial ought to work, the victim's brother hired a bunch of guys from Lib to break into the police station and kidnap the murderer. The guy's drowned body turned up in the waters by Rosa the next day and everyone pretended to have *no idea* how that might have happened.

But here's the other thing: the murder victim was a citizen, not a guest worker.

Something complicated like this—everyone would pretend they thought it was *coincidence* that all these people were developing kidney failure. Or maybe they'd blame Clark's. The doctor at the clinic clearly thought it was Clark's.

I did know one person who was powerful enough to actually make a difference, though: my father.

My father scared me. Especially when he was angry. But he was my father. I ought to be able to go to him with this.

"Dad?"

Our apartment was mostly dark; light spilled from my father's office. "Come in here, Beck."

"I need to talk to you about something," I said.

He must have heard the seriousness in my voice because he pushed himself back from his work and gestured to the chair. My father's office had one visitor's chair, which sat directly in front of his painting. He had a painting on his wall of two girls playing a piano and singing to a person who seemed to be listening. I'd wondered a few times why he liked it; he wasn't all that interested in music.

"I was trying to find something kind of unusual this week," I said. "I was trying to find a person."

His eye twitched. "Really."

"Well, I started out trying to find a pair of size eight sparkly strappy sandals. But the woman who had those wanted me to try to find her sister." He didn't answer. I swallowed hard and went on. "So, okay, I'm going to skip all the intervening steps and tell you what I realized today, which is that Mr. Gibbon, Mr. Janus, and Mr. Butterfield are conspiring to poison bond-workers, so that their contracts can be sold for skin farm work. It wasn't an accident that L—" I broke off, suddenly not wanting to give my father any names "—the woman I was looking for got sick."

"Mmm," he said. "Do you have any actual *evidence* for this story you're telling me?"

"No," I said, honestly. "I mean, I'm not a police officer or a doctor. But I bet if you examined any of the bond-workers who've been treated for kidney failure in the last month—"

"Yes, most likely you'd find traces, if a poison was involved. Well. Yes." He pondered that. "I assume your, ah, your *date*, this afternoon . . . was the woman you were searching for?"

He heard from the ADs already. "Yes."

"You are *remarkably* tenacious."

"Thank you," I said, even though I could tell this hadn't been a compliment.

"And just what do you expect me to do about this, Beck?"

"Go to the police and make them investigate?"

"You must realize that you've overlooked a wide range of alternate possibilities. These individuals might have eaten or drunk something dodgy, first of all; that's the simplest explanation. It might be pure coincidence. Or perhaps most likely of all, they might have all ingested something *recreational* that displayed questionable judgment on all their parts."

"And *coincidentally*, Butterfield bought up all those people with kidney failure?"

"Oh, I'm sure that wasn't a coincidence. He has an arrangement with the man who holds the patent on the kidney regeneration technique and can have it done at a discount. Undoubtedly, he has a standing request at the hospital for notification when anyone has significant kidney damage."

"How do you know this?"

"I know a lot of things, Rebecca." He fell silent and watched my reaction. I tried hard not to give him one. "Now," he said, "I received several interesting calls today. Apparently you were pestering Rick Janus outside of his dining hall, after talking your way in. You had nothing wrong with you this morning at the clinic, although you did cost me a fair sum what with all the tests they ran. And you went to Lib this afternoon."

He hadn't heard about Embassy Row. I didn't tell him.

"All, apparently, to find—and eventually to *personally rescue* this particular bond-worker. Surely the rescue wasn't in your original agreement with the owner of the sandals."

". . . No."

"No." He leaned back. "So? Explain."

"When I was down by the locker rooms today someone attacked me, grabbed me from behind and hit me, and told me to mind my own business." I glared furiously at my own feet. "I was *done* but that made me think I must have missed something important. Something worth hiding."

"I see."

He fell silent. I lifted my chin and stared out the window. Or at the window, since it was dark.

"Well," he said, "you've demonstrated that you are stubborn, disobedient, and disrespectful."

"I'm sorry, sir."

"No, you're clearly not." He tapped his desk with a pen. "I'm going to have to think on how best to use you. In the meantime, I'm grounding you for the next month. If Jamie still wants you as a Finder when the month is up, that's between the two of you."

I swallowed hard. "What about Gibbon and . . . what about the bond-workers?"

"I expect there won't be any more mysterious kidney failures," my father said, turning back to his computer screen. "I'll pass the word along that if their plot could be unraveled by a persistent *teenager* they need to knock it off. I expect they will. Also, I don't like people manhandling my daughter, especially considering how thoroughly the tactic backfired. I'll see if I can identify the thug."

"But—what about L—I mean, my date from this afternoon?"

He looked back at me and raised an eyebrow. "Don't go looking for Lynn Miller again," he said. "I doubt that you will like what you find."

Back in my room, I turned on a mainland streaming show, laid out my homework, and changed into pajamas. When I took off my jeans, they crinkled; the letter I'd been handed at the Institute was still in my pocket.

My father hadn't mentioned *that* particular bit of disobedience. I smoothed the letter out, then opened it.

> *Dear Becky,*
>
> *Happy birthday, darling. This is the twelfth of these messages I've written. Every year I send a new one to the Services Bureau on Rosa, in the hopes that eventually you will come in, and they can deliver it.*
>
> *I'm not sure what your father has told you about me. I just want you to know that I love you, and I would like to see you. If you're not willing to come stateside, I would like to speak with you by phone or correspond by letter. Whatever you're comfortable with. If you'd like to leave New Minerva, the Bureau will provide you with transportation to San Francisco. I'll meet you there, and take you home—to my home.*

I just want you to know I haven't forgotten you.
I'll never forget you.
I hope to see you again someday.
Love,
Mom

My first thought, staring at this, was that someone was confused. This couldn't be a letter from my mother; my mother was dead. She died in a drunk driving wreck years ago, before my father had brought me to the seastead.

Then rational thought caught up with what I *thought* I knew, and the truth hit me like a breaking wave. My father had lied. My father had *lied.*

I stared into the darkness, wide awake, my heart pounding.

What else had he lied about?

PART TWO
HIGH STAKES

CHAPTER THREE

DEAR MOM,

I was really surprised to hear from you, because Dad told me you were dead. ~~Should I have thought of a more tactful way to say that?~~

I'm sorry about my handwriting. I don't handwrite very much but ~~there's no way to send you email without Dad seeing it~~ this way I can have someone leave it at the American Institute so they can send it back to you. I don't know exactly how I'm going to get this to the Institute, but if you get this, I figured it out, so if you write to me again that way I should be able to get it.

I'm thinking about what you said about coming to California. ~~I just can't imagine leaving I've lived here for so long that~~ All my friends are here. I'm not sure about leaving them behind. Also I have a job. Or I used to, anyway. ~~I'm grounded at the moment~~

It feels weird going on all chatty. Like I'm saying, "Here's what's new with me!" I can't very well tell you everything that's new since I was four.

I wish I could send you a picture of me now but I don't have any prints. ~~Could you send me a picture of you?~~

~~Sincerely Yours Truly Love~~
Your daughter,
Beck

CHAPTER FOUR

THE SEASTEAD HAD NEVER FELT SMALL TO ME BEFORE.

My father grounded me for a month. Thirty days. I was only allowed out of our apartment to go to school: all my meals were in the apartment, even lunch. He knew when I needed to leave, and he knew when I'd get back if I didn't loiter. If he was out, he checked the door logs.

He also took away my gadget. For schoolwork, he gave me the sort of locked-down half-gadget you'd give to a six-year-old. With the locked-down gadget I couldn't watch TV, read mail, listen to music, or even get any books that weren't on my school list.

So I was really, really bored. By the end, I even missed Shara and Maureen's company.

On the thirty-first day, my father grimly told me I was free to go where I liked again. So after school, I went for a long walk—I went to the far end of Min, crossed the bridge to Rosa, and made my way through Rosa to Pete, where I paid some of my hard currency for access to the sun-deck and leaned against the rail to stare west over the open ocean.

After a month of being shut in, I thought the seastead would feel *enormous*. Instead, it felt as shrunken and constricting as our apartment.

*

When I got home that afternoon my father was in a cheerful mood. He came out of his office and sat down with me in the living room to ask me how my schoolwork was going and quiz me on the economic theories of value used in the creation of the Brazilian monetary system. Then he pulled out a box and handed it to me. "I took a look at your handheld while I had it," he said, "and I realized it's quite old, nearly obsolete. So I ordered you a new one, and conveniently enough, it arrived today."

I opened the box and looked at it, a little disbelieving. It was the newest new thing, or close, with a larger, higher-res screen and high-speed biometrics so it would work seamlessly for me but shut down for anyone else. "Thanks," I said, wondering if he'd found out I knew my mother was alive, and if this was a bribe to keep me here.

"Also," he said, "I'm wondering if you're interested in a new job."

"What do you mean?" I asked, feeling a surge of suspicion.

"You might have heard there's a studio from Los Angeles that's coming to film a new reality show on the seastead for stateside broadcast."

I *had* heard rumors about this, but without my gadget I hadn't been able to read them for myself. ". . . Yes?"

"Well, they're coming, and they're looking for an intern—they want someone young and savvy, apparently. You've got a month of school vacation coming up, and I was asked if you'd be willing. I said I thought you'd be excited about the opportunity."

"Sure," I said, still feeling suspicious. "That sounds great. Why me?"

He shrugged. "Your father knows the right people, that's all."

Yes, I concluded. *Bribe.*

*

"You must be Rebecca. I'm Janet." Janet was a tall, thin, blonde woman with tan skin. She stood up to shake my hand, and we sat down together. "Am I *really* allowed to smoke in here?"

"What are you smoking?" I asked. She held up her pack of cigarettes. It must have been bought in the States because I could read the word CANCER even from across the table. "Yeah, that's fine. There are dining halls that ban tobacco but Gibbon's is fine with it."

We met up in Gibbon's dining hall, over lunch, and people were covertly staring at us. I could almost hear a thousand rumors pinging their way from gadget to gadget.

She lit her cigarette with a lighter and then left it to smolder on the ashtray. "I'm the Location Czarina for 'High Stakes,' a reality show we're filming here." She handed me a business card, which did, in fact, say *Location Czarina*. "One of my many responsibilities is liaising with the seastead," she said. "I have liaisons with the various steader governments—for the seasteads that have them, I guess?—and from the Chamber of Commerce. But I decided I wanted a local assistant I could choose myself, sort of a Girl Friday. Someone who grew up here, and I specifically wanted a teenager. I want someone very candid, and I think teenagers are typically more honest than adults, don't you?"

Janet's tone was breezily confrontational—like what she really wanted was someone who would candidly *agree* with her. Still, there was something weirdly flattering about a grownup offering to pay me to be her right-hand yes-man. I smiled broadly and nodded. She watched me nod, and nodded back. She picked up her cigarette, tapped the ash off it, and put it back down.

"Your father signed off on the contract, but we like your agreement, too." She slid the contract across the table. Payment was in U.S. dollars, but would be deposited into an account held jointly with my father. The account was set up so I could only draw out scrip, which I could then only spend on Min, and only on certain items. (You could trade up for hard currencies, but the exchange rate sucked.) It was a pretty standard arrangement for money held by teenagers, not just something my father had set up for me, but I still didn't like it.

"I know you negotiated this with my father," I said, "and he's agreed to this. But I think you'll agree that you don't just want my father to twist my arm, you want my *enthusiastic cooperation*."

"Absolutely," she said. She leaned back and picked up her cigarette again. She looked expectant now, and a little bit pleased, like I was living up to her personal stereotype of the wheeler-dealer stead kid. We settled on $50 US cash per week, in addition to what she was depositing into the account. "It's going to be hard to put this in the written contract without your father finding out," she said.

"We'll do a handshake deal," I said, and held out my hand.

She set her cigarette down and we shook. "So," she said. "Let's talk about your rules of contracts, anyway. Because they're pretty central to the concept of the show."

The show was called *High Stakes* because people had to "buy a stake" to become a citizen of the seastead. "Is this sort of like buying into a condo association?" Janet asked. I had to have her explain the concept of a condo association. It wasn't a terrible analogy. The seastead doesn't have any taxes, but the money to keep us all from sinking into the ocean does have to come from somewhere, and it can't *all* come from visa fees for tourists.

"So, your father brought you here?" she asked. "Was he ever a bond-worker?"

"No!" I said, a little shocked. "He wasn't even a guest worker. He came with enough money to just buy in right away."

"What's the difference between a bond-worker and a guest worker?" She started taking notes on her gadget. "And what are you, exactly?"

"I'm a dependent." Which was why my earnings were all supposed to go into an account my father controlled, but the term "dependent" seemed to satisfy her so I decided not to explain that. "If someone pays their own way to get here and lives here without a stake, they're a guest worker. They have a sponsor and that makes them kind of like a dependent but not exactly. If someone else paid for them to come and they have to pay back their ticket out of their earnings, they're a bond-worker. It's sort of like being an indentured servant." *Except not really*, I thought, even as I said it. Mrs. Rodriguez had described it that way when we were learning about the establishment of the American colonies. But indentured servants served for a particular length of time, not until they earned out a particular amount of money.

"So," Janet said, and lit a fresh cigarette, "we want to recruit twenty bond-workers and have them compete on our show. The winner has his debt paid off *and* receives enough money to buy a stake. The runner-up just gets his debt paid off. The rest, well, they'll get a salary for being on the show so that'll pay part of their debt, and I guess we'll sell their contracts again." She set her cigarette in the ashtray. I wondered why she kept lighting them when mostly she was just letting them burn down to nothing. "The thing is, we tried an initial set of auditions and *no one came.* We didn't publicize them well at all, because my thought was, we wanted people who were motivated enough to follow up on rumors. I thought at first maybe we just muffed it and no one knew, but one of my other assistants did some asking around and *that* wasn't it. So I don't know."

I knew the answer to this, because after my father told me about the job, I did my own research right away. "What are you planning on having them do to win?"

"Oh . . . well, contests, you know? Stuff they have to race to finish, puzzles they have to solve, there'll probably be a popularity-contest element . . . it needs to be hard enough to be interesting."

"The rumor that *I* heard," I said, "is that you're going to make them gladiators, and have them fight to the death."

Janet nearly started out of her chair. "Are you fucking *kidding*

me? No! Contests of strength and guile, not fights to the goddamn death." She reached for her cigarettes, then dropped them
on the table and filled up her water glass instead. "Would that
even be *legal*?"

"You're setting up a new stead for the show. And you're apparently the Czarina of the stead, so it's legal if you say it's legal."

"*Jesus Christ* you people are weird." She slammed her water
glass down and stood up. "Attention, everyone!" The only people
in Gibbon's that time of day were there to gawk at her, so she
pretty much had everyone's attention already, but the room went
quiet. "As Czarina of Lifepoint Television Island, I hereby decree
that *no gladiatorial combats shall take place there and murder is
illegal*." She sat back down. "Think that'll do it?"

"I have no idea."

"Well, see if you can stir up some interest for me, okay? BIG
PERSONALITIES. Drama queens. Attention whores. You know
the type, I'm *sure*."

I did.

"Bring me some names the day after tomorrow. That's your
first job."

So, I was finding again. Finding attention whores. Who wanted to be on her show. And believed it wouldn't involve battles to
the death.

How hard could *that* be?

As soon as I showed up for afternoon tutoring, all eyes turned
toward me. "Is it TRUE?" Shara asked.

"Is what true?" I asked, mostly to bait her.

"That you're going to be working for the reality show they're
filming here? The REAL one, I mean."

Oh, *Stead Life*, how quickly you are cast aside by your alleged
fans. A homegrown reality show could never compete with something brought in from the shore. "Yes," I said.

"Lucky." Shara sighed.

"Is it true that it's all about bond-workers?" John asked. "They're going to have bond-workers competing to earn out and buy in?"

"Yeah," I said. John hadn't treated me any differently in the last month, which made me think his father, the owner of the skin farm, hadn't told him about Lynn's assisted break-out.

"They should do one about teenagers," Maureen said. For once, she looked envious instead of contemptuous. "You know, because we don't have a stake, either! That would be totally awesome. You should try to convince them to do a show like that."

"Mm," I said, pouring myself coffee and then sliding into a seat on the couch next to Thor.

"So why is this such a big deal, anyway?" Thor asked. "Don't bond-workers earn out and buy in all the time? I mean, isn't that the whole point? Why else would they come here?"

"Sometimes they're in legal trouble," I said, thinking about Thor's parents and their tax issues.

"Well, I suppose, but surely some—"

"Can you think of anyone who's earned out?" Mrs. Rodriguez asked, looking around the room.

"Davy," Shara said at the same moment that Andy said, "Dave Alonzo." Everyone nodded. Davy Alonzo was one of those legendary stead residents, like the Founders. He come over here on a bond ticket fifteen years ago, earned out in five, and earned a stake in another five. He was sort of unusual in that he was an educated bond-worker—he'd been a software developer, not a dishwasher, and his contract included provisions for bonuses. Still, he was proof it could be done.

"I know one other," Mrs. Rodriguez said. "Some of you know her, too—Mrs. Lindsey."

"The day care lady?" Shara exclaimed, scandalized. "She was a bond-worker?"

"Yeah, and she came over as a nanny. She *married* out. You

may have noticed there are more men here than women . . ." Everyone nodded. "So, when they recruit people to sign bond agreements, they tell the women they'll probably find someone who wants to marry them, and that person will buy out their contract."

"But if they just *buy* it you're their bond-worker, not their wife," I said.

"Oh, I know this one!" Thor said. "There's a law against marrying your bond-worker. Or even, uh, dating them. At least there is on Rosa."

"Yes," Mrs. Rodriguez said. "It's the law on both Rosa and Min. And even on Lib it's likely to garner some disapproval from your neighbors. Anyway, Mrs. Lindsey married out. Her husband didn't buy her a stake, though; she kept working as a nanny for a few years to earn it. So it does happen."

For the first time, I wondered why Mrs. Rodriguez had come to Min, originally. Whether it had been her idea, or her husband's idea. It wasn't done to ask that sort of question; of *course* they'd wanted to move here, wouldn't anyone? I bit my lip and looked down at my Economics text and didn't say anything as Shara loudly asserted that she would *never* be a bond-worker *ever* and people who signed that sort of contract were mostly pretty stupid. Eventually we moved on to the History lesson.

When we broke up for lunch, Thor lingered as I packed up my bag. "Hey," he said. "Where do you go to eat?"

"Sandwich shop, usually. If I don't feel like walking back to Gibbon's. Um . . ." He was staring at the ground and I wasn't sure if he was trying to hint that he wanted to come with me, or not. "Do you want to join me?"

"Yeah! Thanks." He brightened and fell into step beside me. We walked down the hallway to the place with the cheap tuna subs I liked, and then sat at one of the tables, drinking pop and eating our sandwiches.

"I wish they'd hire me, too," Thor said wistfully. "I'm new here, so, like, I have an insider *and* an outsider perspective. I can explain all the stuff that confused me so much when I first got here. All the stuff I wished I had someone to explain to me."

"What do you miss, about life on shore?" I asked.

"Oh . . ." Thor pushed a lock of dark, curly hair out of his eyes. "A lot, actually. I miss being able to get whatever I want at the store. I miss milk. I mean, we have it here but it's the ultrapasteurized kind in boxes and it doesn't taste the same. I miss *hiking*. Dad said he'll take us hiking in Thailand sometime but it won't be the same as going to Torey Pines. That's a park outside of San Diego, where we used to live. It's on the ocean, and the views are great. Not that you can't see the ocean here, but at Torey Pines you could see *other* stuff, too."

"I was born on the shore," I said, "but I haven't been back since I was four. I really don't remember anything about it except this playground I think I might have gone to when I was little. It had slides."

Thor laughed a little. "All playgrounds have slides."

"I remember there were a *lot* of kids who would go there."

"Yeah, sounds about right."

I looked over my shoulder to make sure Shara and Maureen weren't in the sandwich shop, and then leaned over the table to speak quietly. "I have a proposal to make," I said. "I'll tell Janet—that's my boss on the reality show—that she should consider hiring you, too. I mean, I can't guarantee that she'll agree with me, but I can *suggest* it. In exchange, I want you to deliver something for me."

Thor looked at me silently, one eyebrow raised.

"You won't get in trouble," I said. "You know practically nothing's illegal here, right? This isn't illegal. It's just that my dad will be angry if I go to Embassy Row. I want you to drop off an envelope for me at the American Institute."

Thor looked at me, and I couldn't quite read his expression. I thought he was trying to figure out the catch. Then he held out his hand, and I took my folded, taped letter out of my pocket and laid it in his palm. I'd written *from B. Garrison, to my correspondent* on the outside; I wasn't entirely sure if I wanted him to know who I was writing to.

"I think we have a deal," he said.

Embassy Row was off-limits, but my father hadn't told me I couldn't go to St. Peter's Church. I went every evening at 10:20 until, on the third day, a heavy man in a kitchen worker's uniform turned up. He crossed himself and slid into the folding chair next to me. "Father Tim thinks you're discovering your faith and has been wondering if he should come talk to you," he said.

I stifled a laugh. "I'm an atheist," I said. "I was coming here because I wanted to talk to *you*."

He nodded. "Good strategy. Is this about the poisonings?"

"I guess I could have saved myself a trip if you know all about it already."

"Word got around—not that Janus got in any trouble. Or Gibbon, or Butterfield. But the disappearances have stopped. For now."

"Good. I'm sorry I couldn't come tell you earlier, I was—"

"Imprisoned," he finished for me. "Yes."

"I was just going to say 'grounded.'"

The man tilted his head and looked into my face, his eyes much more intent than I had expected. "You refused to be intimidated, you pursued the trail to the end, you saved Lynn, and you got the word out. When someone's locked away for doing the right thing, that makes them a prisoner of conscience. Not merely a *grounded teenager*."

I didn't know if I liked the direction this conversation was going, and he quickly shifted gears. "I heard you were hired to work on that new TV show," he said.

"That rumor's really gotten around," I said.

He chuckled. "I also heard you were recruiting."

"Yeah," I said. "I'm supposed to find people with 'big personalities' and reassure them that no gladiatorial combat will be involved."

"People don't trust Janet," he said. "But if *you* vouch for the contract—they trust you."

"People trust me? Which people? *Why?*"

"I think you know why."

My cheeks grew warm. "Well. I haven't read Janet's contract but I really don't think she's going to have anyone killed. She comes from the States, you know, and she was genuinely shocked that anything like that would be legal."

He smiled broadly. "Since you are vouching for Janet . . ." He handed me a folded slip of paper. "I have a *very large* personality, Rebecca. And I would be *very* interested in being on the show."

I looked at the slip of paper: *Miguel Garcia* was written inside, along with Gibbon's phone number and Miguel's bond ID number. I opened my mouth and Miguel gestured for me not to speak. "The walls have ears," he said, and folded my hand over the paper.

"I'm supposed to bring her a lot of names," I said. "Do you have any other suggestions?"

His eyes danced with amusement. "I suggest you go down to the locker rooms again and do some recruiting there. It'll be good for your spirits."

I hadn't been down to the locker rooms since my grounding. When I last saw Debbie, Lynn was alive; now, she might well be dead. I had no idea what Debbie would know, or how much she'd blame me for. I slipped in a puddle as I trudged down the grubby stairway, and had to grab the handrail to keep from falling on my butt. I caught my breath and wished I'd demanded a bit more information from Miguel.

Debbie spotted me as I was walking into the locker rooms. "Rebecca!"

"Hi," I said, already feeling like I shouldn't have come.

To my surprise and embarrassment, she swept me into a hug. "I'm so glad you came down so I could thank you properly."

"But—I didn't—did Lynn . . . ?"

"I heard what happened from you-know-who." She let go of me and tapped her left shoulder with three fingers of her right hand, nodding.

You-know-who? Did she mean Miguel? What was up with the Significant Gesture? I had learned how to finger-spell in American Sign Language back in my elementary tutoring, along with "good morning" and "excuse me" in Spanish and Russian, but she'd formed a W, not an M. Or maybe that was a non-ASL number three.

She dropped her hands to waist level, rapidly finger-spelled M I G U E L while saying, "You know, William." I nodded, although I thought probably my confusion showed. She tapped the wall and pointed at her ear. *The walls have ears.*

Miguel hadn't wanted me to speak his name aloud, either. I nodded. "I'm actually here because of my new job," I said apologetically. "I'm working for Janet—"

"Oh, yes, the *reality show*," Debbie said with a broad grin. "It's been the talk of the locker rooms."

"No gladiators," I said. "No one's going to fight to the death."

"Yeah, that's the latest thing people are saying."

"Janet sent me to find people who want to be on it. People with big personalities." Was I grasping the whole Signing thing? I laboriously finger-spelled ATTENTION WHORES and Debbie almost choked as she laughed out loud.

"Honey, you came to the right place," she said. "We've got some fantastic big personalities around here."

"Janet is only interested in people who *want* to be on the show," I said. "That's why she sent me—she wants me to clear it with individuals before they start negotiating for contracts. Only, of course there will be auditions—"

"I think I get it," Debbie said. "Let me introduce you to a few people." FRIENDS, she spelled. OF MIGUEL.

"Next," Janet said.

We were in the office suite Janet's network had rented for the auditions. It was windowless, but there were so many lights it was almost as blinding as actual daylight, and there were cameras *everywhere*, because some of this footage would be used in the actual show. Janet was sitting at a long table, with a casting director of some sort and a couple of other production people. I was at the far end of the table, so I could run errands if anyone had any for me.

They were making everyone sing, even though it wasn't a singing show. Janet had told me this was just to get a sense of their personalities. Confident singers (even if they were terrible) probably had big personalities.

When Debbie came in, she smiled broadly and looked startled when she was asked for a song. Her eyes flicked over to me. As discreetly as I could, my hands still on the table, I spelled, LOUD. She belted it out with an off-key flourish, and got the longer interview that I'd realized was Janet's indication she was seriously considering that person. "Where are you from, originally?" Janet asked.

"Mobile, Alabama," Debbie said.

"How long have you been here?"

"Three years."

"What brought you to the seastead?"

"My sister and I got caught with a hundred tabs of T-13." T-13 was barely even a real drug, to my mind—but it was enough in Alabama to get them a ten-year prison sentence, and on impulse they'd jumped bail and come to the seastead. I swallowed hard, lowering my eyes, thinking about Lynn. She should've just served the time. Debbie was smiling ruefully, and I wondered if Janet could see how forced her smile was.

"Is your sister auditioning?" She looked down at her notes.

"No. Just me. My sister and I are out of touch right now. I believe she's working on New Amsterdam. Or Amsterdarn, as we usually call it."

"Any dreams for the future?"

"Earning out my bond and buying one of the apartments with a window," Debbie said, unhesitatingly.

Janet made a note. "Thank you. We'll be in touch. Next!"

We had a run of people who clearly didn't like singing, and then Miguel. He smiled broadly when she asked for a song and sang "Love Me Tender," the Elvis song, with great dramatic verve. Janet smiled, and I knew she was thinking, *Oh, perfect.* She raised an eyebrow and shot me a triumphant look, clearly happy with my recommendation. Miguel had only been here 18 months, and had come, he said, because he had no future back in Mexico and dreamed of a better life on the seastead.

Janet happily made notes for a minute or two after he'd stepped out and then leaned over to ask me where I knew him from. "He works in the kitchen at the dining hall where I eat," I said. "He just seemed like a good fit for what you're looking for."

Of my other suggestions—the "friends of Miguel" Debbie had pointed me toward—two were also judged perfect, one was a "maybe," and three weren't comfortable enough in front of a camera to make the cut. Janet had a list of thirty when she was done and gave me the job of buying the contracts. "Tell me if anyone gives you trouble," she added, "though you understand how business works here better than I do."

"You know," I said, "I have a classmate named Thor who suggested you might like someone who has both an insider *and* an outsider perspective. He's new here—newish, anyway—and had to get used to all the ways the seastead is different from the shore."

"Oh?" Janet was looking at her own to-do list and only half-listening. "Do you work well with Thor? I'll hire him on as your assistant if you want."

For a fleeting minute it occurred to me that I could win back Shara's loyalty by offering her the job. But I wasn't even vaguely tempted. "That would be awesome."

"OK. Fifty a week, directly from petty cash."

"I'll have to talk to him but I imagine that'll be fine."

"Filming starts in a week. Try to have at least twenty of the people on my list ready by Monday."

CHAPTER FIVE

BUYING BOND-WORKER CONTRACTS WAS A LOT LIKE NE-
gotiating for turquoise-blue cashmere sweaters or vanilla-scented
bath bubbles or potting soil. The trick was to shrug and act like
it was all the same to me whether the person sold or not. If they
balked at my "final offer" (which was always 10% lower than the
budget Janet had given me for each contract), I'd tell them I'd
have to clear it with Janet, and warn them that if I could find
someone cheaper before my meeting with her, we probably lose
interest. They all caved, because when it came right down to it,
from a bond-broker's perspective all these people were basically
widgets, and the TV studio was offering really good money.

I was a little worried that Mr. Gibbon would balk at selling
Debbie or Miguel's contract, but I had a list of six people I wanted
from him, and he perused it, made me a counteroffer, and we
came to terms. He didn't bring up Lynn, and neither did I. He
noted that he'd be interested in buying back his staff after filming was over (at a discount, obviously). Unlike some of the other
bond-holders, he refrained from making any jokes about how he
was only interested in buying back the people who survived to the
end of filming.

Thor was delighted at the prospect of being my assistant and didn't even try for a higher wage. "Do you want me to get you coffee?" he asked as he fell into step beside me after school. "I could *totally* get you coffee."

"Yeah," I said. "See if you can find me a coffee. I'd like an *Americano.*"

"Oh," he said, and raised his eyebrows. "I'll see what . . . I'll see what they have, all right?"

Dear Rebecca, my mother's letter said, *I don't think you can imagine how overjoyed I was to hear from you.* Like me, she clearly felt a little awkward about being chatty, but she told me a little about her job as a nurse in a Los Angeles hospital. She had enclosed a picture of herself and a stack of crisp US $100 bills. *I know a little about how the seastead works,* she added in a PS. *Money is power. Forgive me if this is an imposition, but I'd like you to have a little bit of power your father doesn't know you have.*

Of course, money my father didn't know about required a hiding place he wouldn't be able to check, and since my alcove had no door, he could search it any time he wanted to. I tucked it into my pocket.

Janet was delighted when I handed her a roster of names by Saturday morning, and kicked out a chair for me. "Okay, kid, I need some more names from you."

"Of bond-workers?"

"No, not this time. Movers and shakers. Big shots. The muckety-mucks of the seastead." She handed me her gadget, a list of names already up. "I got started without you, but surely you can add some names here."

I looked it over. "Why's Joe Wiley on here? He likes to *think* he's important—"

"The Seastead Governing Council appointed him as my *of-*

ficial liaison." She caught my eye. "You can see why I hired you."

"Oh. Yeah." I pushed my hair behind my ear and kept reading. The others looked okay; she'd gotten all the official people and a few of the unofficial ones, like my father. I came up with another twenty names, which she noted down.

"Do you know how to find these people?"

"What do you mean?"

"Can you hand-deliver something to them?"

"Well, some of them. I'm not allowed to go to Lib. Sal and Amsterdarn aren't connected by bridge and anyway I'm not really supposed to go to them, either. But most of these people live on Min, Rosa, or Pete, or spend enough time here that I can find them. What are you having me deliver?"

"Party invitations," she said. "I'm hosting at the Winter Palace."

"Where?" I said, trying to remember if there was a dining room somewhere—Amsterdarn, maybe?—called Winter Palace.

She sighed. "If I'm the Czarina, I must live in the Winter Palace, right? Our *yacht*. The one the studio sent."

"Oh," I said, feeling stupid. "And . . . you're actually writing the invitations on *paper*?"

"Don't you think that'll get people's attention? Although actually, I was going to have you and your assistant take care of the writing, if you can at least print legibly."

Thor and I split them up. I saved my father for last, since I could give him his when I went home. He was working when I got there, and nodded when he saw the invitation in my hand. "Just leave it on my desk," he said. "I don't have to RSVP by way of you, do I?"

"No. Although you can if you want. Joe did."

"Joe *Wiley*?" He looked up at me, a little incredulous, as I put the invitation down on his desk.

"I know," I said, sighing. "But apparently the Seastead Governing Council made him Janet's *official* liaison. I don't know why."

"Probably to get him out of someone's office." My father gave me a restrained grin. "Well, considering that Joe's going to be there, I'll have to ponder whether I want to tolerate his company."

"It's going to be on a visiting yacht," I said. "The one the network sent."

"Will the food be good?"

"I would think so. They're having Primrose cater."

"Primrose is overrated, but it'll be an interesting change." He stretched and cracked his knuckles. "You can tell Janet I'll come."

The *Winter Palace* (that was the actual name of the yacht) wasn't the biggest yacht I'd seen tie up by the stead, but it was respectably big, at least 50 meters long, and I was pretty sure it had been built at the Perini Navi shipyards. It wasn't Janet's yacht, and when I asked around I discovered it wasn't even really owned by her network—they'd rented it. Janet let Thor and me walk around some before the party started, explaining that the losers from the show would be housed in the yacht cabins while they waited for things to wind up.

There was a big party room with enormous walls of windows on both sides. I felt almost a little exposed, even though the sea was very calm that day. The floors were gleaming wood and the ceilings were high enough to hold chandeliers, which swayed slightly with the movement of the waves.

Some staff were setting up tables at the far end, and I realized they looked familiar. "I'm having the cast members serve the food," Janet said.

"Oh, that makes sense," Thor said. "I mean, you bought their bond, and filming doesn't start until tomorrow."

Janet shook her head very slightly, a hint of a smirk on her face, and pointed at a pin clipped to her scarf that I'd thought was jewelry. "We're rolling already."

"Are you expecting anything interesting to happen at the party?" I asked.

"You never know! But mostly this will give us some back-story that might be fun to seed in—about what the bond-work-ers might be doing the rest of the time." She whipped a scarf out of her pocket, along with a pin. It was shaped like a spider but when I took a closer look I could see the lens of a camera. "Time for some accessorizing," she said, arranging the scarf around my shoulders and fastening it with the pin. "You can turn it off if you need to go to the loo. Some things *none* of us need to see." Thor's hidden bodycam was a tie clip.

Guests started arriving an hour later. Janet sent me and Thor to work at the door, with instructions to greet everyone by name if I recognized them, get their name to check them against the list of invited guests if I didn't, then point them toward the bar and the food. They had all sorts of fancy fruit as part of the spread, as well as vat-grown lobster meat and more ordinary stuff. I pilfered some strawberries before Janet sent me over to start door duty.

People mostly arrived in groups, since they needed a speed-boat or hovercraft to get to the yacht from the stead. The yacht it-self had one twelve-person hovercraft, so when people arrived in a group of twelve, I knew they were the ones who were too cheap (or broke) to pay for a taxi even if it was more convenient. Joe, the irritating "liaison," arrived in the very first group of twelve. My father arrived with two other men—one was a friend of his who has his own speedboat. Dad was dressed in a sports coat, which is about as dressed up as anyone ever gets on the stead. He was laughing, which made him look younger. Shana once told me that my father was good looking. I found it hard to really assess, but I could imagine someone seeing him that way, especially when humor sparked in his eyes.

Once everyone had arrived, Janet let me and Thor wander around with the instruction to eavesdrop on interesting conver-sations. We went to the buffet first; we both wanted more straw-berries. There were kiwis, too, and watermelon. "You know another thing I miss?" Thor said a little mournfully, surveying the options. "Raspberries. Have you ever had raspberries?"

"I've had raspberry jam," I said.

"The fresh ones are better." He ate another strawberry.

My father was talking to a couple of men in the corner; it looked like an interesting conversation but I decided I didn't want to go eavesdropping on it. People were gawking at my father because he hardly ever went to parties, but most of them were keeping a respectful distance.

I listened in on Joe for a while. He cornered a woman named Annie near the bar and was holding forth on how he was going to make sure this show portrayed the seastead fairly and accurately and not as if we were a bunch of monkeys in a zoo on display. Annie caught sight of me and used me as an excuse to make her escape, whereupon Joe latched on to me, instead. I wondered if I could get him to say anything interesting enough to use on the show. He clearly didn't know my pin was a camera, or he'd be looking at it.

"Hi, Joe," I said. "It's Beck Garrison, remember me?"

He looked me over with faint disdain. "Yeah," he said. "Paul's kid."

"Yep! Anyway I was listening to you talk to Annie because what you were saying was *so interesting*." He brightened a little, despite himself. People respond to flattery—it's really funny, even if you're a teenager and they think they're better than you they *still* like it when you tell them how smart and interesting they are. "I totally know what you mean, I mean, *Stead Life* really has an educational mission, right? And they're *us* talking to the rest of the world, not outsiders coming in to talk about us."

He nodded. "Exactly."

"But what are you going to do, I mean as far as controlling what they show? It's not like they have to even let you preview footage, and they're not a recognized part of Rosa or Min so our rules don't apply."

"Oh, we have ways of exerting pressure if we need to," he said. "That's all *you* really need to know."

"Come on, give me a hint, at least?"

He looked past my shoulder. "Oh, I see your father!" he said, enthusiastically, and strode off.

I looked over at the bar. I didn't recognize the guy tending bar but Miguel was working off to the side, replenishing snacks and bottles of cold beer. I ambled over to him. "Do you have any pop back there?"

"What's your pleasure?" Miguel said. There was no smile of recognition, no warmth, and I suddenly felt very conscious of my scarf pin. I took it off and stuffed it in my pocket as Miguel filled a glass with root beer and handed it to me. (I know, it's a little baby-ish, but beer is *gross* and real mixed drinks are *even grosser*.) He saw the missing camera and this time his face lit with a real smile. "Enjoying the party?"

I shrugged. "The buffet's pretty awesome. Janet's making me work, though."

"Me, too." He gestured at the glasses. "But I don't mind. I think I'm on to her clever plan."

"What sort of footage do you think she wants? If I knew I'd probably do a better job finding it for her."

"Just encourage people to be *themselves* around you." He winked.

"Hey," I said. "What do bond-workers do with their money? I mean, if you get some money you don't want your bond-holder to know about. Do you keep cash in your locker?"

"Sometimes," Miguel said, "but that's risky, because lockers aren't hard to break into. There are private options." He laid his hand on the table and slowly finger-spelled the word GENEVA.

I looked at his hand and then back at his face, a little baffled. "You use a *Swiss Bank Account*? From *here*?"

He laughed. "That's a person. Ask around."

*

Geneva was a woman, it turned out, and she ran a secret bank with some other women named Lucerne, Bern, Basel, and it wasn't until I found out about Zurich that it dawned on me these were code-names. I was given an address on Rosa that turned out to be a beautifully appointed apartment with a window and a *deck*. Geneva had two-year-old twin boys who were climbing on the sofa as she talked to me. She turned on some loud children's music for her kids and then bent her head close to mine. "Who should have access to your account?" she asked.

"No one but me," I said. "That's the point of coming to you, isn't it? I don't want my father to be able to get in."

"Is there anyone you want to be able to access it if you get into trouble?"

I shrugged. "Thor? But only if *I* can't access it for some reason."

"You can set up a password, and require that he tell me the password."

"Okay," I said. She scanned my thumbprint and gave me a number to identify my account; I set the password as *he lied to me.*

"Here's how it works," she said. "You'll have a phone number that reaches me, Lucerne, Bern, Basel, and Zurich. If you need cash urgently, you leave a message saying 'hit me' and the sum you want, and we'll get it to you within an hour. There's a $10 fee for that, assuming you have the money in your account to cover it. If it's a loan, there's an additional fee. I have a printed schedule you can take a look at before you go. If you need cash less urgently, the message is 'pat me,' and we'll have it to you within a day—there's a $1 fee for that. If you have a deposit the message is 'pull me,' and you'll be told where to go for the handoff, which is free. I pay no interest, I just guarantee your deposit won't get stolen and *no one* will *ever* hear about it."

"Are your files encrypted?" I asked.

"Of *course* they're encrypted. And that reminds me of something else—if we run into each other at a dining hall or something, you don't know me, and I don't know you. Especially if my husband's there." Her eyes glinted faintly and I saw her glance at the toddlers.

"Okay," I said, and handed her my money.

Filming started the next day.

The network had set up its own sea platform, next to the yacht. I'd never actually seen a bare sea platform before—Rosa and Min had been built on them originally, but the platforms were all thoroughly built up now, and the last time Rosa had expanded, the investors had found it more cost-effective to buy a retired cruise ship, chain it up to its neighbors, and build skyways in and out. This one wasn't quite like the base platforms the steads had used—it was smaller, for one thing—but it was still a big, wide patch of open space bobbing on the water.

"This must have cost a lot," I said, looking at it from the hovercraft.

"Amsterdarn is going to buy it when they're done," Thor said. "I heard one of the accountants talking."

"Why a bare platform?"

"We're re-creating the early days of the seastead," Janet said. "The teams are being given the sort of sparse environment the earliest seasteaders would have had to cope with."

I tried not to scoff out loud at that. "They came on yachts, you know."

"Yeah, well. Sea platforms make for better TV. It's all about the story."

We settled in on the yacht. There was an observation deck, and although there were sets of binoculars for people to pick up and use, the best view was provided via camera feeds to a bank of twelve screens. We were only about 200 meters from Rosa, and when I looked up I could see people clustering on the observation deck with binoculars. They wouldn't be able to hear a damn thing, though, while we got full audio.

The host was a guy named Jef Jefferson, which apparently was a TV name and not the result of parents who thought "Jef Jefferson" was a reasonable name to give a kid. Jef had a booming voice and a wide smile. I liked Janet a lot better than Jef, probably for the same reasons that Jef was the host and Janet the behind-the-scenes Czarina.

I watched on the screens as Jef divided the bond-workers into two teams, and then told them they'd be competing to build shelters. There was a pile of miscellaneous stuff in the center of the platform, and they'd be dividing it—he flashed his wide smile as he added, "By whatever means you choose."

Thor and I exchanged glances. Maybe they weren't *officially* turning the bond-workers into gladiators, but they were clearly hoping to get a fight or two out of this process.

"You're not going back to your rooms tonight," Jef warned them. "You'll be sleeping in this shelter for the next few weeks, so you might want to take that into account. But this is also a race. Whoever is done first will win the first challenge."

The bond-workers were looking at Jef warily and I could see more than a few glancing at Miguel. Miguel's fingers flicked—whatever he was signing was more complicated than finger-spelling, and I couldn't read it, but I saw someone else spell FAIR.

"On your mark," Jef said. "Get set. Go!"

Someone from each team stepped forward and each held out a fist. For a second I thought they were issuing some sort of challenge, and then I realized they were playing Rock-Paper-Scissors. Paper covered Rock, and he pursed his lips, looked down at the materials, and grabbed a sheet of corrugated tin. He handed it off to his team, and someone carried it to the other end of the island. The woman who'd thrown Rock picked out a sheet of corrugated tin as well, which made sense; it looked like it would make a good roof.

Piece by piece, the building materials got divided up. A few times there was some discussion: "We'll let you have all of those if you'll let us have all of these." There were a bunch of plastic jugs which got filled with water and used as bricks.

"Were you expecting them to be more dramatic?" I asked Janet nervously.

"It's all about the story," she said. "Good stories have conflict. But if we can't do man-vs-man there's always man-vs-nature. We'll shoot more than we can ever use and then craft what we want with editing." She pointed at one screen, where a man had just dropped a brick on his foot. "We could play that bit a thousand different ways. Do you know what the difference is between comedy and tragedy?"

"Tragedy is when it happens to me. Comedy is when it happens to you," Thor said.

"Not bad, but on TV it's always happening to someone else entirely. The difference between comedy and tragedy is the music we play while it's happening." She lit a cigarette and looked around for an ashtray. "Anyway, a good part of the show is going to be the interaction between the contestants. They're on camera 24/7."

It took about an hour and a half for the groups to get their shelters built. They determined the winner with Rock-Paper-Scissors, too: the other team won this time, and the losing team dawdled a little over finishing their shelter. "Okay," Janet said, watching. "*That's* weird." She took a drag on her cigarette. "This might be a more interesting story than I was expecting."

I didn't stick around for the evening activities, which apparently involved a set of campfire cookouts, bottles of whiskey to pass around and loosen everyone's tongue a bit, and a fresh camera crew, but Janet greeted me quite cheerfully the next morning and showed me highlights of some of the footage.

Debbie had kicked things off, suggesting a game where each person could ask a question and everyone else had to answer. Hers was, "Where did you grow up?" It got steadily more personal as questions and answers moved around the circle. Who's owned your contract? What's the worst job you've had since coming to the seastead? How much do you owe? I was a little shocked to realize that about half of them owed *more* than they'd owed when they arrived.

"I was most of the way paid off," said a heavily tattooed young man named Tom. "Then I slipped at work and messed up my ankle. Now, it says in my contract that if I'm injured on the job, the contract holder is supposed to pay for my care. But he said that this only counts if I'm injured due to *someone else's* actions. Since no one pushed me—I just slipped—I was out of luck. I wound up pretty much where I'd started by the time I was healed enough to walk again."

"I've got a better one," Debbie said, and told her sister's story—a little edited, but she did mention that the kidney failure was suspicious.

Janet was chewing her lip and looking thoughtful. I wanted her to say something, but she just lit another cigarette and sent Thor and me to start a fresh pot of coffee.

The second-day contest involved some combination of fishing and platform maintenance and again was rendered rather less dramatic by everyone taking the high road. "Let's go get some lunch," Janet said as the contestants painstakingly divided up the fish they'd caught. "Rebecca, Thor, I think I want both of you. Are there any restaurants here or just dining halls and sandwich shops?"

"There's a woman on Rosa who cooks for people in her apartment when they want something a little more cozy than a dining hall. And there are a bunch of restaurants on Amsterdarn, because of the tourists," I said.

She chewed on her lip some more. "Will your parents kill me if I take you to Amsterdarn? I want sushi, and I know they've got a place."

Thor lit up. "*Sushi.* It's *so crazy* I haven't had any since I got here! I mean, we're like, *surrounded* by *ocean.*"

"I'm not supposed to go there by *myself,*" I said, fudging the truth only a little, "but you'd be supervising so I'm sure it's fine. I mean, you're hardly likely to send me off to entertain myself at a brothel or an opium den, you know? We're just going to get sushi."

New Amsterdam—Hedonia to the tourists, Amsterdarn to the locals—isn't connected by bridge to Min and Rosa and the rest because no one really wants to put up with tourists. Tourists still come, but at least they have to hire a speedboat to get over from where the plane drops them off. Hedonia is actually really *big.* It has the airport, which is on a decommissioned aircraft carrier, and a hospital that specializes in plastic surgery, including the sort of weird stuff that a Stateside doctor won't do. (A doctor on Hedonia figures, it's YOUR BODY. If you want a healthy limb amputated, or if you want your face altered until you look like the offspring of a human and a cat, or if you think you'd look better without a nose . . . they live to serve.) And there are brothels and opium dens and that stuff Debbie got busted for back in Alabama can be bought by ten-year-olds if they have spare cash and inattentive parents. (Not a lot of families live on Amsterdarn, actually. In part because of things like the T-13 you can buy along with your toothbrush and tampons.)

You're probably wondering about bond-workers and brothels. It's illegal to sell someone's bond to a brothel, even if they consent to it. But (you knew there was a but) there are plenty of *guest workers* who work for brothels, and if you're a guest worker at a brothel and you're forced to take on a bond (to pay for medical care, say) they decided it wouldn't be fair to insist that someone lose his or her job in that situation, so . . . yeah.

Also, to be honest, although Amsterdarn has more in the way of law enforcement than Min, the main thing the cops care about is crimes against tourists.

I'd only been to Amsterdarn a handful of times. It was really different from Min and Rosa: no one on Min bothers with neon-light signs, but they're all over on Amsterdarn. The floors are a lot cleaner, and there's a lot more shopping for weird useless stuff like novelty holographic T-shirts. The sushi place was on a sun-deck on one of the retired cruise ships. I let Janet order for me—I'd never had this stuff before, although as excited as Thor got when she said "sushi," I figured it had to be pretty good.

"So," Janet said. "The stories the cast members are telling, that you've heard—do they ring true to you two? Or do you think some of them are bullshit?"

The question surprised me. "I haven't heard anything I thought was made up," I said, cautiously, "but I haven't watched all the footage so I couldn't say for sure."

Thor half-nodded, half-shrugged.

"Why do people sign these contracts?"

"Sometimes they're jumping bail," I said. "I mean, Debbie told you that at auditions. She was caught with T-13."

"Right, but she'd have gotten ten years for that, and served five. She's going to be in debt here for . . . how long, do you think?"

"When they recruit women they say you'll probably be able to get married," Thor said, "since there are so many more men here than women."

"Okay, but coming here for a better life?"

"*That* might have been a lie," I admitted. "They wanted to tell you what they thought you wanted to hear."

The sushi arrived. Some of it was little round things that Thor called rolls. There were also strips of pure raw fish pressed onto little rice balls. I eyed a piece of rich pink fish with a little unease, but at Thor's insistence I tried it. I *like* fish, and this was like . . . all my favorite things about fish, distilled. He watched my face and visibly brightened. "See?" he said. "It's *awesome*."

"It's still a man-vs-man story," Janet said, half to herself. "I just need to work out a way to bring the bad guys into the show."

*

Dear Mom,

I've never seen a TV show up close before and it's pretty weird. By the way, if they show you the bit where Debbie talks about her sister—that's the woman I took to the Institute, only I couldn't talk her into going back to the States.

I decided to leave out "and she's probably dead now."

Also, if they show you the fall Tom took today— he's the bond-worker with the really awesome tattoo of a dragon on his back, he's been taking his shirt off every day so we've got a LOT of footage of that dragon—you should know he hurt himself really badly.

Tom's fall probably wouldn't have hurt him particularly badly except that he re-injured his ankle. And therein was the problem.

Janet had me take him to the hospital, draping me with a scarf and adding the camera pin. She gave me a letter of authorization and instructions to get Tom and his awesome tattoo back on the set ASAP.

I was expecting this to be quick and easy. But somehow Joe got wind of it and bullied his way into the room where Tom was being examined. Worse, Dr. Luciano made a point of noting that Tom had *re-injured* his ankle. The injury that sent him deep into hock would have healed more completely if he'd used something high-end, like nano-grafting and a microsplint to repair the torn ligaments. Instead he'd just immobilized it, and he'd gone back to work too quickly, setting him up for this injury.

Since it wasn't original to the incident on the show, it wasn't covered by his current contract. That meant the network could legitimately refuse to pay, and Tom could get stuck with the bill—which would be added to his bond. Tom told them to just wrap it: "If I get stuck with the bill for a nano-graft," he said, "I'm going to *die* still bonded."

Back on the set, I explained the situation to Janet and she nodded, a faint smirk on her face as she unpinned my scarf. "I wasn't watching the live feed but I watched the footage as you were walking back. No worries. Tomorrow I'm going to run a reward challenge where the prize is medical treatment. I think we can count on them to pull together and make sure Tom wins. Should be great."

"Oh," I said. "Good idea."

The next morning, though, the cast pulled together in a way we didn't expect.

"This is creepy as hell," one of the camera guys said to Janet when we got there. "About an hour after sunset last night, all the cast members quit talking. We thought maybe they'd all turned in early, but no. This morning they're *still* not talking. They'll follow directions from Jef but no one's saying a word."

"What the fuck?" Janet turned around to stare at me, wide-eyed.

"I have no idea," I said.

"Let me see the footage," Janet said.

It started with Tom turning his ankle again. There was concern from the other bond-workers about whether they should call the producers for another trip to the hospital, which clearly they hadn't done. Someone re-wrapped it for him and fetched instant ice from the first-aid supplies. We could hear the murmur of conversation, but people had their heads together; they didn't want this to be for the cameras. They all moved into the shelter, where there were fewer cameras and the light wasn't as good. I saw Debbie look furiously directly at the camera and then tap her shoulder with her three fingers. The gesture spread slowly through the room.

Then another gesture started: an upraised arm with a fist, first showing the back of the fist, then whipping it around to show the front. It spread through the room, until everyone was making the gesture in unison with one hand and slapping the floor with the other.

"What the hell does that mean?" Janet said. "Is that *sign language*?" Someone from the crew came and looked.

"Yeah," he said. "That's the ASL sign for 'strike.'"

"Why ASL? All of these people hear just fine!" She looked at me for an answer and I started to shrug, then realized that I *did* know this one.

"The walls have ears," I said. "If you use Sign, you won't—you *can't* be overheard."

"Let me look back through the footage," Janet said grimly. Now that we were watching for it, it was obvious that the bond-workers were using finger-spelling almost as much as conversation, although they were covert enough about it that even the cameraman with the Deaf brother couldn't actually pick up what they were saying beyond a few things here and there.

"Well, this is just great," Janet said.

"They probably want to force your hand," I said. "Make you pay for Tom's surgery."

"They're more likely to trust you than me," Janet said. "Go tell them we have a plan. If that doesn't work—figure something out, for heaven's sake." She handed me the pin, and I dutifully put it on as I climbed into the speedboat. I wondered if they'd talk to me or if this would be entirely in Sign, too. If they had to slowly finger-spell everything our conversation could take a long time.

On the bond-worker island I was met, very solemnly, by Debbie. She pointed at my camera-pin and held out her hand. I took it off and gave it to her. She escorted me into the shelter. Every single bond-worker had crammed inside and was sitting, looking at me. Debbie pointed at the cameraman, then at the door.

"I think she wants you to leave," I said, apologetically.

"Are you sure you'll be okay?" he said.

"They're bond-workers, not cannibals," I said. "They just want a little privacy. Okay?"

Debbie handed him my camera-pin. He looked at it, then at me, still hesitant. I gave him an encouraging nod. "Okay," he said finally. "I'll be right outside if you need anything."

There wasn't any electricity, but the summer sunshine filtered through the jugs of water that had been used as bricks. Debbie pointed at something written in sand at my feet: DON'T USE OUR NAMES. She looked at me, eyebrows raised. I nodded. Fine. The walls really might have ears if the cameraman was pointing his recorder at the door.

Miguel stepped forward. "Rebecca," he said with a nod. "I'm glad they sent you to negotiate."

"Janet wants you to know that she has a plan to get T—" Wait, was that covered by the "don't use our names" rule? Or since they all knew who I meant, did it not matter? "Er, the person with the broken ankle, she has a plan to get it fixed properly."

"Well, that's something," Debbie said.

"What's the plan for Tom's ankle?" Miguel asked.

"It'll be a reward challenge. She says she thinks she can count on you making sure Tom wins. It'll be a good story, you know?"

Miguel shook his head. "No. We think it's the network's moral obligation to get it fixed."

"Janet agrees, but the doctor said they might refuse and stick Tom with the bill," I said.

"We want them to sign a contract addendum, not just for Tom but for all of us."

Debbie tilted her head. "It might do more to raise awareness if we go through the show, like she wants."

"Off-stead, sure," Miguel said. "On-stead—" He switched to Sign. I could see people around me nodding.

"When did you all learn ASL, anyway?" I said.

"During the last six months," Debbie said, with a sideways look at Miguel, and tapped her shoulder with the W.

"What does THAT sign mean?" I asked.

"You have to be a Fellow Worker to be let in on *that*," Debbie said. "Anyway, tell Janet that until Tom's ankle is fixed *properly*, none of us is going to speak on camera. On the other hand, if they sign the contract addendum and get Tom's ankle fixed *today*, we'll provide some bonus drama, and she can take her pick between a big fight or a romance between Tom and one of the pretty young girls. Or if she's got something else she wants, we're up for it."

"What if she wants to know who instigated the strike?"

"We're not telling." Debbie glanced at Miguel, then back at me. "I suppose it's up to you if you decide to *speculate*."

Miguel met my eyes and gave me the same intense look he had when he'd called me a "prisoner of conscience." "She won't," he said. "I trust Rebecca. You should, too."

Janet took Tom back to the hospital and told them she wanted his ankle fixed—quickly and efficiently, with the nano-grafts or whatever they thought would actually *fix* it. It should have been easy, but *this* time Dr. Luciano put in a call both to Joe *and* to Uncle Paul. Min has an Athenian-style democracy where major issues are voted on directly by all citizens, but the thing about that is you really don't want to have to call an assembly (even online) and vote on every barnacle you need scraped off the underside of the seastead. For day-to-day stuff, you want someone to just take care of it, and on Min, that's Uncle Paul.

His official title is "administrator" but everyone calls him Uncle Paul, even the grownups. He been hired into that job so long ago I pretty much couldn't remember anyone else in it. His job was on Min, not Rosa (which had its own administrator) but he had a lot of influence. He been invited to the party on the *Winter*

Palace but hadn't come, and when he walked into Tom's hospital room, Janet leaned over to ask, "Who is that?" I suppressed a groan and told her. "Why is he here?" she asked.

"I'm not sure," I whispered back.

Janet smiled at him brightly and shook his hand, and said, "To what do I owe the honor of this particular visit?"

"I heard a rumor you're getting pressure from your bondies regarding that boy's medical care."

Janet gave him a puzzled look and said, "Pressure? I'm not sure what you mean."

"You know perfectly well what I mean," he said, his voice hardening. "I heard your bondies decided they're not going to perform the work they've agreed to. I just wanted to make sure you understand we have *ways* of dealing with that sort of thing."

He wasn't just threatening the bond-workers, I thought. He was threatening Janet. For a moment, I wondered if I could tell Janet this somehow—with a note? Maybe she knew the finger-spelling trick?—but I looked at her face, and the way she'd raised her chin, and knew she was fully aware of it.

"Ways of ealing' with it?" she said, with a bland, unflappable smile. "I really don't understand how you do things around here, so do you think you could spell that out for me?"

She was wearing a camera-pin, I noticed.

Uncle Paul leaned back against the wall and folded his arms. "Ordinarily, a bond-worker's contract can't be sold without their consent," he said. "But there are exceptions to that rule, and one of them is, you can sell a bondie contract if they refuse to do the work they're contracted to do. I *assure* you that even if you didn't spell out *talking* in your contract, our mediators would agree that it's assumed."

"The contract we signed also assumes liability for medical care," she said. "The addendum merely clarifies what we already agreed to."

He tightened his lips. "I don't think you realize how many

bondies have something or other wrong with them," he said. "Old injuries. Unless you want every person in your cast throwing themselves off ladders to put you on the hook for rebuilding them from scratch with platinum bone-marrow or whatever, you don't want to open this door."

"Ah," she said. "Well, given that we're going to have to sell their contracts—other than the winner and the runner-up—at the end of the show anyway, I'm not sure how big a threat 'we'll sell your contracts early' really is."

"You're not quite following," he said. "Although they've agreed to be sold to *someone* they can still veto something like a skin farm. Normally. But they're in violation of their work agreement."

"I know someone told me what a skin farm is, but I can't remember," Janet said. "I know it's not prostitution, so . . . what makes it so bad?"

"Skin-farm employees work with dangerous chemicals," he said. "They tend to die of cancer. It's not a job anyone wants. You turn a tidy profit, I expect, since the skin farms have a hard time recruiting."

"So what you're suggesting is that instead of paying for medical care, I scrap my entire cast and start over from scratch?" she said, laughing. "I may not know how the seastead works, but you clearly have *no* idea how television works. The schedule is far more important than a few dollars here and there on medical care." Uncle Paul started to interrupt and she held her hand up. "Excuse me! You have also misunderstood. The bond-workers did not *threaten* me to get medical care for Tom. They *offered me something*, something that'll give us a better story. You want Tom to suffer on camera? I'm open to the idea, but you'll need to make it a good story. Tom's a cutie. Our audience wants to see him bouncing around the way he did before his injury. And it's all about the story." She raised an eyebrow at him.

He started to speak again and she whipped out a hand gadget. "You know, it occurs to me this whole conversation would make a *great* story. Do you mind repeating everything you said, maybe a bit more slowly and clearly?"

He snapped his mouth shut, turned on his heel, and walked out.

Janet breathed out and stuck her gadget back into her pocket. "Rebecca," she said. "What do the laws here actually say? Does he have any authority to give me trouble—I mean, could he revoke some permit or . . . whatever?"

I shook my head, then hesitated. "You're not going to put me on your show, are you?"

Janet grimaced and turned off her pin-camera.

"By our rules, you're an autonomous country—you don't need a permit from anyone. And the laws on Min and Rosa aren't set up to refuse you entry, and as Tom's bond-holder it's totally within your rights to pay for his ankle to be fixed, even if they don't like you setting that precedent. If you wanted to pay for a nose job for him you could do that, too, though if you were getting it done over his objections you'd have to take him to Amsterdarn."

"I could—" She stopped. "Tom's nose is fine. Okay. I think I've had enough of Dr. Disapproving. Do you know if there's another orthopedist?"

"No, but I know how you can find out."

It turned out the other orthopedist was on Amsterdarn, so we did have to go over there for Tom's treatment. Tom looked a bit puzzled when Janet hastened to reassure him that she wasn't going to have them do an involuntary nose job on him.

It was really late when I got home. The living room was dark but my father was still working. "Beck," he called. "Come in here a minute." I went into his office. "Have a seat." I sat. Cautiously.

"You should know," he said, "that there is a dangerous terrorist group that may be operating on the stead right now. It may even have infiltrated the reality show you've been working on."

"Oh?" "Dangerous terrorist group" sounded bad, but given that I was not a *complete idiot* I was not inclined to take what my father was saying at face value.

"They're allegedly a union, but they're known for promoting sabotage and other violent acts. They were behind a series of riots in San Francisco about five years ago—you probably weren't paying attention to that news story, but I was. And while the other so-called unions have generally stayed off the seastead, the Wobblies are apparently here."

"Wobblies?" It was a ridiculous-sounding name.

"They're also sometimes called the IWW."

Oh. Suddenly I knew what the "WW" shoulder-tap meant. *You have to be a Fellow Worker to know that.* Oh.

I was pretty sure those thoughts hadn't shown on my face.

"Wow," I said. "Okay."

"The person sent by the IWW might be posing as a bond-worker," he said, "and we think it's someone *on the show.*"

I shook my head. "I negotiated their bond releases myself," I said. "They all really are bond-workers."

He rolled his eyes. "I'm sure our mystery man—or woman—is *really a bond-worker* but it's a pose because the Wobblies will buy him out if things get too hot for him here. He's undoubtedly got some way of sending messages back. They wouldn't strand him."

"Huh," I said.

"I believe you know who it is," my father said. "I'd like you to tell me."

I blinked at him. "What, you seriously think they'd tell me who it is? I'm *Paul Garrison's daughter.* The bondies on the show like me well enough—I mean, I got them a really sweet contract—but they don't *trust* me."

"You were the one sent to negotiate when they went on strike. Who was it you spoke with?"

"Everyone on the whole show was in that shelter. I don't remember everyone who had something to say."

He narrowed his eyes. "*Speculate*," he said.

Speculate.

My gadget's bugged.

I tried to keep my face still, but I felt myself go cold with shock and then hot with rage. My blood pounded in my ears as I pieced it together. He had given me this gadget *because he could use it to spy on me.* Had he found me the job so that he could use me to spy on the bond workers? *I was a tool. I was his tool.* And yet, despite the bug, he needed me to divulge the actual names, because everyone had been so careful. *The walls have ears. No names out loud.* I was dead certain Miguel was the undercover organizer, but my father still didn't know.

Well. *I* certainly wasn't going to tell him.

My father let out a long breath. "Beck, I know you'd like your own money—to buy your own stake when you turn eighteen. Before you go to college. Anyway, I'd like to support you in that, and so I think you should know that a consortium of influential individuals are offering an *extremely sizable* reward for the name of the IWW organizer. Just the name. If you can't remember the name, we could run some of the raw footage of the workers and let you point him or her out. If you do that for us, that money will be *entirely* yours. It's enough to buy in with some left over; it'll go into a private account, not one I cosign, as recognition of you making your first truly *adult* decision." He smiled at me, a friendly, generous, loving smile.

I gave him a tentative smile back. A totally false, carefully crafted smile.

While he was talking, I'd imagined all sorts of great things I could say: "Go to hell," for instance. "I can't be bought, you son of a bitch." "I have just one question: When were you thinking of telling me that you lied about my mother?"

I decided to keep that card in reserve, at least for now. "Thanks," I said. "You know what, you'll have to give me a little more time. I want to be *absolutely sure* I don't give you the wrong name."

CHAPTER SIX

I WRAPPED MY HANDHELD IN A T-SHIRT, THEN STUFFED IT into a purse, which I left in the far end of Miscellenry since I was the only one in there. "Hey, Beck," Jamie said. "Nice to see you. What are you looking for?"

I held up one finger. "Discretion." And another. "And a gadget. It doesn't have to be shiny. Just a basic one will do."

"Huh." He pulled one out from under the counter. It was older than my old one, but good enough. "Like this one?"

I checked the price and asked him to hold it for me, then stepped outside and called Geneva. "Hit me," I said.

As tempting as it was to find a railing somewhere and drop-kick my bugged gadget over the side, I knew I couldn't afford to do that; it would tip my father off that I didn't intend to cooperate. But I made it a special carrying case with supplies I bought from Miscellenry —a large purse with a taped-together nest of sound insulation inside. (Sound-dampening curtains were quite popular in stead apartments, and I found a tatty one with a funny smell that Jamie let me have cheap.)

I would need to figure out what to do in a few days, when my grace period was up. I alternated between imagining myself telling my father to go to hell and trying not to think about it.

In the meantime, filming continued. We got our promised romance. I tried to come up with a way to get word to Miguel that the authorities were on to him, but couldn't think of a good excuse to go over and talk to him. "Have you thought about hiring security?" I asked Janet. "Like, the Alpha Dogs or something? They're the most bad-ass private security force on Lib."

Janet lit a cigarette. "Yes," she said. "I've been thinking about it. I guess the thing is, though—will they stay hired, if I hire them? Because I'm pretty sure Uncle Paul's friends could outbid me. So I'm not sure there's much point."

When Thor arrived that afternoon, he brought me a cup of coffee, a letter from my mom, and a data chip. "What's this?" I asked.

"Some guy gave it to me to give to you," Thor said. "He said you were compromised, whatever that means, so he didn't want to come to you directly."

"Was it a bondie?"

"Maybe? Yeah, probably."

I popped the chip into my clean gadget and took a look. It was camera footage and after a minute or two I realized it had been taken inside a skin farm. Looking at the pulsing screens and the grim faces of the workers, I could almost smell the chemicals and the sweat. The camera panned around the room, zooming in to make sure the viewer could see that a lot of the workers were chained to their benches.

There weren't any interviews. I was damn sure everyone knew the camera was there, but no one wanted to have to admit later they knew the camera was there, so even though everyone conscientiously made sure the camera had a good view, no one looked directly at it. There was a long conversation between some of the workers about the risks of the job, and two others had a chat about how they'd wound up at the skin farm (both had gotten seriously ill—one had consented to having her bond sold to the skin farm, the other had been sold over her objections on the grounds that her medical situation was truly dire).

"Ugh," Thor said, looking over my shoulder. "I wonder why the guy thought you'd want *that*?"

I froze the image, suddenly wondering if I should have let Thor see this. He was already keeping secrets for me, though. And I didn't think he was going to run to my father to tattle. I unfroze the image. "I don't think he thought *I'd* want it," I said, and walked over to Janet and nudged her. "Hey," I said. "Do you want to see some pictures from one of the places you're *totally* not allowed to go?"

The next morning I got up early so that my father wouldn't stop me on my way out. I'd have to talk to him sooner or later, and I'd pretty much settled on "When were you going to tell me about my mother?" as a response.

But when I got to the filming site, things were in turmoil and Janet was in shock. "There was a murder," she said. "One of the cast members was killed last night. Miguel."

The killers came at 4 a.m. We had footage, of course, because the cameras were left running.

Four masked men had arrived on a speedboat. They sent the night camera crew off to one side; the cast, they'd lined up on their knees, shining flashlights into faces one at a time. "Are you Miguel?" they asked when they'd identified him.

"Yes," he said.

BANG.

They shot him in the head, twice, then jumped back into the speedboat and disappeared into the night.

When Janet realized what Thor and I were staring at, she hit the pause button, which froze the screen on Miguel's outstretched hand, limp against the platform. "Sorry," she said. "You shouldn't have seen that."

Thor looked sick. I didn't know how I looked; it was hard to believe that what I'd seen on the cameras had been real. Until I looked at the hand again, and thought, *He died for this. Died.*

Janet had been up since 4:05—the night camera crew had called her the second the killers were gone. She called the police, but the police officers on Rosa (all three of them) considered her domain to be out of their jurisdiction. "If you can find the killers and get them on your island," they'd said, in a reassuring tone, "you know you can mete out whatever justice you like. There's a private security force on Lib you could hire to look into it . . ."

"It probably WAS the Alpha Dogs," Janet said furiously, telling me and Thor the story. "I mean, don't you think it was the Alpha Dogs who did the murder?"

It might have been. Or the Tigers. Or freelancers. Looking at a clip of the killers getting out of their speedboat, I was at least certain that my father was not among the actual killers. I was just as certain he'd known this was going to happen, even if he hadn't hired the killers himself. I shrugged. "I don't know," I said.

"I need a drink," Janet muttered.

"I could go get you a bottle of whiskey," Thor offered.

She looked at his baby face skeptically. "I keep forgetting you don't have a drinking age here. No. I want a real bar, and that means Amsterdarn again. Let's go."

Janet took us to a bar called Tiki Top, which had tiki torches, umbrellas, models of Easter Island heads (who knows why?), and a beverage menu full of drinks with names like the New Minerva (ouzo in ginger ale), the Rosa (raspberry liqueur, cream, and vodka), the Pete (I think most people call that one a White Russian), and the Lib (sort of a bartender's surprise).

Janet ordered scotch for herself and something called a Shirley Temple for me and Thor. It turned out to basically be pop with a maraschino cherry at the bottom and a little umbrella on top. I fidgeted with the umbrella, making it go up and down, up and down.

"Why Minerva?" Janet asked. "I mean, no offense, but I wouldn't say you folks are exactly devoted to the Roman Goddess of Wisdom."

"It's *New* Minerva," I said. "The first Minerva was a much earlier attempt at seasteading." I put down my miniature umbrella. "Some settlers built up a sandbar into an island and named it the Republic of Minerva. Then it got invaded by Tonga."

"Tonga. *Tonga?*"

"Yeah, I know what you're probably thinking—these were libertarians trying to colonize a sandbar, didn't they bring any guns? But yeah, Tonga sent their Navy or whatever and said that since they'd owned the sandbar, the island was also theirs, no matter how it got there. They cleared everyone off and it washed away. So we're New Minerva, named after that early experiment."

"Got it." She sank back into morose reflection. Thor and I sipped our Shirley Temples. "I thought this was going to be so much fun."

"Filming here?"

"Yes. And the show itself. It was supposed to be bright and cheerful and funny." She narrowed her eyes, staring at her whiskey. "*Stead Life* is bright and cheerful and funny. And people all over the world watch it—we were shooting for that demographic."

"*Stead Life* never covers bond-workers," I said.

"Yeah." She looked at me. "I've watched *Stead Life* for years. I think that's part of why I liked the idea of focusing on the bond-workers—we could show the other side of life on the stead."

"You have," I said.

"I can't do a *game show* about this. I can't."

"So don't," I said. "You want a story, right? You've *got* a story. The other side of *Stead Life*."

"God, they'll be pissed," she said. "The council from Rosa—"

"You're totally not in their jurisdiction," I said. "They won't even investigate Miguel's murder. You don't answer to them."

"I suppose that's true."

"Do you want to *really* piss them off?" Thor said. "Release some bits and pieces of the footage *now*."

Janet raised an eyebrow. "Any particular bits you're thinking of?"

"The murder." Thor stared down at his drink.

"Also—" I dropped my voice. "The strike."

"Mm." Janet finished her whiskey and signaled the waitress to bring her another. "If that's the story I tell, how do I end it? Is there any *light* at the end of this shit-stained tunnel we're in?"

Miguel was the light at the end of the tunnel, I thought, and I was pretty sure Janet was thinking the same thing.

"No," Janet said, drinking her whiskey in a single gulp and slamming down the glass. "I know. We'll find the darkest of the darkness. I've got footage of a skin factory. I've got footage of a goddamn *murder*. Show me something worse." She looked at me and Thor with grim expectancy.

"Okay," Thor said, and stood up. "We're even on Amsterdarn already. It won't take long to get there."

So, you know how I mentioned that it's *mostly* illegal to sell someone's bond to a brothel? But also the cops on Amsterdarn don't really pay that much attention to stuff when it's not going to hurt tourism?

You probably already figured this out, but there *are* brothels with bond-workers who had their bonds sold. They're not on the official Red Light level, with the neon signs and the hot babes posing in windows in lingerie. There's a lower level that's dingier, smellier, more cramped, and much, much less likely to get inspected by anyone who would care whether the ladies in the windows are free to leave.

So we took Janet to the Black Light district.

*

On our speedboat back from Amsterdarn, Thor stared out across the water. "I knew it was there," he said. "People talk about it. But it's not what I expected." He looked at me, his eyes bleak. "It was *crowded*."

"Yeah."

"I kept thinking—you know all those bondies who skipped bail? That's *exactly* what my dad did. Skipped bail to avoid jail time. Only in his case we had enough money to just buy right into the top shelf. But you know, I kind of lied, it wasn't *just* tax evasion, even though that's what my father likes to tell people. He embezzled, too, from his company. He stole money. The money we *used* to buy in here was *stolen*. And here we are, living in a deckside apartment with a bathtub and a kitchenette. Is selling tabs of T-13 really worse than stealing? M-51, *maybe*. But T-13?"

"Yeah."

"Sometimes I wish I could burn this whole place down."

We docked at Min and climbed off the speedboat. "So who's going to win?" I asked Janet. "Somebody has to win a stake, right? And someone else gets their bond erased? How are you going to pick winners?"

Janet gave me a dumbfounded look and then a manic grin spread across her face. "I've got it," she said. "I know how to end the story."

Jef arrived on Bondie Island with a big jar full of plastic eggs. He explained that the producers had decided to determine the winner randomly. "One of these eggs contains a gold marble and one contains a white marble. If you draw the white marble, your full bond will be paid off. If you draw the gold marble, your bond will be paid off *and* you'll receive a cash prize sufficient to buy a stake. Everyone will choose an egg, and then everyone will break open their egg at the same time."

The bond-workers silently lined up and drew out their eggs. Then they fell back, nudged by Jef and the camera crew into positions that would allow every reaction to be caught on camera, and opened their eggs.

There was one gold marble, as promised. Tom of the awesome tattoo got that one.

Every other marble was white.

There were shrieks of delight and then a hush of puzzlement. Jef said, "And now your Czarina has a few words she would like to share with you," and Janet stepped out of the speedboat.

Janet, for once, was not holding a cigarette, probably because it was illegal (she'd mentioned) to show them on TV back in the States. "We're canceling everyone's bond. I'm also concerned that you'll be in danger if you stay; we'll be pulling the yacht out later today, and anyone who wishes to leave with us is welcome to do so. We'll be happy to drop you in either Mexico or the US."

"When's this going to air?" Debbie asked.

"Soon," Janet said.

Debbie turned around, to face the other bond-workers but also the cameras. "Listen," she said, and I could hear the rhythm of a speech she'd thought through carefully. "Miguel's murder wasn't random. Miguel was murdered because he was organizing a union.

"The IWW warns its organizers to keep their heads down. If employers know that their workers are organizing, they'll harass you. They'll fire you. It's only here—only in this haven of freedom!—that they can *murder* you with impunity. Not that murder is technically *legal*—it's just that it happened outside everyone's jurisdiction! There's nothing they can do!"

The bond-workers made derisive noises.

"They silenced Miguel," Debbie said. "They may silence me next—I know the risks. But they can't silence all of us. And you know why they can't silence all of us? Because they depend on us! We cook their food. We scrub their floors. We paint the bridges and scrape barnacles off the bottoms of the steads. We do every

scrap of unpleasant work that's too dangerous or boring or unpleasant or demeaning for the wealthy and privileged here to
dirty their hands with! If they silence us all, *they'll be stuck doing
it themselves.*"

There was a wave of laughter with some scattered applause.

"I'm not leaving," she said. "I'm going to stay and fight. It's
time for direct action. It's time for a slowdown." She made sign
I hadn't seen before—fingers drawing a whisker. *Cat.* "We're not
demanding that our contracts be cancelled—though we certainly
considered it. We're not demanding a stake, though we've certainly more than earned it. We're demanding fair pay—enough
to actually *earn out*, like we were promised when we came here.
And we're demanding a health benefit. Our bond-holders need
to start bearing the cost when we're sick or injured, not tacking
it onto our bond so that injuries *they can cause* plunge us deeper
and deeper into slavery."

She made the cat sign again. "*It's time.*"

Janet pulled out her own gadget and started keying in a message. "We're leaking that last bit," she said. "Right before we pull
out. Consider it a parting gift."

Tom walked over and handed the gold marble to Debbie.
"We'll share," he said. "Everyone who's staying."

One by one, the bond-workers made their choice. In the end,
only two went with Janet.

Back on the yacht, I watched all of this on the monitor screens.
Janet had heavily hinted to Thor and me that she was going to
cancel everyone's bond, so I was excited to see that celebration,
but when everyone decided to stay and fight—I hadn't seen that
coming and I was pretty sure Janet hadn't either. It was thrilling,
and also very worrying, because I liked Debbie.

Janet came back with her two passengers and sent them off to
the salon with a camera guy to keep filming, because they might

as well. Then she turned to me and Thor. "I can't take you," she said, regretfully. "I think technically it would be kidnapping."

"Yeah," Thor said.

"Actually," I said, "according to a US court, it's my mother who has custody of me. She lives in San Francisco."

Janet lit a cigarette and stared into the smoke, considering.

"She can't take you," Thor said. "Your father could hire the ADs to go after her, and he would, don't you think?"

He would. Thor was right. I hadn't decided about whether I wanted to go to California to live with my mother, but it didn't matter because I knew I didn't want Janet to get hurt trying to protect me. It made it an easy decision, in some ways. I'd stay, like Debbie.

Janet's eyes focused on me, through the smoke. "They might not catch us."

I shook my head. If Debbie could stay, I could stay. "Good luck," I said. "I hope your show is a huge success."

Janet paid each of us for the last time. I started for the speedboat and then turned back. "Hey," I said. "One more thing." Janet looked at me, waiting. "Take my picture," I said, "and send it to my mom. She doesn't have any recent photos of me."

A slowdown, Debbie had said.

By the time I made it up to Gibbon's dining hall, there was already a huge line down the hall just waiting to get in. The tables were laden with dishes and the food, once it came out, was terrible.

I saw one of my father's friends go stomping back through the kitchen door and a little while later Gibbon, red-faced, came out to clear plates.

Gibbon caught my eye before I got up to leave. "Are you still looking for a job?" he asked.

"Nope," I said.

*

I braced myself for a confrontation with my father as I walked back to the apartment. I imagined him telling me that I should have taken his offer while I had the chance—since obviously, they didn't need information now—and tried to think of a good response. Was he going to blame me for the slowdown? Surely he'd assume it was Janet's fault, not mine. Unless he'd been eavesdropping on me even with my bugged gadget muffled.

But when I got to the apartment, the door was locked and my thumbprint didn't open it. I knocked, thinking at first there was some sort of technical glitch, but I got no response.

I took out my gadget—maybe my father wasn't home?—and found a note in my e-mail account.

> Beck.
> You seem to find it entertaining to defy me—to play games with me—to act like you think I'm an idiot.
> I'm done with your games. Call me when you're ready to act like my daughter: respectful, obedient, and responsible.

I swallowed hard. For a minute, I thought about banging on the door, apologizing, begging him to let me in.

Then I took the gadget he'd given me, shoved it through the delivery slot, and walked away.

PART THREE
SOLIDARITY

CHAPTER SEVEN

FINE, I THOUGHT FURIOUSLY, STRIDING THROUGH THE corridors. *This is just fine. I don't want to live with him anyway.*

The seastead has some big hotels, but they're all on Amsterdarn, for the tourists. On Rosa and Min, we have a couple of guest houses—just a few small rooms, comfortable and private, with attached bathrooms. When someone has a guest visiting from shore, they stay in a guest house, because no one's apartment is big enough to comfortably house guests.

When I went to the guest house on Min, the guy said they were full. The guy running the Rosa guest house said the same thing. It was possible they really were full, but it was just as possible my father had paid them to turn me away. Or just *told* them to turn me away.

My father doesn't hold any of the elected offices and he's not on the Business Council or even the Seastead Governing Council, but his word carries a lot of weight. Even on Amsterdarn; even on Lib. People know who he is, and care what he thinks. And prefer not to cross him. He didn't have a title, beyond "Mr. Garrison," but that was true for a lot of the most powerful people on the seastead, because it wasn't a *title* that gave you power here, it was money and influence.

With nowhere else to go, I went to the Catholic church to sit and think. The knowledge that I would *not* see Miguel there was nearly overwhelming. I was a little worried the priest would try to talk to me, but everyone left me alone. The church was crowded, and a lot of people were crying; clearly, I wasn't the only person grieving Miguel's death. Most of the people there this time seemed to actually be praying. I found a spot in the shadows and tried to consider my options sensibly.

I could take a boat to Amsterdarn. It was unlikely that my father had bought off every taxi driver and every hotel owner, so that would probably work. Amsterdarn was large, though, and honestly it kind of freaked me out, since I didn't know anyone over there. I could go to Thor's apartment and see if they had a couch they'd let me sleep on—except his parents would call my father, and turn me away if he asked them to.

I didn't think the American Institute was likely to be open this time of night. But even if it was, leaving like this—now—felt cowardly. All the bond-workers had stayed (well, almost all) and they were in a lot more danger than I was.

And that brought me to my final option. I could go rent a locker to sleep in, like a bond-worker would. I stayed in the church for a long time after that idea occurred to me. The third time I pulled out my gadget to check my mail, I had to admit to myself that I was hoping my father would change his mind. He wasn't going to. I stuck it in my pocket and found the stairs down to the lower levels.

It was late enough by then that I wasn't certain I'd be able to find a landlord. I tried Debbie's old room, but of course she'd given up that rental while she was on the show and no one knew where she was staying now. A woman named Elaine recognized me, though. "Why do you want our landlord?" she asked bluntly.

"I need a place to stay. My father kicked me out."

"Oh! That's terrible. I'll find him for you."

It turned out that lockers could be rented only by the week, which meant I had to spend a lot more than I'd expected. Then it turned out that mattresses and blankets were offered a la carte and had to be paid for separately. Oh, and so was the lock. If I stayed there for more than six weeks it would cost more to rent the mattress and blanket than it would have to buy them, but surely by then . . .

The locker was exactly long enough for the mattress, with half a meter of clearance overhead. It felt a little like crawling into my own coffin, an image I tried desperately to push out of my head. Elaine showed me how to lock it from the inside. It was pitch black, and I realized that the only light source I had with me was my gadget. I turned it on, trying to glean some reassurance from the dim glow. But the "battery low" light was lit, and I didn't have the charging cable. I turned it off and tried to settle in.

The mattress was so hard I wasn't sure why I'd bothered to rent it, and the blanket was thin. I had no pajamas or even a toothbrush, and I'd forgotten to get a pillow.

When I focused, though, I could feel the movement of the waves: the gentle up-and-down rocking that had been part of my life since I was four years old. That, at least, was the same down here as it was in my father's apartment. I closed my eyes and focused on the waves until I fell asleep.

I woke up desperately wanting to pee. It took me a second to remember how to work the lock, and I mis-remembered the distance to the floor and stumbled. Three women were standing around talking, but they fell instantly silent and stared at me, wide-eyed.

"Elaine helped me rent this locker last night," I said. "My father kicked me out. And I have to pee. Can you tell me where the bathroom is?"

It was down the hall, but you needed to swipe an ID card to

get in. "I'll swipe you in," one of the women said grudgingly, "but you'll owe me the charge."

". . . it costs money?"

There was a round of derisive laughter. "You sound like a foob," one of them said. "Fresh on the boat. There ain't no such thing as a free lunch, honey, and there's water in those bathrooms. Desalinated water. You don't think that's free, do you?"

Of course. In our apartment, the water was simply billed to my father. "I have an ID card," I said, hesitantly, "but I'm not sure it'll work. And I don't want my father to know where I am."

"You can get a cash-basis card if you want to stay anonymous," the woman said. "They cost more, though." She swiped her card and let me into the bathroom. "Don't waste water," she called after me. "It's all getting billed to me."

I peed. The toilet would be saltwater, so at least I wouldn't be charged as much, but it flushed itself twice while I was sitting on it. I'd run into toilets before that did this and it had startled me, but never *infuriated* me. When I was done, I rinsed my mouth, since I had no toothbrush. I carried a hairbrush in my backpack, and I wet it to brush my hair and then put my hair in a ponytail. I would have liked a shower, but I had no towel, plus I didn't want to abuse the woman's generosity.

"The stupid toilet flushed itself three times," I said when I came out. "But I used less than a gallon from the sink. Can I pay you later today? I need to get money from Geneva."

"Yeah," she said, and told me how much I owed her.

Now that I'd peed, I realized how hungry I was. The last time I'd eaten was on Amsterdarn, yesterday, with Thor and Janet. Clark's was the dining room on this level: it was cheap and offered meal plans by the week. The line was really long, probably due to the slowdown the union had organized. I was standing in it when I remembered that this was the dining hall that had poisoned Debbie's sister Lynn. What if they poisoned me? What if my father had *paid* them to poison me? What if the whole purpose of throwing me out was to set me up to get so sick that they could blackmail me with medical care?

I went to the sandwich shop near my morning tutoring group, instead.

"Hey, Beck!"

It was Thor, waving me over to his booth. Seeing a friendly face gave me a jolt of hope and relief—a sense that everything would be okay, maybe. I slid in across from him. "You look a little frazzled," he said.

"Yeah. My father kicked me out. He said I could come back if I agreed to 'act like his daughter' which I think probably means spy on whoever he wants me to spy on, and tell him anything he asks."

I wanted to sound tough and defiant when I said this, but looking at Thor's face—which was worried and concerned and sympathetic all at once—broke my resolve. I started to cry. Thor moved over next to me and put his arm around my shoulders as I sobbed.

"Hey," he said. "Beck, it's not that bad. You can go to California, right? And live with your mom."

"I don't *want* to leave." I tried to explain, but I could tell from the noises he was making (the sort of "uh-huh" that means, "You can keep talking, I'm still listening," not the sort that means, "I totally agree with you") that he thought I was nuts.

"I can't wait to go back," he said. "If I had a parent on shore who wanted me, I'd be in the Institute right now saying, 'Get me out of here!'"

"Shore's *home* for you, though," I said.

"I asked Tyrone—you know, the guy at the American Institute—about whether I could become an emancipated minor. He said no, probably not, at least not yet. But the day I turn eighteen, he said he can help me. I might enlist."

"Enlist?"

"In the military. Which admittedly is a little like being a bondworker, since you can't quit, but they pay for *everything*. Housing, food, clothes, all your medical care . . ."

I had seen a few movies where people were in the Army. I pulled away and looked at Thor, trying to imagine him with all his pretty curls shaved off for boot camp or whatever they called it these days. I must have made a face because Thor laughed.

"Anything but the Navy," he said. "I've had enough of the ocean."

He put his arm around me again and I leaned my head against his shoulder.

"Go to California," he said. "That way when I get there in two years, I'll have someone to visit."

But I didn't want to leave. I didn't want to leave *Thor*. And I knew from the way his arm tightened as he said "go" that he didn't really want me to go, either.

I got money from my underground off-the-official-books bank and went to Miscellenry to buy the stuff I needed most urgently—a toothbrush, a towel, a change of clothes. A second blanket. A charge cable for my gadget. A flashlight. Jamie took my money and avoided my eyes. I could feel my father's influence as if he loomed over Jamie's shoulder, glaring at me. I thought about asking Jamie if he wanted to hire me back—he'd said just the other day he'd hire me back in a second—but I was afraid I'd start crying again when he said no. So I didn't ask.

"I need a cash-basis water card," I said.

Jamie looked over his shoulder, like he really did expect my father to be standing there, and said, "I don't sell those," a little bit too loudly. Then he pulled one out from under the counter and slipped it to me. "Don't tell anyone," he whispered. I reached for my wallet and he shook his head. "It's on me."

I tried to calculate how long my savings would last, paying for bed, food, water, and all the things I was probably still forgetting to account for. Not long, was the answer. Maybe a month. And then . . . what?

For now, I decided, I wasn't going to worry about it.

It was supposed to be my first day back at school, but I was pretty sure I couldn't go—if my father was cutting me off, he'd surely have canceled with my tutors. The day stretched out in front of me, empty, so I went for a walk, Min to Rosa to the far edge of Pete. I didn't go to Pete very often, because about the only thing I can say in Russian is, "Sorry, I don't speak Russian." (I had a Russian tutor for a while when I was little, but then my father got pissed off at some collective decision made on Pete and switched me to Spanish. Which I don't speak very well, either.)

Pete does have a few cool things, though, including a good-sized stretch of open deck that you can get onto for a really small fee—you don't need an ongoing subscription. Unfortunately, I realized only after I'd paid my entry fee that the weather was lousy. It was overcast and drizzling, but at that point I felt obligated to go stand in the open air for a little while anyway, because otherwise I'd have wasted my money. I looked out over the rail. I could see Sal, which was about a kilometer away. Sal is short for Silicon Waters, and it's separated from the rest of the seastead because they do nanotech experimentation and the rest of the steaders are nervous about the dangers. Of course, people go back and forth by boat all the time. It's where my father's business is, although mostly he works from home.

Amsterdarn was on the other side of the stead from here, so I couldn't see it. Aside from Sal, I could see a couple of speedboats and someone who looked like he was out fishing. One of the signs said (in English, Spanish, and Russian) that on a clear day, visibility from this point was 11 kilometers, but I certainly couldn't see that far right now.

". . . funeral of the rabble-rouser," someone said, in English. I stiffened but didn't look around.

"What about the press? I'm thinking of *Stead Life*, in particular, since they have a significant following." The voices were male; there were two of them; they were standing a short distance away. I resolutely stared out to sea.

"They're already not going."

"Heh. Good. The last thing we need is someone making more of this than it is."

"At any rate, we hired the ADs for the actual action. Your people are for the perimeter—we want you to make sure no unacceptable targets even make it to the funeral in the first place. Ideally we like no one who isn't a bond-worker, but for sure, absolutely no minors are to be allowed in."

"Understood."

My ears were burning, and even though I hadn't meant to, I glanced at the men. One of them was the operations manager for the Scoundrels, which is a security firm on Lib. I recognized him because he puts up a lot of ads. People call the Scoundrels the Cut-Rate Bastards behind their backs. The other guy I didn't recognize, and to my relief, he looked at me blankly. "Hey, girl," he said. "You planning to go to the big funeral tomorrow? Are all the kids going to be there?"

"Mne ochen zhal, ya ne govorit po angliyski," I said. *I'm sorry, I don't speak English.*

He shrugged and turned back to the Scoundrel. "Payment will be in cash. Since your job is to keep people *out*, I was going to suggest a base payment with a large bonus that goes *down* for every citizen and dependent who's missing afterward . . ." When I heard there was a list of citizens they were to make *particular* effort to keep away from the funeral, I decided I'd been out in the rain long enough. I might be on that list. My picture might be on that list. Hopefully they wouldn't look at my ID photo and recognize the damp, bedraggled Russian teenager who had been standing right by them a minute earlier. Anyway, I knew the part that mattered, which was that they were planning to do something horrible at the funeral. I had to tell someone! But Miguel was dead, and I had no idea where Debbie was.

After dithering as I walked across the bridge from Pete, I went to the church where I'd gone to meet Miguel. Miguel said the priest had noticed me, and had wondered if he should talk to me about my faith—since he knew Miguel, maybe he'd be officiating at the funeral. Maybe he'd have some idea what to do.

The church was open and less crowded today. I looked for Debbie but didn't see her. I didn't see the priest, either, but there was a door at the far end and I thought it might lead to an office. I tried knocking, and when no one answered, I tried opening it. It led to a hallway, and one of the doors off the hallway was labeled "Fr. Timothy Esposito."

It occurred to me he might not be here. Priests sometimes got called out to visit sick people, didn't they? And . . . actually, I had no real idea what priests did all day. I knocked. The door was opened by a middle-aged man in a black suit and one of those weird white collars that goes straight across. "Oh," he said, surprised. "It's you. Rebecca, isn't it?"

"Yeah," I said, and wondered if I was supposed to add "Father" or if only Catholics were supposed to do that. "I want—can I talk to you for a minute? Mr. . . . Father . . . Mr. Esposito?"

He opened the door a little wider and gestured for me to come in. "Call me Tim."

Tim. Okay. I took a deep breath and entered.

Tim's study was crammed full of books—old-fashioned bound books. Some of them were Catholic, or at least religious, but as I looked around I noticed he also had *Lord of the Rings*, a shelf of books by Ursula K. Le Guin, and *The Secret Garden*.

"Have a seat," he said, gesturing to a chair, and sat down across from me. I'd sort of expected him to sit behind his desk, but he had two visitor chairs and he sat in one of them.

"I'm not here to talk about my faith, just so you know," I said. "I'm an empiricist."

He gave me a slightly quirked smile. "That's fine."

I was waiting for some sort of religious sales pitch; it didn't come. After a minute of expectant silence I realized he was waiting for me to go on.

"Okay," I said. "I'm coming to you because I think you were Miguel's friend and might know what to do. I heard some people talking an hour ago, over on Pete. One of them was the guy who runs the Scoundrels, and the other I don't know who he was. They're planning to do something horrible at Miguel's funeral. I don't know if they're going to blow up the church, or what, but it's going to be bad."

Tim's brow furrowed. "The funeral isn't going to be here," he said. "They're holding it on the sea platform that was built by the network for their reality show. Apparently, instead of selling it to Amsterdarn, as originally planned, Janet handed it over to the bond-workers who'd performed on the show."

"Oh. *Oh.*" Well, that explained why they thought they could destroy it without sinking part of the stead. "Tell them not to! I mean—*can* you? Can you warn them?"

Tim pondered this. "Given this information, I might be able to persuade people to move it here. They have to put it off for another day or two, though, while I negotiate with my neighbors for some additional space. Part of the reason it's being held on the sea platform is to enable more people to attend. The other reason is because Catholic funerals aren't set up to allow for speech-making." He shrugged. "I can turn a blind eye to that, but there's a limit to how many people you can fit in here. The biggest church is the Methodist church, which is a level up from here and about four times the size. Whether they'd be willing to host—who knows?"

"Were you going to be there on the platform?"

"Yes." He raised an eyebrow. "So apparently the gentlemen you overheard on Lib consider me entirely disposable. They may be hoping the next priest will be more willing to dance to their tune."

"But you'll tell people," I said.

"Yes, I'll try to get the word out."

"Okay," I said, standing up. "Do you think there's anyone else I should tell?"

"Feel free to warn anyone you like, although rumors of danger may only make people more stubborn. It's hard to know."

"Thank you."

"Thank *you*." He stood up. "Feel free to come by and talk anytime. About anything. Empiricists and rationalists are welcome here; I'm a Jesuit, after all."

I smiled, although I didn't really get the joke, and went back out.

I wasn't sure whether I could trust the priest or not—I didn't know if he'd actually try to get the funeral moved, and for that matter, I didn't know if he actually had the necessary influence. Maybe, I thought, I should spread the word, too. Although, I wasn't sure how to persuade people to trust me. Debbie would, but I had no idea where to find her.

I passed a dining hall; the lines coming out were unreal. The sandwich shop I'd planned to buy dinner at was just as bad. If I went to Clark's, I could warn people, and surely they weren't actually organized enough to poison me under the current circumstances. I went back down to the locker-room level and got in line.

"Miguel's funeral's been delayed," said the man in front of me. "Pass it on."

Well. Apparently the priest *was* the guy to go to.

Clark's, when I finally made it in, was crammed full of people. Instead of chairs, the tables had long benches, and people sat shoulder-to-shoulder. I took a plate and held it out to the servers, who gave me four scoops of . . . stuff. There was a scoop that looked sort of like animal protein, but I couldn't tell what kind. The second was beige, like mashed potatoes. The third was green and on inspection I thought it was broccoli. The fourth was brown and was ice cream. To go with all that I got a small glass of water. I looked around for somewhere to sit; I didn't see any spots. But a man saw me looking and scooted over, making a small space, and I sat down. I was hungry enough that it all tasted okay.

"Miguel's funeral's been postponed," I said. "Pass it on."

He grunted. "I know."

The staff here didn't appear to have slowed down—or maybe it was just that customers were expected to do more of the work. We had to carry our own food to the table and bus our own dishes. The dishes went through an automatic washer, but the person who put in the last dish had to give the rack a shove toward the sprayer. I copied the people around me and made my way back to my locker. My gadget's battery was almost drained; I needed to find somewhere to plug it in.

But when I got to the locker room that night, I was locked out of my unit. There was a notice of eviction taped to the side. I pulled it off, blinking away tears of frustration and bewilderment. The letter said that because I was a *dependent*, and neither a citizen nor a guest-worker, I was not legally permitted to engage in commerce my guardian had forbidden. The money I'd paid—for the locker, the mattress, the blanket, all of it—had been refunded. To my guardian.

I felt like screaming and kicking the side of the locker. Or throwing up. I knocked on locker #6, because I still owed her money. She slid the side up; she'd been watching TV on her own gadget. "I'm *not* passing you in again."

"No, I don't need you to. I just want to pay you back for this morning," I said. "I couldn't wait, you see . . ." I held out the letter of eviction. My throat was already closing.

She took it from my hand and looked at it. "Well, isn't *that* a load of boiled shite," she said. "He took your money, and now he's saying it's not good enough? What, he couldn't tell *looking* at you that you're a teenager?"

"I don't know," I said. "The lighting in here's pretty bad. Maybe he couldn't tell."

She handed me the letter. "Don't worry about paying me back for the water, kid."

"Can you tell me . . . do you know if there's anyone who wouldn't care? Who let me stay? I'm so tired," I said, and my throat started closing again. "I just want somewhere I can *sit*."

The locker door by my ankle slid up and another woman looked up at me. "I'll tell you," she said. "Keep going down."

The woman in six started to say something but the woman in the lower unit shook her head. "You really think she ought to go home right now? Go down. Dodge the authorities. And don't piss anyone off." She slid her door shut again.

CHAPTER EIGHT

GO DOWN. DODGE THE AUTHORITIES. DON'T PISS ANY- one off.

A good portion of stead is actually below the waterline. The old cruise ships generally have a draft of about 30 feet, Lib's freighter is closer to 40 feet, and to provide stability, there's actually 50 to 60 feet of stead underwater for the main sea platforms that make up Min and Rosa. Some of this is used for habitation— a lot of the locker rooms, for instance, are in the underwater portions of the sea platforms—but the further down you go, the more it's utility stuff, like generators and desalinators.

I'd never been below the locker rooms, but I knew the stairs kept going, even if the elevators didn't.

I shouldered my backpack, glad that I hadn't left any of my possessions behind to be confiscated and given to my father. I had a blanket, a snack, and a flashlight. *Everything I really need.* I found the stairs and started going down. Below the habitable levels, the doors were supposed to be locked, but when I got to the bottom level, I found that the door's latch had been taped open. Around the edge of the door frame someone had taken permanent marker and scrawled *welcome to the free land, the glad land, the fair land, the no-man's-land, the lost land, the you-and-me-*

and-thee land. It was a song lyric I recognized, from a stateside musician, about a guy being locked up in a hospital after murdering a bunch of people.

I was under a desalination plant. It was cool down here, and damp. I could hear water dripping and hoped it was condensation rather than a leak. There were supposed to be alarms for things like leaks, but there were also supposed to be locks on doors like the one I'd just come through. Dim lights shone through a tangle of wires and pipes overhead and the ceiling was low. I had to duck a lot to pass under low-hanging pipes and I'm not actually that tall.

Dodge the authorities. Don't piss people off.

I had no idea where I was going, but I kept walking for a while. Presumably if you were near the door, you were more likely to be found by the authorities. If they ever actually came down here. I wasn't sure they did. Surely they'd rip the tape off the latch if they came down.

And then, off to the right, I saw a brighter glow. I followed it, only to be stopped with a blast of brilliant, dazzling light in my face. I flung up one hand and flinched back. "I'm sorry!" I said.

The light left my face. "Not a cop," someone said.

I couldn't see anything but spots. "No," I said. "I'm not a cop." *Don't piss people off.* Too late, I wondered if I should have tried harder to sound friendly.

Someone grabbed my arm. "Over here," the voice said. "You can sit down. You'll be able to see again in a minute. Next time don't sneak up on us."

"I wasn't trying to *sneak*," I said. "All I knew was, if I went to the bottom level I might find somewhere I could stay. I rented a locker but got evicted, because . . ." Should I tell these people I was a dependent? They could probably guess. "Because the guy was an asshole."

I was sitting on something hard, but it wasn't the floor. I patted it with my hands and concluded it was a concrete block. I could smell food cooking, and as my vision slowly returned I looked around.

Yes, there were people living here. I could see blankets spread on the floor, marking out beds. Someone had a little stove going: they'd cut into one of the wires running past our heads and added a spliced-in makeshift outlet. It looked like a fire hazard. I could see the dripping water now: it was dripping from one of the pipes, and being caught in a bucket. One of the men got up to swap in a fresh bucket, and carried the full bucket over to the circle. He ladled water into cups. "Do you have a cup, kid?" he asked.

I had a water bottle in my backpack. "It's fresh?" I asked.

"Straight from the desalinator."

"Do I need to pay you?" I asked a little nervously.

"Yeah," he said and held out his hand. "In advance. In *gold*."

"Shut up, Leo," the woman next to me said, laughing. "I think she believes you." She turned to me. "It's free as long as you're down with receipt of stolen property. You could get a pretty hefty fine for taking that water, you know."

"But they'd fine you just as much for being down here at all," someone else added.

I held out my water bottle and Leo filled it.

"My name's Jen," the woman said. "The water boy is Leo."

"Shut up," he said.

"Water boy *of the day*."

"I'm Rebecca," I said, wondering if people would recognize me. If they'd throw me back out. Or over the side. That last would be tricky, though, since we were several stories below the waterline.

No one reacted to my name. I was just a grubby nobody, apparently, and grubby nobodies were okay.

"Soup's up," someone said, and they gave me some of the soup, too. I offered my trail mix to the meal, and that got a round of approving nods; I appeared to be following the rules.

Jen showed me around the encampment. They drew water (a trickle at a time) out of the fresh pipes; they drew electricity from the wires and yes, they were willing to let me charge up my gadget. The thing I thought was most impressive was the latrine; they'd hung a shower curtain to provide privacy, and the latrine went straight to a waste pipe. Jen showed me how it worked: you unlatched the top part to use it, then re-latched the top part and pulled on something near the bottom to flush. "Be *absolutely sure* the lid is latched when you flush," she warned me, "or we will be *swimming* in shit."

When the meal was over, everyone settled in for the night, leaving one person awake to empty buckets and watch for cops. "If anyone comes," Jen said, "you'll need to grab your bag and get out as fast as you can. Keep your flashlight off if you possibly can—light will lead them to you."

"What happens if you're caught?"

"They fine you for trespass and theft."

That didn't sound *too* bad, but Jen raised an eyebrow and added, "Could *you* pay a fine? Because if not, they bond you for it till you pay off the debt."

"You'll still come out ahead, if you're not caught too often," Leo said from his sleeping spot a few meters away.

"What if you're a dependent?" I asked. "Theoretically, I mean." It's illegal to sell someone under 18 into bond—everywhere that has laws, at least.

"Then your parents get the bill. And the bond, if they can't pay. You're their responsibility. *Theoretically*."

"Okay," I said.

"Sleep tight," she said.

My gadget was charged, and as I started to stash it, I wondered if I'd be able to get a signal down here. I could, it turned out. I wrapped up in my blanket and tried to check my mail. I couldn't get into any of my accounts—not even the one I thought my father hadn't known about. It was a good thing I hadn't used that account to contact my mom.

On the stead's "trending" page, where you could see all the

"hot right now!" links, I saw that the first episode of *High Stakes* had been released. I pulled it up to watch.

It was weird to see which scenes they put back-to-back, telling the story. They focused a lot on Debbie, and there was a long clip of her telling the story about getting arrested with her sister when they were caught with the T-13.

From that, they segued into a scene of one of the people from the network staff at a shop—it was on Amsterdarn, I was pretty sure, because it was well lit and I didn't recognize the owner. They bought a toothbrush, a tube of toothpaste, a bottle of aspirin, and ten tablets of T-13. There was a brief interview with the shopkeeper, who looked utterly baffled when they asked him about the legality of T-13.

Then a scene stateside: Janet was interviewing a lawyer who said that for a first offense, if the person had the money to pay for drug treatment, he could almost always get the sentence knocked down to probation. "If someone can't afford that, though, and if they're using a public defender they usually can't, they might get three years, five, even ten. And I mean prison time, not probation."

I wondered what a public defender was and moved over to the sidebar to see if they had notes. They did: it was a lawyer who worked for people who couldn't afford lawyers. Weird. I switched back over to the show.

Now they were showing video of people getting off a plane on Amsterdarn while a voiceover talked about laws on the stead, and how the differences between stead and shore had led to all sorts of fugitives taking up residence on the stead. I thought maybe they'd segue to Thor's father, but no. They switched to a picture of a little girl with pigtails, hanging from a bar, a big grin on her face.

"My name is Lenore Garrison," a new voice said. "This is my daughter, Becky. I haven't seen her since she was four years old, when her father violated the custody order and took her to New Minerva."

It was my mother. *That's my mother.* I looked around wildly, wanting to show someone—wanting to show *Thor*, actually, but of course he wasn't there. She looked older than my father, because her hair was mostly gray. She was tense. I could see it from the way she held her hands.

My mother pretended, in the interview, that she hadn't heard from me; she was protecting my secret. She spoke in a composed, calm way, although the camera angle changed a few times and I could tell they'd edited out bits. I wondered if she'd told Janet that she could only interview her if she didn't show her crying.

"I kept my married name," she said near the end, her lips twisting into a faint smile. "I'm hoping that she'll have an easier time finding me, if she ever comes looking. I'm not sure whether she even knows I'm alive."

After the interview with my mother, Janet's voice talked about how they ran a database check on all the heavy-hitters of the seastead and found that it wasn't just the bond-workers who were often on the lam. I thought they'd mention Thor's father for sure now, but in fact there were *fifteen* people on the stead who'd committed embezzling and tax evasion, plus another twenty-two who'd done one but not the other, and a bunch more who'd been either convicted or charged with fraud. There were eleven sex offenders, four men who'd been involved in human trafficking (I had to look that one up: apparently they'd been selling people somewhere that bond-workers were illegal), and two who'd jumped bail after being charged with felony assault. One man had been charged with murder. Probably the creepiest people on the list: *nine* of the doctors practicing medicine on the seastead had lost their stateside medical license due to ethical violations, including someone who'd been *experimenting medically on his patients.* That got them curious about seastead medicine and they'd done some checking; four *more* doctors on the seastead may never have actually gone to medical school at all.

Cut to the lawyer. "The fact is, here in the U.S. we pay a lot in taxes, but part of what we get from that is oversight. We have people who check to see whether the food we eat is safe, whether our water is safe to drink, whether our doctors are licensed to practice medicine. On the seastead, it's caveat emptor for every-thing. Let the buyer beware. But the fact is, most of us are not in a position, on a day-to-day basis, to check every bite of food and make sure it's not contaminated with pesticide or E. coli."

Back to the stead, and Debbie was talking again.

"My sister was poisoned," she said. "I don't know if it was on purpose or by accident, but it destroyed her kidneys. The cost of treatment was so high, the only way to get a loan to cover it was to allow her bond to be sold to a skin farm on Lib. She said no, but there's a loophole. If you're dying, your bond can be sold without your permission to anyone willing to pay for the treatment. And that's how she wound up chained to a bench in a skin farm."

I knew what was coming next: the recording I'd gotten and passed to Janet, of the skin farm. I didn't need to see that again. I shut my gadget off before I killed the battery, and lay down to try to sleep. The floor was hard, and even wrapped in both my coat and the blanket I was chilly. I rested my head on my backpack. *I want my mom,* I thought, and drifted—finally—to sleep.

When I woke up, the camp was quiet around me, and when I sat up, I realized that everyone was gone.

The whole camp was gone, in fact. Bedrolls had been packed up and carried away. The curtain around the latrine had been tak-en down and the waste pipe closed back up. Even the water leak was patched (with what looked like a wad of gum). Next to me, someone had written in chalk, TONIGHT: L-38.

I wondered how to find L-38. Probably Jen could have ex-plained it to me.

Someone had filled my water bottle for me before closing

up the water pipe. I wondered what time it was and reached for my gadget.

It was gone.

I went through my bag, double-checked the spot where it had been plugged in to charge the night before . . . nothing. My money, which was deep in the bag I'd had under my head all night, was still there, but the gadget had been in my hand when I fell asleep and someone had taken it. *Stolen* it.

It probably shouldn't have surprised me as much as it did. These people routinely stole water and trespassed rather than pay rent. Stealing from a person is different, but I doubted swiping my gadget had been some sort of *collective* decision. Although leaving me sleeping surely had been.

If I could find my way to L-38 tonight, I could ask for it back. That might work. I sighed heavily and headed for the stairs.

Upstairs, I went to the sandwich shop, hoping to find Thor. He jumped up when he saw me and pulled me into a hug.

"That was your mom, wasn't it?" he said.

"Yeah," I said into his shoulder. "It was."

"She pretended—"

"She knew I was keeping it a secret," I said. We sat down. "They sort of mentioned your dad, too."

"Yeah, guess he's not the only lowlife on board, huh?" Thor had already bought two sandwiches, and passed one over to me, along with a soda. I would have liked to refuse on principle but I was too hungry.

"Yeah, it gets worse, too. Who do you think the sex offenders are?"

"Uncle Paul," Thor said. "I don't trust any man who wants me to call him 'uncle' when he's not actually my relative."

"Huh." I couldn't talk; too busy eating.

"And I totally bet that jerk doctor who didn't want to treat Tom's ankle properly was one of the ones who had his license yanked."

I swallowed. "I don't know where Janet looked this stuff up. Can *we* check?"

"I bet we could from your dad's computer. But database access like that costs money, and some of these people are probably using false names here—someone would have noticed the license thing, otherwise. Also, digging for this information takes time. Janet has assistants." He looked a little wistful. "Someone else will do it, though. It'll get around."

"Ha. We could start rumors about people we don't like. My dad, for instance."

"True. I mean, he's already a kidnapper. Maybe he's also defrauded people, molested children, and eaten kittens."

"He never eat a kitten. Too much work for too little meat."

"Wait, are you quoting something he's *said*?"

"He was kidding around at the time." I looked at Thor. "He's not *always* awful, you know."

"Well, I'm glad he's not always horrible to you."

"He's not."

"Good."

I finished my sandwich and was thinking about buying another one when the shop owner brought over two banana splits.

"Dammit," I said, between bites. "I *have* money, you know. I could be buying my own breakfast. Lunch. Whatever this is."

"I was kind of thinking of this as a date," Thor said, looking at his own banana split and turning bright red. "So I'm paying, okay?"

A date.

"Well, okay," I said, taking another bite of banana split.

When we finished eating, Thor said, "Hey, I had a message for you. *Not* from your mom."

"Oh?"

"Or your dad, either. Someone from *Stead Life* wants to talk to you. They tried reaching you by phone and mail and couldn't get you, so they came to me. They said you could go straight to their office, if that would be easier than calling. They're on the

Cruise Ship part of Rosa, level thirty-two, west edge."

"*Stead Life* wants to talk to me?" This made me unaccountably nervous. "Do you think it's about my mom?"

"No, actually, they called yesterday before *High Stakes* went live."

"Weird. Well, I'll go see them, I guess. What time is it? Are you late for anything?"

"I don't care," he said.

"Don't get yourself in trouble," I said, and squeezed his hand. He squeezed mine back.

"Are you sure you don't want me to walk you to the *Stead Life* office?" he said.

"Do you think I actually need protection?"

"I mostly just think it would be fun to walk with you."

"How about halfway, then you go to class?"

He grinned. "Okay."

The *Stead Life* offices were a lot smaller than I'd imagined them. Just like *High Stakes*, they had a producer who was not one of the people who appeared on camera. Her assistant buzzed me in and then went for coffee. The producer's name was Leah; I'd seen it in the credits a million times but I'd never seen her face. She was the opposite of Janet—scruffy where Janet was polished, nerdy where Janet was slick. "You're Beck Garrison," she said, before I could introduce myself. "I'm glad your friend found you. You disappeared *really* effectively."

Huh. Good.

"We can interview you on camera if you want, but mostly I was hoping you could help me find that woman, Debbie. We *really* want to interview her."

I laughed out loud. "You're hiring me for a finding job?"

Leah blinked, confused for a second. "Oh, yeah, you found stuff for the Miscellenry, didn't you? I heard that when I did background on you. Well, so. Yes, we want you to find Debbie and help us arrange an interview. She's disappeared even more thoroughly than you did."

"Probably because she doesn't want to get killed."

"If necessary, we can give a camera and list of questions to the person of her choice. You, for instance. Surely she'd want to get the word out on the stead. That's what we do: get the word out."

I bit my lip and looked up at Leah. "So why weren't you planning to go to Miguel's funeral?"

Leah looked down at her desk. "We didn't think it fit our show. Funerals aren't very interesting."

"Oh? Really? Is that the reason?"

"More or less."

"Yeah. If Debbie gives you an interview, will you actually *air* it? Even if—say—Paul Garrison tells you not to?"

"We don't take orders from your father, Beck."

"That's good, because you'd probably be surprised by just *how many people on this stead do.* And the ones who don't are easily cowed by his goons."

Leah tilted her head. "I live on Min because I don't like people telling me what to do. I run a reality show because I like asking questions. And I carry a gun because I don't like people trying to intimidate me."

"Good to know," I said. "If I find Debbie, how shall I tell her to reach you?"

"Let me give you a disposable phone—"

I shook my head. "I've had a bad experience with gift gadgets. How about just a number?"

"Fine." Leah wrote a number down on an index card and handed it over. "You can also feel free to come back here. I'm hoping to interview her before tomorrow morning. Let me know if you hit a dead end."

*

It kept coming back to finding.

I started with the locker rooms, because maybe someone knew where she was, enough to pass the message along, but no luck. I tried Clark's, plus similar low-end dining halls on Rosa and Pete. I tried the real estate office, on the off chance that she'd used her money to buy a place to live straight off.

When I went to St. Peter's, Father Tim looked happy to see me. "I assume you heard the funeral got moved," he said.

"I heard it wasn't going to be on the sea platform anymore," I said.

"Yeah. We've fixed things with the Methodists. It'll be tomorrow, in their church. I'm *hoping* it will at least be a harder location to attack. They certainly won't be able to blow it up without destroying a lot of stuff they'd rather not destroy." I must have looked uncertain because he added, "We can't *not* hold a funeral."

"I guess not."

"Any news on the slowdown?"

"I'm not the one to ask," I said. "Do *you* know anything new?"

"I've heard rumblings of a caveat to the 'medical care' thing, after the broadcast last night. No one wants to be packed off to a doctor who didn't go to med school."

"Or who might experiment on them? I can't *imagine* why they'd object."

In any case, Father Tim hadn't seen Debbie and didn't know how to get a message to her. "Actually," he said a little sheepishly, "I was thinking of asking you to try to find her for me. I want to make sure she's okay with the current funeral plans. If you could give her this note . . ." He handed me a paper envelope. "She can send a message through you, if she doesn't want to come up."

Come *up*. Of *course*. She was hiding at the bottom of the stead, the same as I had last night.

*

So, the problem now was this: the thought of endlessly wandering around that dimly lit maze of pipes and wires with no destination, trying to find someone who was hiding on purpose when I'd already been warned that plenty of groups down there weren't "friendly"—frankly, that didn't sound like a good plan. I mean, I'm not exactly a coward, but when I went to rescue Lynn from the place on Lib, I took an Alpha Dog with me. I *could* actually hire a bodyguard, but going down there with a hired gun was the most certain way possible to ensure that no one trusted me and I *never* found Debbie.

I pondered whether I knew anyone who was big enough to make me feel like I had someone with me, but also nonthreatening enough that he wouldn't make things worse, and went to see if I could find Thor. I caught him as he came out of his afternoon class. His face lit up when he spotted me. "I wasn't expecting to see you again today."

"Yeah, well, I want company for something." I was trying to avoid specifics where people could overhear.

"Awesome." Thor put his arm around me and his head close to mine. "Do you need help getting to the American Institute?"

"No," I said. "I want company while I hunt for Debbie."

"Why do you need her?"

"*Stead Life* wants to interview her."

He raised his head and glanced over his shoulder. Shara was coming out of the tutor's apartment as well, and he waved. "See you later," he said cheerfully, and we picked up the pace.

"Okay," he said, "I'm in."

"Are you sure?"

"Of course. Do you want to stop and get something to eat first?"

"Yeah," I said, "but you have to let me treat, because it's not a date when I'm kind of basically using you for your height and gender."

"Sure it is," he said. "As long as we're spending time together, I'm good."

"You haven't seen where I'm taking you!"

"I should tell you, I'm still jealous of that Alpha Dog who got to hang out with you on Lib."

"You should be more jealous of Lynn. After all, she was *officially* my date—that's how I got the Alpha Dog to rescue her."

"True, but since she's either dead or somewhere awful, that felt like sort of a tasteless joke for me to make."

"Sorry."

"No, it's okay for *you* to make it. I just didn't feel comfortable going there."

I bought us both sandwiches. The line was kind of long; a lot of the people with dining hall contracts had realized the one-person operations like sandwich shops were mostly not affected by the slowdown.

"We should make sure you're not being followed," Thor said. "I mean, if other people are after her, you probably don't want to lead them to her by accident."

"Good point," I said, and we took a circuitous route to the locker-room level. If anyone was following us, they were good enough that we didn't see them when we looked over our shoulders repeatedly.

The door to the utility level was still taped open. On the other side, Thor looked around in wonder. "I can't believe you didn't think this was a romantic destination," he said. "It's dimly lit, mysterious, and our parents would *never* find us down here. What more could you ask for?"

"*Not* being slapped with a massive fine if you're caught during your date?"

"That just adds to the element of excitement."

Walking down the row, I realized that the whole place was labeled on a grid with letters and number: A-Z in one direction, 1-99 in the other, which undoubtedly was the key to finding L-38, that number I'd seen written when I got up this morning. Debbie hadn't been with last night's squatter crowd, but I went to L-38 anyway, thinking I could ask if anyone knew how to find her. I could ask about my gadget, too. But no one was there, so either it was too early, or someone (like the gadget thief) had written down entirely the wrong location to send me astray.

We kept walking down that aisle, past holding tanks with AIR BALLAST CHAMBER stenciled on them in orange, and something with a sign saying DANGER: HIGH VOLTAGE, and a locked cage that held a bunch of switches that looked sort of rusty.

"Password!"

It was a male voice, but not one I recognized. I froze and held up my hands to show I didn't have a weapon. Thor did the same. "Sorry, I'm not with your group," I said. "I'm looking for someone I have a message for."

A light exploded in my eyes and I covered them, too late. When my vision started to come back I found myself nose-to-nose with a man in a black leather jacket, with a blue tattoo of a lightning bolt down his cheek. "What sort of message?"

"*Stead Life* wants to interview Debbie. Union organizer Debbie. They want to put her on their show. I said I'd try to find her and let her know."

"Can't help you," he said. "But pass freely."

"Okay," I said. "Uh. How freely? Any areas I should avoid? I hate to get shot, you know?"

"Hardly anyone down here has a gun," he said dismissively. "Just don't act like you're a cop, you'll probably be fine."

"Thanks," I said. "But if *hardly* anyone has a gun . . ."

He shrugged.

I turned to Thor as we walked away. "We can go back, if you want."

"We haven't found Debbie yet."

"I feel guilty about getting you into this."

"You're not making me do anything."

"Yeah, but I *asked* you to come . . ."

Thor put his arm around my shoulders and gave me a sideways hug. "Quit it," he said. "If you're here, I want to be here."

If Debbie were here, she was surely as far as possible from the stairway in. The next encampment we passed wasn't guarded at all, but abandoned. It looked a lot more established than the place where I'd slept last night; there were bedrolls laid out. I couldn't tell if everyone who normally lived there was out for the day or if they'd scattered when they saw us coming. "Debbie?" I called, tentatively. "It's Beck." No response.

"Do you want to wait here and see who comes?" Thor asked.

"No," I said. "If we can't find her, we can try this spot again."

The next camp found us before we found them. We were approaching a corner when I felt something hit me in the back. I was starting to turn to look behind me when every muscle in my body seized up; I fell, hard, unable even to catch myself.

"What the hell are you doing here?" someone was yelling at me. No, at Thor.

I struggled for breath. The shock—it had been an electric shock, I was pretty sure—had stopped, but I was still having trouble making things work, and that included my mouth. "Stop, wait," I said, struggling for coherence. "Don't blame him! I made him come!" *I need to tell them I want Debbie,* I thought, *but in a way that doesn't make me sound like a threat.* Whoever it was shocked me again; this time it felt sort of like the numbness that shoots down your arm when you hit it between the bones of the elbow. Thor was yelling something, too. I didn't know what. "It's not Thor," I said when I could talk again. Which was not exactly helpful, but I was terrified that they would hurt him even worse, because he was big and more of a threat. *Why did I bring him? Why did that seem like a good idea?*

Hands grabbed my shoulders and yanked me upright; I could see nothing but a dazzling light. "Oh, her," someone said.

"Let her go." This time it was a woman's voice, with a southern accent. "She's one of us."

"Debbie?" I said, hopefully.

"Yeah, hon, it's me. Put her on one of the cots. The boy, too. Good God, y'all, can't you tell an Alpha Dog from a jumpy teenager?"

"Is Thor okay?" I asked.

"Yeah, he got the same as you. Just relax, you'll feel better in a few minutes."

My vision slowly cleared, although my fingers and toes still felt weird. I sat up and looked around. We were in the far corner, as far as possible from the stairs, and this camp looked downright permanent. They had plastic sheets tacked up all over, with labels written on them in permanent maker: men's bathroom, women's bathroom, kitchen, do not disturb.

The most startling thing—I mean, beyond finding Debbie and getting shocked—was that there was a *child* here. A little girl, three years old, watching TV.

"Holy crap," Thor said, sitting up next to me, looking at the little kid. "Do you think she *lives* down here? I mean, all the time?"

Bond contracts typically required contraceptive implants for workers—male or female, it didn't matter. They usually further specified that if a child was born *anyway*, that child would be taken away and placed for adoption unless either the mother or the father could buy out within one month of giving birth.

It's pretty harsh, but it's not like you could keep a kid in the locker rooms. I wouldn't have thought you could keep a kid down here, either, but clearly someone had managed it.

Once we were steady on our feet, Debbie led us behind the "do not disturb" plastic sheet to a room with an actual table and chairs. "Welcome to my office," she said. "Have a seat. You must have had a pretty big reason to go to the trouble of tracking me down."

"*Stead Life* wants to interview you," I said, and laid out their proposal.

"What do you think, Beck?" she asked when I was done. "Should I do it?"

"I think it's a good idea," I said. "It'll give you another chance to get the word out, both on the seastead and elsewhere."

"Maybe." She ran one hand through her hair and sighed. "I wish I could talk this over with Miguel. He had a much better sense of strategy than I do. He probably have come up with a better idea than hiding down here."

"Yeah, well," Thor said. "He also got killed. So maybe not."

"Hmm," Debbie said. "Tell them this, Beck. Tell them I'll do it—I'll meet them down here, in A-15, right near the stairs. I'll give them a half-hour interview. But in exchange, they *have to* cover Miguel's funeral, too. I heard they aren't coming. I want them there. That's my condition."

I nodded. "Yeah," I said. "I'll tell them."

Miguel's funeral was held the next day.

I knew what Debbie was thinking: getting *Stead Life* to cover the funeral would be good for the movement and would build sympathy for the people doing the slowdown, but it would also provide them with human shields. Uncle Paul or my father or whoever it was that was behind the man I heard hiring the Scoundrels—they might have been able to get away with sinking a sea platform full of bond-workers, but killing journalists guarantees that their friends will make you look as bad as possible in the stories that run afterward.

I liked that idea, but I thought they could do with a few more human shields. I had Thor pass the word to Shara and the rest of our classmates; I told Geneva about the funeral when I met her to withdraw more money; I told Jamie at Miscellenry. Father Tim had been sympathetic, so I stopped in at the Baptist Mission Outreach Center, the Mormon Mission, and the Russian Orthodox church over on Pete. The Mormons were not initially sympathetic—I think they were annoyed about the slowdown—but when I told them about overhearing threats of violence they said they'd come.

I went to the funeral an hour early and saved Thor a seat. No one stopped me entering. Once I was in the church, I borrowed a phone and called my father.

"Hello, Beck," he said when he picked up.

I looked over my shoulder. "How did you know it was me?"

He sighed heavily. "You're the only person who has my private number. Besides, you're coming in from the Methodist church's data node. I'm not surprised you decided to go to the funeral."

"Well, I was calling to let you know I'm here," I said. "I know the ADs were going to do something horrible to the funeral the first time around, and the Cut-Rate Bastards were supposed to keep any minors from getting in. I'm here, Thor's coming, and so are most of the other teenagers. All the religious leaders are coming, including the Baptists and the Russians. *Stead Life* is coming. If anything goes down, it's not just bond-workers who will die."

There was a pause. Then he said, "You know, I was expecting you to bring up a more personal issue first."

My cheeks warmed. "Mom," I said. "I saw her on TV."

"Yes. 'Mom.' I suppose it won't do much good to give you my side of the story at this point, but she was trying to keep you from me, she was telling you lies about me, and it was clear that it was her or me—we could never *both* be your parents."

I didn't really want to argue about this. Not here, not on the phone. So I sat there silently, waiting to see if he had anything else to say.

"Come home, Beck," he said. "Please? You don't . . . I don't want you to feel like you *have* to go to her. To give up the sea, the stead, your life here. I'm sorry I turned you out. Just come home."

"Settle the strike," I whispered. "I know you can make it happen. Negotiate with the bond-workers, find a deal that everyone's satisfied with, and when the slowdown's over, I'll come home."

The Methodist church was a lot like the Catholic church, only bigger: one of the stead's large interior rooms, structural pillars here and there, folding chairs. They borrowed extras (probably from St. Peter's) and jammed them together, with standing room in the aisles and in the back. Thor came early, and sat down next to me.

The Methodist church had elaborately painted walls: they'd created twelve arched windows that looked out on various made-up scenes. One showed the sea on a sunny day; another had gardens. The window painting next to me depicted a playground filled with children. I wondered if children on real playgrounds all looked as joyful as the kids in the painting, or if in real life they squabbled a lot over whose turn it was to go down the slide.

Father Tim and the Methodist minister both appeared to be presiding. I wondered if Tim was nervous. He didn't look nervous. He welcomed everyone and then drew a cross in the air and blessed the crowd. Some of the people near me crossed themselves, but most kept their hands at their sides, so I didn't feel too conspicuous.

There was a series of readings. Some of them were religious: Father Tim read a passage about Moses saying "Let my people go." Some of the people in the crowd shouted "Amen!" to that, which appeared to startle Tim a little. The Methodist minister read a bit about tending vineyards and flocks and getting grapes and milk. "Is it about OXEN that GOD is concerned?" he thundered. ("No! Amen, brother, no!" someone near me said, half under his breath.) "Surely he says this for US. Whoever plows and threshes should share in the HARVEST." ("Amen!" the person near me said, louder this time. It didn't seem to startle the Methodist as much as it had Father Tim.)

There were also some poems, and then songs, but I didn't know enough of the words to sing along with them.

Then Debbie got up to deliver the eulogy. I was tired by now, and hungry, and it was hard to concentrate. Next to me, Thor took my hand and we laced our fingers together.

"Miguel is gone," Debbie was saying, "but the fight is anything but over."

There was something of a commotion and for a second I thought that despite all the kids, all the religious leaders, and everyone else who'd come, there was going to be violence. But it was someone with a note, which was passed up to Debbie to read.

She stared at it wordlessly for a moment.

"This says that a consortium of business owners has agreed in principle to providing health care as a standard part of every contract, effective immediately and retroactively," she said. "They're requesting a meeting to discuss details."

She started to go on, probably to say that the details might be important (for one thing, presumably the bond-workers would want it spelled out that they'd be seeing REAL doctors and not someone who got his medical degree by printing off an official-looking certificate) but her voice was lost in the ecstatic cheer.

Thor clapped, but he was looking at me, and I could tell that we were thinking the same thing: *that was way too fast. Too easy. What are they playing at now?*

Thor walked me back up to my father's apartment.

"Are you sure about this?" he said. "I still think a night down on the bottom level would be a pretty cool adventure."

"Have you ever slept on a concrete floor?" I asked. "It's *really uncomfortable.*"

"Who said anything about sleep?"

My face flamed and he looked a little stricken. "I meant *talking,*" he said, hastily. "We could just, you know, hang out." He lowered his voice. "And I don't care what you said to your father, I still think you should get off the stead."

"He's worried about losing me," I said. "He wants me to come home. If I leave, I lose any power and influence I have."

"I don't trust your father," Thor said. "Not to keep his word, and not to keep you safe."

"Me, either. But I don't think he'll *hurt* me."

"Well," Thor said, "at least the stuff about eating kittens was always a joke, right?"

"Right."

We were about to turn down the corridor where my father lived, and Thor stopped dead. When I looked up at him to ask what was up, he bent down and kissed me. Then he broke the kiss and looked embarrassed. "Sorry," he said. "I just realized, once we're by your father's apartment . . ."

"Yeah, he has a camera," I said. "Good thought." I wrapped my arms around Thor's neck and kissed him back.

The entry code let me into my father's apartment this time. He was waiting for me in the living room.

"I wondered if that would be good enough for you," he said.

"Well," I said, "it sounded like a good-faith effort."

He didn't smile. Instead, he let out a long breath and studied me in the dim light.

"Do you have any questions about your mother?" he asked.

"Where does she live?" I asked.

"California somewhere. I'm not sure exactly."

I thought about asking if I could write to her, but I knew if he *knew* I was writing to her, he'd be monitoring the mail. It might be easier just to keep sending letters through the Institute. I could have asked him why he lied, but we already covered that by phone, and I didn't really believe his answer anyway.

"Well," I said. "Now what? Do I go back to living here, sleeping in my own bed, going to school?"

"Yes," he said.

"Okay, then," I said, wondering why he was still looking at me that way.

"You'll be attending classes by video for now, though," he said. He had an abstracted look on his face—not angry, not the way he'd looked when he was grounding me. *Worried.* He raised an eyebrow at me, probably reacting to the look on my face. "I'm not punishing you," he said. "There was . . . there may have been an accident on Sal."

"What?" I whispered.

He laced his fingers together. "As it happens, the bond-workers' demand was something we begun to think we would need to provide anyway. There's an illness on the stead. It may be contagious, and it may be spreading. I'm not grounding you, Beck. I'm quarantining you."

PART FOUR
OUTBREAK

CHAPTER NINE

WHEN I WOKE UP THE NEXT MORNING, MY FATHER HAND-
ed me a suitcase and told me to pack.

"Are we leaving the seastead?" I asked, in shock. I had literally
not set foot on shore since I was four.

"No," he said. "Rosa's got the best protocols for keeping people from spreading the disease, so I've made arrangements for
you to stay on Rosa until the illness is under control."

"For *me* to stay—aren't you coming?"

"This will also allow me to spend my time elsewhere," he said.
"I'm going to Silicon Waters, to oversee the research into a vaccine personally."

It didn't take me long to pack. My father loaded my suitcase onto a little hand truck, along with two heavy plastic crates.
"What are those?" I asked.

"Your rent," he said. "MREs."

The connections between Rosa and the other steads were
too permanent to simply be collapsed like tents, but there were
men out disassembling one of the bridges with wrenches and a
crowbar. The bridge we crossed was being watched by guards, but

my father passed the supervisor an envelope and they waved us through. The corridors were quiet and nearly deserted; we passed my Humanities tutor's apartment, and her *now accepting students* sign had been taken down and replaced with a sign saying *all lessons will be online until further notice.*

"That reminds me," my father said, and handed me my gadget. "You'll need this for school."

I'd expected a room in a guest-house, but instead he led me up to a level of deck apartments and knocked brusquely. To my surprise, it was Thor who opened the door.

My father peered at him impatiently. "Where's your father?"

"Oh, uh—Dad!" Thor called over his shoulder.

A short, gray-haired man came to the door. "Mr. Lundquist. We spoke," my father said.

"Yes."

"This is Rebecca. Here are her things, and the food." My father passed everything, including me, through the door. "I assume you will be running a *tight* quarantine from now on, and not allowing your son to fling the door open to all and sundry?"

"We were expecting you," Thor's father said defensively.

"Good. Let me know if there are any problems." I wasn't sure if that last sentence was addressed to me, or to Thor's father. The door closed behind me.

Thor looked at his father, alarmed. "*Quarantine?* You told me Mrs. Rodriguez was *sick,*" he said. "You said *that's* why I had no school today. *What's going on?*"

Mr. Lundquist started yammering about how some people would believe every rumor that came along and maybe someone somewhere was sneezing. I said, "There was an accident on Sal."

Mr. Lundquist rolled his eyes. "Even if there was an accident on Sal, I don't think we're actually facing the Omega Plague. But quarantining does seem prudent, so the MREs . . . should come in handy, since they'll allow us to eat here, rather than in the dining hall."

Thor was flushed and furious. "We should leave," he said. "Quarantining on the stead is a *joke*. We should get out of here." He looked away from his father, and I realized his mother was standing in the living room doorway; he was making his appeal to her.

She shook her head, her face drawn. "There's a U.S. Naval blockade," she said. "They were dispatched from San Diego during the night. Apparently we're surrounded."

Thor sat down on the couch, looking utterly appalled, and Mrs. Lundquist shook my hand stonily. "You must be Rebecca Garrison," she said. "I made some space for your things." She gestured for me to follow her.

The Lundquists had one of the biggest apartments I'd ever seen. They had a kitchenette, first of all, with a good-sized fridge and a pair of burners you could actually cook a meal on, if you wanted to. They had *three bedrooms*—one for Thor's parents, one for his brother and sister, and one, the smallest, was Thor's. They had a huge main room and a deck. The bathroom had a *tub*.

Thor had mentioned that his father had jumped bail after being charged with tax evasion and embezzling. Apparently the criminal life paid well.

The rooms were all crammed full of stuff, and I made a mental note that if I ever got back to Finding for Jamie, I should start here the next time I needed *anything*. Seriously, Mrs. Lundquist had a big shelf full of actual books, and framed photos on all the walls, and dressers and boxes full of clothes that couldn't possibly fit anyone who lived here, and a full set of dishes, and toys everywhere for Serena and Erik, and a shelf displaying little china figurines, and I was pretty sure I saw a box of yarn and knitting needles sticking out from under the couch.

Thor's room was even more cluttered than the rest of the house. More books, a bunch of games, golden cups with little figurines of runners and *State Champion* engraved on the side, stacks of folded T-shirts. Thor looked deeply embarrassed.

"I swear I got rid of a *lot* of stuff when we moved here. I mean, I had to, we left town kind of fast. But you cram it all in a space this size and it looks pretty ridiculous."

"What are those cups for?" I asked.

"They're trophies," he said. "Running trophies. I did cross-country, back at my high school." I must have given him a blank look because he explained. "You know how there are sports teams? You've seen them in movies, right?" I nodded. "I was on the running team."

"And you won stuff?"

"Yeah, I—Yeah." He picked up one of the cups, then put it back on the shelf. It said *State Champion* at the bottom. "I wish I'd just left these behind, though. They really aren't *for* anything."

"Did you like running?"

"I loved it," he said. "We have a treadmill. I get it out some-times, but it's not the same."

One thing Thor's family had that my father was *never* going to get us was a balcony. When Thor realized how excited I was by the prospect, he found a gingham tablecloth in one of the boxes stacked up in the living room and spread it on the floor of the balcony. "We can have a picnic," he said.

The weather wasn't great, and any thoughts of private conver-sation were squelched by the prompt arrival of Erik and Serena, Thor's younger brother and sister. Erik was six and thought a pic-nic was the best idea ever. Serena was two and toddled out be-cause if both her brothers were outside, then outside was clearly the place to be.

"I miss picnics," Erik said. "We used to go for picnics at the park all the time back in San Diego. Balboa Park. Have you ever been to Balboa Park, Becca?"

"Nope," I said.

"You should go sometime," he said with the knowledgeable air that only a grade schooler could properly pull off, and proceeded to tell me in detail about the zoo and the weird assortment of museums. Apparently they had one that showcased antique cars. Thor heaved a sigh, leaned back against the railing, and let his kid brother talk. Erik barely touched his MRE and once it was clear that he wasn't going to eat any more, Thor finished it off.

Mrs. Lundquist eventually called Erik and Serena inside, Serena for a nap and Erik for a reading lesson. Erik still got school from his mom, so lessons weren't canceled.

"Sorry our picnic got crashed," Thor said, stretching his legs out and looking up at the sky.

"It's okay," I said. "Can we eat out here for dinner, too?"

"Maybe," he said. "You don't have a balcony, then? You have an outside apartment."

"We've just got a window. And it's in my father's office."

"Huh." Thor glanced inside. His mother and Erik were nowhere in sight. We could see his father, who was watching TV in the living room. "When my parents bought in, they picked this place because it was the biggest unit available on Rosa or Min. They didn't want to get rid of anything they didn't absolutely *have* to leave behind."

I glanced toward the piles of boxes in the living room. "Do you think they'll get rid of stuff eventually? Most of us—I mean, people who live on the seastead long-term—don't keep a lot, because we have so little space. That was sort of the whole point of my job for Jamie. You don't keep stuff around just in case you need it; you hire someone to track it down for you if you find you really do need it."

"That would be a good idea," Thor said. "I'm really one to talk, though, you know? All those stupid trophies."

It seemed tactless to agree. They clearly *meant* something to him. "Do they ever fall on you during storms?" I asked.

"Only one time," he said. He grinned. "I duct-taped them to the shelf." His smile faded. "Here's the thing," he said. "My father thought we could throw a lot of money into getting established here and then he'd find a job. No one's hired him, though, because they *know* he's a thief. They don't care about the tax dodging, but the embezzling? They're not cool with that. Mom, she's tried to get Dad to switch our meal contract somewhere budget instead of Primrose but he's convinced his best chance of finding a job is to look like we're doing just fine."

"Your mom could go to the American Institute if she needed a way to get back to California, couldn't she? I mean, *she* didn't commit a crime."

"She thinks they'd come after her for the tax stuff. She signed the returns, too."

"They really do that? Lock your mom up for something your dad did?"

"No. Yes. I don't know. There are laws that are supposed to protect innocent spouses—I've checked—but maybe she *did* know stuff and she doesn't want to say." He heaved another sigh. "You know, sort of the opposite of the people who earn their way out of bond and become citizens are the people who start out citizens and then have to sell themselves into bond. It does happen. I checked on *that*, too."

"I didn't know it was even legal."

"Sometimes it's teenagers," Thor said. "Tyrone—you know, the consular officer at the American Institute—told me about this guy whose parents kicked him out when he turned eighteen. He didn't have any way to make a living and wound up selling into bond. He said he brought it up because he was hoping I'd spread it around to the other teenagers to come to the Institute if that happened to us. If they're not U.S. citizens, they should 'ask for asylum,' there's some weird loophole that's related to the fact that the U.S. doesn't recognize the seastead as a sovereign country. Anyway, he could help."

"That's really nice of him."

"I've told you I like him, right? Anyway, he *said* he wanted to get the word out to all the kids our age, but I think seriously he wanted to tell *me*. I think he was worried my parents might pressure me to sell into bond. To help the family. Especially my little brother and sister."

I looked at him, horrified. "You wouldn't, would you?"

"No. I might send money back here, but I would *swim* to California before I'd sell into bond." He squinted up at the sky; there was a bird, very high up, circling. "My mom, on the other hand..." He sighed. "There *have* been people who were citizens, grownups, but they hit some bad luck and spent all their money and wound up taking out loans, first against their stake, then against their labor. Tyrone said there was one who came to the Institute and asked for transport back to the states, and he was able to arrange it, and as far as he knows the guy's doing OK. Another, though, was a true believer. He wouldn't go, no matter how bad it got. He was sure things would turn around for him. Tyrone's not sure what happened to him."

"It sounds like you've talked to him a lot."

"I've, um, run a few errands there. And he's really friendly, when he's not too busy."

I could imagine Thor leaning against the counter, letter in hand. Probably Tyrone was willing to let him talk about his homesickness. I looked at Thor's face now, staring out to sea, lost. We been sitting on opposite sides of the balcony, facing each other, and I scooted over to sit next to Thor. "Tell me more about Balboa Park," I said. "Is there *really* a whole museum just for old cars?"

We didn't get a picnic for dinner: Thor's family ate MREs together, tense and mostly silent, in the living room. Erik barely touched his, again. The TV was on, tuned to a satellite U.S. station that was showing re-runs of a stupid comedy.

"I want to see what's on the Stead channel," Mrs. Lundquist said.

"It's always garbage," Mr. Lundquist said.

"I want the Stead channel, too," Thor said.

"Yeah? Well, I want Erik and Serena not to have nightmares."

"You could go read them a story in their room," Mrs. Lundquist said.

"Whatever," Mr. Lundquist said, and relinquished the remote.

Stead Life is best known for its uploads, but Leah also uses it for a stead-wide local channel. When she's not airing stuff like *Stead Life* she tends to rent the studio to people who use it to push some idea or product or political candidate. The Mormon missionaries rent it for an hour a week to talk about their religion.

It was not Mormons today, or the *Stead Life* hosts, or the potted plant that sits in the studio when it's empty. It was Leah herself. There was a sign behind her that said, in large hand-printed letters, WE ARE BRINGING YOU ONGOING REPORTING OF THE CURRENT CRISIS. CALL OR TEXT 5556071 IF YOU HAVE FACTS TO ADD.

Leah was interviewing someone over the phone. Apparently the interviewee's wife was hallucinating. She thought she was back on shore, at a job she'd had years ago. Leah seemed to be assuming that everyone watching had been glued to her for the last few hours because she wasn't really going back to explain anything, but it was clear that a lot of people were sick—the illness, at this point, was not really disputed. Most of the sick people were running fevers. Some were hallucinating. Others apparently had violent diarrhea or were racked by violent muscle spasms. Early symptoms included headaches, or maybe dizziness, or possibly loss of appetite. Leah noted helpfully that the thing about headaches is that if you're worried about getting one, and trying to decide if maybe you have one, it's rather easy to give yourself one. I rubbed my own forehead in silent agreement.

Lots of people calling Leah insisted they knew the cause.

Someone suggested it was cholera, and everyone should boil the hell out of their water because something had gone wrong with the water purification. Someone else thought it was a novel flu epidemic. The most popular theory, though, was that it was Sal's fault and this was from nanotech. That only raised more questions, though: was this germ warfare? Some medical tech that got loose half-finished? Or something else entirely? Leah had called and e-mailed everyone on Sal she knew, but no one was answering.

Everyone in the Lundquist living room looked at me.

I had no idea what to say.

On the screen, Leah announced, "We're going on a five-minute break because I have to pee and there's no one here to take over. Back in a minute." The TV went quiet as the cameras automatically focused on the potted plant.

"Well," Mr. Lundquist said. "I am *so* glad that we decided to watch the news. I feel much better knowing all that, don't you?"

Mrs. Rodriguez had promised online classes, and the next day we actually had one, or tried. Thor and I sat on his bed, leaning against the wall, with our gadgets on our laps. "Has anyone done the reading?" Mrs. Rodriguez asked.

"I can't concentrate without coffee," Shara said. "Rachel, *be quiet.* I'm having *school.*"

"Is Rachel your little sister?" Thor asked.

"Yes, and she's—MOM!"

"Is Maureen coming?" I asked.

"I haven't heard from her," Mrs. Rodriguez said.

"Her family tried to bolt," Andy said. "They took off in their yacht."

"There's a blockade, isn't there?" Thor asked. "I mean, the U.S. Navy is blockading us?"

"Yeah, well, maybe they're not going very *far* but that doesn't mean they have to stay here."

I wondered why my father hadn't bought my way onto someone's yacht, instead. Surely a case of MREs would have gotten me a lot of options.

"Is anyone sick?" I asked.

"Me," Shara said. "I have had the worst headache for the last two days."

"Well, none of you can catch anything through your handhelds," Mrs. Rodriguez said. "So—"

"I heard the headache thing was a lie," Andy said. "They told us that deliberately to get us focusing on the wrong body part. I've heard *really* it starts with a stomach ache."

"I've had one of those, too," Shara said. "And no appetite at all."

"Look," Mrs. Rodriguez said. "Since you haven't done the reading, I was thinking—"

"Rachel, NO!" Shara shrieked.

Thor glanced at me, a rueful look on his face, and quietly pulled down two decks of cards from his shelf. He silently laid out a game of Spite and Malice as Mrs. Rodriguez tried to get everyone to shut up and focus on her lecture. She did, finally, get people to mostly stop talking, and Thor and I listened with half an ear while playing cards.

"Why do you think they're having us boil our water?" Shara asked when Mrs. Rodriguez paused to take questions.

"What does that have to do with the U.S. Civil War?" Mrs. Rodriguez asked, sounding tired.

"No, really, though—if it's escaped nanotech, would boiling our water help anything?"

"Sal's not admitting it's escaped nanotech," Andy said. "Maybe it's really just a water contamination problem."

"Beck might know," Sarah said. "Whether it's actually nanotech, or not. Her dad works on Sal."

"Normally he works on Min, actually," I said. "He works *with* Sal, though."

"Yeah? Well, is he working on Min *now*?"

People actually fell silent, waiting for my response.

"No," I said. "He's on Sal. At least, that's where he said he was going. He didn't outright say that *for sure* this was being caused by nanotech, but he seemed to think it was."

"ALL RIGHT," Mrs. Rodriguez shouted. "I'm going to talk about the U.S. Civil War, and the rest of you are going to listen." She muted everyone—Thor tried to say something but it didn't come through, and there were no further interruptions for the rest of the lecture. Thor and I finished three games of Spite & Malice and switched to rummy.

"Well," he said, mimicking his father's voice when Mrs. Rodriguez had ended the lesson and given us a reading assignment that she clearly didn't really expect we do, "I am *so* glad we decided to tune in that lecture, aren't you? There's nothing like the American Civil War to take my mind off an impending plague."

Thor had sneaked some of the MREs into his room, so when the lesson was over we kept the door shut, had lunch, and watched Leah some more on our gadgets. Her voice was getting hoarse and her callers were getting weirder. At some point she stopped taking calls and said to just leave messages, she'd listen to them later.

The illness was making people crazy. And not in the sense that everyone was paranoid and talking themselves into symptoms—the people who *had* the illness were going crazy. There were the hallucinations: those had been a rumor yesterday, but today everyone was treating them as established fact. But then once those passed, people were acting very strange. Someone's sister had been sick, and was now emptying their cabinets and shelves and lining everything up alphabetically, getting utterly hysterical when anyone interfered. Someone else had talked to a friend who was trying to unravel all her clothing into its component threads.

"I'll be back at nine," Leah said, finally. "I need to listen to my messages and take a nap. Nine, people, I promise."

We looked for news about the seastead outbreak on the satellite stations. We found a news report from California somewhere that said we were having a cholera outbreak and that seasteaders were panicking and then went into a long explanation of what cholera was (it sounded nothing like what Leah was describing) and how we basically brought it on ourselves with our lack of governmental oversight and regulation.

Thor scowled and shut off his gadget. "This isn't cholera," he muttered. "I think they're lying to keep people stateside from freaking out."

I thought Shara had probably talked herself into the headache and stomach ache but the next day she did not turn on her gadget for the online class.

"They were still eating in the dining hall, you know," John said.

"They were?" Andy said, shocked.

"Well, they don't have any windows anyway," John said. "All their air comes from the vents. So her mom said, it's not like they were even really quarantined, they might as well go get the food they'd paid for. They don't have anywhere to cook, either."

Thor's parents had been keeping the door open to the balcony and they'd taped sheets of plastic over the ventilation ducts that usually brought in air-conditioned air. And they were boiling water, like we been told to do, and we hadn't opened the door to the outside corridor since I had arrived.

"How sick is she?" I asked.

There was a long pause. No one knew.

There was a knock on the door in the middle of the night.

Mr. Lundquist stumbled out into the living room, shirtless in PJ bottoms, and peered through the peephole. "I thought you said you wanted us observing quarantine," he shouted.

"Let me in." It was my father's voice.

"We're all still healthy!"

"That's great. Let me in."

Mr. Lundquist opened the door and my father came in. He was unshaven and wearing the same clothes he'd had on when he'd dropped me off, and carrying a briefcase. "I've got the prototype vaccine," Dad said. "Doses for all of you."

Mrs. Lundquist was coming out of the bedroom, settling her glasses onto her nose and tying her bathrobe. Thor, too, had gotten up. "What's the truth about the disease?" Mr. Lundquist asked.

"It came from Sal," my father said. "The vaccine's also from Sal." He took out a plastic pill bottle and shook a set of capsules into his palm. "One for each of you. It's oral. Take it, Beck."

I hesitated. He met my eyes squarely and held out his hand to me. "Pick one for yourself, and pick one for me," he said.

I took two capsules, and handed one to him. He gulped it down without water. "Now you," he said.

Hesitantly, I swallowed mine. I could see him breathing easier, watching me.

He shook the remaining pills back into the bottle. "There's one for each of you. I'm going to get some rest. They're making more, but it'll take days before there's enough for everyone on the stead. It's fast-acting; you should be fully immune by morning." He set the bottle on the end table by the door and went back out without another word.

"We are NOT HIS LAB RATS," Mr. Lundquist shouted.

"Are you kidding me? He gave one to his own daughter. He took one himself. You can't possibly think there's anything harmful in them."

"Yeah? I don't know if you've noticed this, but Paul Garrison is a fucking lunatic. A bona fide mad scientist. He as much as admitted he's the one who loosed this plague on us in the first place."

"I'm taking it," Mrs. Lundquist said, and grabbed the pill bottle before Mr. Lundquist could stop her, taking out one of the capsules and putting it in her mouth.

"Fine. You are an adult; you can make your own choice. *I* am not taking it and you are *not* giving any to the children."

"Mom," Thor said, and held his hands over his head. Mrs. Lundquist re-capped the bottle and tossed it to Thor, who took a pill out and swallowed it before his father could stop him. "Mr. Garrison wouldn't take it himself unless it was the best chance we had."

Mr. Lundquist stared at all of us, red-faced, and then stomped away, saying, "I'm going back to bed."

The vaccine, like the disease, turned out to cause hallucinations.

I suppose I could provide a trippy, rambling account of the hallucinations, like a "Beck Hallucinates" segment of a movie (which of course would have "welcome to the free land, the glad land, the fair land" playing in the background since for some reason that song was playing in my head for most of the time I was out of it.)

Instead I will provide a list of what I remember:

- That song.
- The overpowering sense that I needed to find something.
- A forest that was maybe ferns, or maybe octopi.
- Needing to pee really badly and not being able to find the bathroom.
- Marmots.

- Thor's face. Which was just his face, and not some sort of creepy hallucination of a half-Thor, half-marmot or anything.

Then at some point I dozed off and when I woke up, I was fine, and so were Thor and his mom.

After that, the chances that Thor's father would allow Erik or Serena to take the vaccine (let alone take it himself) were approximately nil. Even though it was over in a few hours, and none of us had even hallucinated anything scary. Thor had put the pill bottle in the pocket of his jeans, or his father would have flushed the three remaining pills down the toilet.

The very first thing Mrs. Lundquist did was leave the apartment. Meanwhile, Thor's father packed up the MREs, Erik and Serena's toys, and the TV set, and moved into the master bedroom with a pointed slam of the door. "Aren't they going to have to come out to pee?" I asked Thor.

"No," Thor said. "There's a master bath. Just a toilet and sink, but they'll be able to pee and run water." He mulled it over. "They can't boil it, though. I guess Dad thinks that infection from Mom is a bigger deal than un-boiled water."

I looked at my watch. "It's ten-thirty," I said. "According to my dad, we're immune now." We looked at the door. "Let's get the hell out of here!"

I had expected empty hallways, but as we got closer to the commercial area we saw a fair number of people out. "Hey," Thor said. "Is that Shara?"

Shara was walking along the hallway with a bucket and a cloth. "Shara?" I called. She turned around and smiled hesitantly.

"Hey," she said. "I thought you were quarantined?"

"We, um," should I tell her about the vaccine? "Not anymore. You aren't, I guess."

"No, I got sick but I'm feeling a lot better. It wasn't that bad, just a day of *crazy* hallucinations and puking." She dipped her rag in the bucket and started scrubbing at a spot on the wall. "Anyway, my apartment is totally cleaned up now, so . . ." She gestured at the wall.

"So?" Thor said, a little blankly. "Why are you scrubbing the hall?"

"Because it's *dirty*?" she said, slowly, like she was talking to a small child or a dumb adult.

"Okay," he said. "Well, um, I'll see you later."

"Yup." She went back to scrubbing.

"What the hell?" Thor muttered as we walked further.

There were other people out with buckets and rags, or buckets and brushes, or mops. Someone was painstakingly washing shop windows with a spray bottle. Now, there *are* people who are hired to clean the corridors on Rosa, but they wear ID badges and they have big rolling buckets to wring out their mops and so on. Some of these people were walking around in PJs and slippers and were carrying around the sort of little buckets you'd keep in your apartment to clean it.

We saw someone else counting ceiling tiles, and making notes on his gadget each time he spotted a damaged one. Another person was out with paint and was painting a wall a vivid shade of aqua. Someone was dusting light bulbs.

"What the fuck," Thor whispered.

"What did you hallucinate?" I asked. "This morning? Was there something you needed to do?"

"I needed to run," he said. "I was trying to find the treadmill and I couldn't, but I needed to run."

"I needed to find something," I said. "I didn't know what."

"Huh," Thor said. We watched someone who was swabbing doorknobs with cleaning fluid and a rag. "How the hell would a disease make you want to clean doorknobs? Or run or find things? Or unravel clothing, or whatever it was Leah was talking about the other day?"

"Everyone knows that Sal does nanotech stuff," I said. "Maybe they did nanotech stuff that messes with brains instead of fixing your busted knee?"

"So what was in the vaccine, then?"

"Probably more nanotech," I said.

"Great."

"My father took it, too."

"How sure are you that he didn't take, like, an antidote or something first?"

"I don't feel like swabbing doorknobs," I said. "Do you?"

"No," he said.

"What do you suppose everyone's doing who's still in their apartment?"

We visited Mrs. Rodriguez, but she didn't answer. The apartment a few doors down had its door standing open, though, and when we cautiously peered inside we saw someone hand-stitching pillows out of clothing. She already stitched a large pile.

"This is way weirder than what Leah was describing on the newscasts," Thor said.

"Maybe we should call her?" I said. "We could tell her about the vaccine, too."

"Do you think we should? Will your dad be pissed?"

"I don't know." I pulled out my handheld and looked to see if Leah was broadcasting. She wasn't. There was a hand-written sign propped up against the potted plant saying BACK AT TEN. Except it was eleven. "I hope she's not sick."

"We could give her one of the vaccine pills. One of the ones we have left over. Do you think they'll work if you're already sick? Or make you worse?"

I thought about it. "They probably don't make you worse," I said, "because my father didn't ask if any of us had been having symptoms. He just gave us the pills and told us to take them. How many do we have? Three?"

Thor took out the bottle and peered in. "Yep."

"One for Leah," I said. "One for Debbie, maybe, if we can find her? And one—I don't know."

"Maybe there's someone who could make more," Thor said.

"Sal's making more—well, that's what my father said, anyway." I wondered how much Sal would *charge*. They might give them out for free—it wasn't just the humanitarian thing to do, it was the option that would reduce the risk of the rest of the seastead showing up on their deck with torches and pitchforks. But would people even trust the vaccine, coming from Sal? What if two-thirds of the steaders had the same reaction as Thor's father?

"Yeah," I said. "Maybe Leah will know."

The *Stead Life* studio was at the west edge of Rosa, and we passed through Embassy Row on our way. Thor knocked on the door of the Institute, to check on his friend Tyrone, but the Institute was locked up, shades drawn. All the embassies were.

"The Americans are going to bomb us," a man said. He was standing in the hallway by the Institute, bouncing nervously on the balls of his feet. "You know you're going to get bombed when they withdraw their ambassador."

"Was he withdrawn, or is he just hiding in there trying to avoid being exposed to the disease?" Thor asked.

"I heard from my brother who heard from a friend that LeBlanc and the other guy both left on a speedboat."

"That doesn't mean much."

"Sure it does. It means he was withdrawn, which the U.S. would obviously do before bombing us. You know this is a nanotech plague; it came from Sal. How do you stop something like that? BOMBS." Someone else was coming and he stopped them. "Excuse me. I think you should know that the U.S. is planning to bomb us."

"It's his compulsion," Thor said. "Talking about this, instead of scrubbing."

"Oh. Yeah," I said. We moved on. As we were going down the stairs I added, "He might be right, though."

"They wouldn't bomb us," Thor said.

"Why not? If we're carrying some doomsday disease?"

"The U.S. doesn't like killing civilians. Especially kids. There are loads of kids here." I must have looked dubious because he added, "Besides, your father didn't seem worried. Not about that, anyway. Would he really be staying here if the U.S. were planning to drop bombs?"

"No," I said. "But he might have been too distracted to know."

"Yeah? Do you think that's *likely?*"

"No," I said. "But it's possible."

There probably wasn't anything we could do about it even if the U.S. was planning to bomb us, but I pondered various options as we walked. Maybe we could steal a yacht and take off. We wouldn't be able to get past the blockade but it seemed reasonable that a small target would be harder to hit with a bomb than the whole seastead. Stealing a yacht would be hard at the best of times, though, and pretty nearly impossible right now since anyone who owned a yacht was probably on it. Had my father put out the word that they'd found a vaccine? Because if there was a vaccine they wouldn't need to bomb us, right?

No one answered when we knocked on the *Stead Life* office door, and for a minute I wondered if Leah was even there. But surely she was holed up inside—if she'd been willing to leave, she'd have had footage of people scrubbing doorknobs. It had been nothing but her and the plant and phone calls. She given me her contact information when she'd asked me to find Debbie for her, so I sat down on the floor outside her door and pulled out my gadget. *Leah*, I keyed in. *Have vaccine. Am right outside Stead Life door. —Beck.*

I heard some shuffling, like someone was stepping over piles of stuff, beyond the door. My gadget pinged. *What do you mean you have vaccine?*

My father made it and gave it just to me and the family I was staying with. I have extra doses, you want one? Let me in.

Pics to prove it.

I waved the pill in front of the gadget's eye, although how she'd know that a blue plastic capsule was the vaccine, I wasn't sure.

There was a crash behind the door. "Hold on," we heard through the door, muffled. "I'll be with you in a minute."

Leah had barricaded herself inside the *Stead Life* office. I mean that she literally *built a barricade* to keep people from coming in the door. Looking around, once I was in, I couldn't tell if she'd had the disease or not. Maybe she had, and it had given her the compulsion to *build barricades* or maybe that was just *her.*

She been camping out in the office; there were gallons and gallons of water in jugs, a pile of food (not MREs; she seemed to have been living off of PBJs and granola bars), and a sleeping bag was spread out in the one clear patch of floor. No one else was here.

"Vaccine," she said. "Tell me the details."

I told her about my father arriving, having me pick a dose for myself and a dose for him, and then leaving behind vaccine for the rest of the household. "Mr. Lundquist won't take it, and won't give it to the two younger kids," I said. "So I thought I'd bring a dose to you, so that you could . . . you know, get out there and do some reporting."

Leah chewed on her lip. "How long until Sal has enough for everyone?"

"I don't know," I said.

"Would your father answer the phone if *you* were the one calling?" she asked.

Her phone rang as I was thinking about this and she picked up. "Is this *Stead Life?*" She put him on speakerphone.

"Yeah, you've got Leah," she said.

"Okay!" The voice sounded excited. Frantic, actually. "We are holding off the invasion but we need reinforcements. Can you get the word out? We're on Min's big dock. We've got lots of guns but we could also use some more ammo."

"It's *not an invasion*, you cretin!" Leah shouted. "You're holding off an *aid ship*."

"Like hell it's an aid ship," the voice said. "It's flying a U.S. flag!"

"That's because it's an aid group that's based in the U.S.! Are you a complete idiot? They're here to help!"

"Oh, sure. Like the old joke goes, 'I'm here from the government, and—'"

"*They're not from the government.*" She looked like she wanted to break something—preferably the phone—in fury. "Have you ever heard of an NGO? A non-governmental organization? This one's called Humanists for Humanity, and—"

"So they're from the UN?"

"*No, they are not from the UN either.*"

"Look, if you don't want to help us, we'll find our own supporters. Bitch." The guy hung up.

Leah dropped her phone on her desk, breathing hard. "This guy's called me, like, twelve times now," she said. "I've been thinking about telling people about the aid ship that's circling the stead, not being allowed to land by the *raging paranoids*, but the unfortunate thing is that they're as likely to get supporters as opponents. And disorganized opponents will just get blown to hell themselves."

Thor was looking at her sideways. "Just how much are you *not* reporting, anyway?"

Leah looked indignant. "I can't possibly report every rumor that reaches me."

"Do you think this guy was always like this, or do you think it's a compulsion from the disease?"

"Does it really matter? He's not going to take your vaccine. Anyway, about your father—"

"I can't call him," I said. "He be furious I've left Thor's apartment." He send the Alpha Dogs after me—in theory they didn't operate outside of Lib, but in practice, right now? For the right price? They find me for him.

It occurred to me, too late, that Leah could blackmail me—threaten to tell my father I'd been here unless I came up with a way to get him to take her calls. But she just looked disappointed and left it at that.

"Well," she said. "*I'm* not a paranoid nutbag and I will *gladly* take the vaccine." She held out her hand. I handed her a pill.

"It's going to knock you on your ass for hours," I warned her.

"Yeah, I suppose it would be nice if you'd stay to babysit me and make sure I don't tear the place apart, but you've already been very kind in bringing it to me. I'll manage."

"You might want to back up your files before you take it," Thor said. "Your editing urges might get *really intense*. Or maybe you'll want to get out and report on stuff, I don't know."

She looked intrigued. "So people's compulsions relate to their *job*?"

"No—maybe?" I mulled that over. "I mean, I wanted to *find stuff*. Thor wanted to run, though, and that's not his job—"

"I don't have a job," Thor said, shrugging.

"No . . ." Leah still looked fascinated. "But maybe that's the pattern." She made a note to herself on some scrap paper. "Hey, before you go, do you want to take a transmitting camera with you? I'm short on good *footage*. Mostly people are staying holed up in their rooms and calling around." She gave us each a camera we could buckle around our wrists like an old-style wristwatch. "Not that this should be an excuse for you to go find the worst mess on Minerva or anything! You're just kids. But if you'll be out, you know, if you see anything interesting . . ."

"People swabbing doorknobs?" Thor said.

"It beats the plant," Leah said.

She dry-swallowed the pill as she shut door behind us.

CHAPTER TEN

"SO, HERE'S SOMETHING I DON'T UNDERSTAND," THOR said. We were walking around Rosa, looking for "interesting footage," since trying to hunt for Debbie down by the desalination tanks right now actually seemed like it might be somewhat suicidal.

"Yeah?"

"There's an aid ship trying to dock here and a bunch of nutbags are trying to stop it. Why don't they go land at one of the other docks?"

"Well, we have some specialized docks. Min has some of the weirder fuel mixes, a crane, and a really big dock. I mean, for something little and straightforward, anyone but Lib can handle it, but if you've got anything weird . . . you might need Min. I assume that either the aid group needs to unload something large, or they need one of the special fuels."

"Why anyone but Lib?"

"Lib doesn't have a dock. They use the other steads' docks plus they have a crane, in a pinch, but mostly it's other docks plus bridges. You know they're on an old Russian cargo ship, right?"

"Yeah. What's it like? My parents won't let me go there."

"My dad doesn't let me go there, either. I did anyway. Anyway, I don't think I exactly saw the scenic parts."

"*Are* there scenic parts? Or do they rent those from Rosa like they rent dock space?"

"There used to be a park deck—you know, lots of plants and you could sit out in the sun. For a fee."

"Used to be?"

"It got sold. It's used for something else now."

"Skin farming?"

"Ha. They couldn't possibly, not unless they installed a roof. You need a controlled environment—temperature, light, everything." I thought it over. "Then again, maybe they *did* install a roof. Lib's comparative advantage is in things that aren't legal other places. Do you know what comparative advantage is?"

"It's stuff you're particularly good at?"

"Well, kind of. It's stuff that you are *so* good at that you're wasting your own money by spending time doing anything else, even if you're making a profit on those things, too. Like if you could make sandwiches for $100 a day, OR you could make customized organs for transplant for $1000 a day, you should go with the organs, right? And that's true even if you have to pay someone else $200 a day for the sandwiches you could make for $100. Because you come out ahead. Anyway. Lib's comparative advantage is in stuff that's illegal other places, like skin farms."

"So do they have a comparative advantage in private security forces?"

"Well—kind of. But those might count more as an operating expense." I thought about the Alpha Dog who'd helped me free Debbie's sister. He been courteous and ruthlessly efficient. Not thrilled with the job I'd given him, but . . .

"You know," I said. "The ADs could totally kick out the paranoid nutbags and let the aid ship land."

"You must have made a lot more money on that TV show than I did, if you're thinking of hiring the ADs. Unless you think your dad might underwrite it."

"I was thinking I might just try to talk them into it."

Thor glanced at me, grinning. "Seriously?"

"Yeah, seriously."

"OK. Are we going to Lib, then? Because this, I've totally got to see."

We had to leave Rosa and pass through Pete to get to Lib, but fortunately no one was really paying attention to the bridges at this point. The guys who'd been guarding the entrances to Rosa a few days ago were all gone—maybe in quarantine, maybe swabbing doorknobs. As we walked, we saw people scrubbing walls and washing windows, counting broken tiles, closing all the propped-open fire doors, cutting paper into strips. Someone had pulled down one of the big stashes of lifejackets and was trying on each lifejacket to test the fit, the buckles, and the straps. We even saw one person who was painting the walls—not with the cream-colored wall paint that you'd see in most parts of Pete but with bright colors from a box of acrylic paints. She was painting a mural. It was beautiful, actually: a landscape with mountains and trees and animals in wild, implausible colors. "Cool," Thor muttered as we passed.

Then we got close to Lib, and were hit by the reek.

We just passed through a set of closed fire doors. Thor pulled the collar of his shirt up over his face. "Do you think the sewer ruptured, or what?" he asked.

"I hope not," I said, trying not to gag. "Wait—we should report this, with those cameras we got from Leah."

"You be the reporter," he said, his voice muffled. "I like my air filter."

"Okay." He held up his wrist camera and I swallowed hard and hoped my hair wasn't sticking out at some stupid-looking angle. "I'm near the Pete side of the Petrov bridge," I said. "It smells *really bad* here. It smells like there's been an accident with the sewer, but we don't see any evidence, yet."

We saw the evidence when we came around the corner. There were people lying in the hallway and the floor was almost running with human wastes.

"Oh my God," Thor said, recoiling. "What the hell is happening here? The plague didn't do this to anyone else we've seen."

The sick people were wedged against the wall, and we could see the evidence of the compulsions, too: there were people scrubbing with water and disinfectant, it just didn't seem to be helping much. Someone else was walking up and down the rows of people, bringing water to the patients. I initially assumed she had a water-carrying compulsion and then felt ashamed as I realized that she might be a good and decent person who wanted to help.

"Okay," I heard Thor's voice say behind me, shakily, as he held up his camera. "Here we are in what seems to be a makeshift hospital. Quite a lot of these people seem to have diarrhea, which is strange because we saw no evidence of this symptom elsewhere."

One of the women who was bringing water around looked up at the sound of Thor's voice, and her face lit up when she saw me. "Beck," she said, standing up. "I need you to find something for me."

I started to say that I wasn't Finding anymore, but she hadn't waited for me to talk. "Sugar and salt," she said. "I'm running out. We're filtering the water to purify it, but we need sugar and salt for proper rehydration fluid." She waved her hand at the bodies in the hallway. "They'll pull through with supportive care."

I looked around and fought nausea again. "What *is* this? I mean—can you tell me when it started?"

"Two days ago," the woman said. I didn't know her name, even though she knew mine. I was pretty sure she wasn't a nurse in her regular life; she was a citizen, not a bondworker or guest worker, that much I remembered. "It's probably cholera. All these people were on Lib—there's something wrong with the water supply."

"Is all of Lib like this?" Thor asked.

She looked around like she was really seeing her surroundings for the first time in a while. "I haven't actually been on Lib. Just here. I imagine it's worse, though."

Thor nudged me. "If she says on camera what she needs, maybe Leah will broadcast it."

I held up my wrist camera to be sure I was getting her on it, and she repeated her request: salt and sugar, and so long as she was giving a wish list, bleach, buckets, vinyl gloves, and clean bedding would be great, too. And more healthy volunteers. As many as would come. She also gave the recipe for rehydration fluid, for anyone suffering in their own apartment: one liter of purified water, one teaspoon of salt, three tablespoons of sugar—"it'll taste like shit, but it'll keep you alive."

The next makeshift infirmary was closer to the bridge to Lib. Here, no one was carrying water, and I was pretty sure that some of the people were dead. I hesitated, wondering if it would help if I brought people water—if there *was* any water—what was it that woman had said about supportive care?

Thor grabbed my arm. "*This* is why we need to get the aid group here," he said.

"Yeah," I said, and let him pull me away.

The Alpha Dogs' door was closed. On the inside of the window into the office, they'd posted a sign saying, OFFICE OPEN ONLY TO EXISTING CUSTOMERS and a phone number.

I dialed it. It rang twice, and then someone answered.

"This is Beck Garrison," I said.

"What the hell are you doing here? Oh, *Jesus H. Christ*," the voice said, and the door opened. Someone grabbed both me and Thor by the arms and yanked us inside, slamming the door after us.

"Jesus H. Christ," he said again. "I suppose this time *he's* your date?"

It was the guy I'd had help me rescue Debbie's sister, Lynn.

"I'm not going to go any further onto Lib," I said, meekly.

He stared at me, turning at least three different shades of red. "I suppose that's something," he said, finally. "Did your father send you here? I guess I should have asked."

"No," I said. "He doesn't know I'm here."

"Of course not," he said.

I'd had my appeal all planned out in my head but he'd completely thrown me off-track and what came out next was, "I have a vaccine."

"Against cholera?"

"No. Against the disease—is it not happening on Lib? The one that's on the rest of the Stead."

"Lib has its own ventilation system and it's been traveling slowly, from what I can tell. Unfortunately, our water-purification system got contaminated, at least that's what we heard. We've been boiling our water and hoping the electricity holds out."

I looked around the small office, wondering how many ADs there actually were, and whether the rest were holed up in the back or if they were scattered all over the stead. I took a deep breath. "Okay," I said. "Here's the thing. I have two more doses of the vaccine. My father says that Sal is making more, but it will take time—I don't know how much time. There's an aid group that came in a boat that might be able to copy it, but they're not being allowed to land because there are Steaders who've taken over the dock on Min, with guns. They think the aid group is the U.S. government, invading." I glanced at the bodyguard for his reaction. He snorted derisively. "Anyway, I was hoping to talk you into helping."

"Helping with what?"

"Helping to retake the dock. On Min. So the aid ship can land, because you know, they'll be able to help Lib, too, all the people with cholera. Or whatever it is people have here. The woman we ran into said people will pull through with supportive care."

The guy's face had returned to a normal color and he looked

speculative, now. "Who are you, anyway?" he asked Thor.

"I'm her date," Thor said.

"No, seriously."

"I'm her bodyguard?"

The AD snorted at that. "My name's Zach," he said, and held out his hand.

Thor shook it. "Thor," he said.

"You two can wait here while I talk to the others. Because we might do this, but there will be conditions. And I don't mean money."

There were a dozen ADs crammed into the back rooms, it turned out, sleeping on rollout mats and living off of frozen dinners and Mountain Dew. After Zach had conferred with them for a bit, they crowded into the front office, bringing with them the smell of unwashed bodies and stale pizza.

"Here's the thing," Zach said. "Min, Rosa, and Pete have laws against 'vigilante actions' that were basically written to keep the ADs out. If we go in there, they could prosecute us later, and although they can't come onto Lib to arrest us, most of us have apartments or at least flops on other steads. Or girlfriends."

"Or boyfriends," someone chimed in, in a cheerful Russian accent.

"Yeah, Evgeni has at least two of those on *every other stead*. Anyway. We're willing to secure the dock on Min so that the aid ship can land, and we will waive our usual fee, which would be *considerable*, for the good of the stead as a whole and because we know perfectly well you don't have it. And the longer we delay, the worse things are going to get. On Lib, and everywhere else. But. We need a signed letter of authorization from Uncle Paul—if he authorizes our action, it's allowed, and we won't have to worry about prosecution later."

"What if we can't find him?" I asked.

Zach snorted. "I don't think there's a man in this room willing to buy that *you* can't find him, Ms. Garrison."

"Okay, well, what if he's dead?"

"If he's dead—call, we'll talk about who would make an adequate substitute. But if there's one thing Uncle Paul excels at, it's surviving. I think if you can find him, he'll be alive. And if you can talk him into putting his thumbprint on the authorization, we'll take the dock. *That*, I think we can assure you, *we* can do."

Around the room, men nodded.

Zach held out his hand. "Do we have a deal?"

We shook on it.

Uncle Paul's office was on one of the oldest parts of Min— one of the original sea platforms, near the base of the platform but with an outside window. It was his office as well as his apartment—I knew that because I'd been there with my father.

This part of Min was eerily quiet and much less clean. The people with scrubbing compulsions were staying away, and it was mostly offices and businesses that had been closed up tight by people who were holing up at home. Some of the lights in the corridor weren't working properly (making the whole thing even creepier) and I could see a thin gleam of light under Uncle Paul's door.

"'What if I can't find him,'" Thor muttered. "*Pfft.*"

"He could have had a compulsion that made him wander," I said.

"No," Thor said. "People are getting their compulsions from their jobs. And Uncle Paul usually does his job in his office."

"Hmm." I knocked on Uncle Paul's door.

"Come in," he called.

I looked at Thor. He raised his eyebrow. Hesitantly, ready to duck if bullets started flying, we opened the door.

The office featured one really big desk, one really big chair, and two much less impressive visitor's chairs. Uncle Paul was seated at his desk, surrounded by what looked like confetti. He had a pair of scissors, and was cutting up a piece of paper into tiny, thin strips. His eyes were on his task. "I'll be with you in a minute," he said.

We waited. He finished cutting up that piece of paper, and shook it out into a single paper loop. He smiled with satisfaction, and then took another piece of paper. "Uncle Paul?" I said.

"Yes, hang on," he said, and started cutting.

"It's a compulsion," Thor said, to me.

Uncle Paul looked up. "God damn *motherfuckers*," he said.

"Who?" I asked, easing my sleeve back from my wrist-camera.

"Just a minute," he said, returning to his cutting.

"Maybe we can talk while you cut," I said.

"No, not really, requires too much concentration. *Motherfuck-ers* on Sal." He slammed his scissors down. "*We can solve every-thing*, they said. *Those bondworkers will line up like children and roll up their sleeves*, they said. It wasn't supposed to be *contagious*."

Thor gave me a startled look. I steadied the camera. "What were the people on Sal trying to do?" I asked.

"Just a minute," he said, and picked the scissors up to start cut-ting again. When he'd finished with his delicate work, he shook it out, smiled at it, tossed it aside, and took a fresh piece of paper.

"Tell me about Sal," Thor said.

Uncle Paul set his scissors down with delicate precision. "They said they had a solution to the union problem. I never liked the idea. Old solutions are always the way to go." He picked them back up. "I was right, too. *Motherfuckers*."

"We've got a vaccine," I said.

"Did it come from Sal?"

"Yes."

"Keep it the hell away from me, then."

Thor had his wrist camera out, so I let him keep at it while I edged over to take a look at Uncle Paul's desk. He left his gadget unlocked: his e-mail popped right up as soon as I flicked the screen. Almost everything was marked *priority* or *urgent* or *emergency*. I'd expected there to be stuff about bombings but the most urgent messages seemed to involve Lib. "What's going on with Lib?" I asked, wondering if he'd attack me with the scissors for reading his mail.

"They want to unship." He looked up at me, his eyes smoldering, but I was pretty sure he was angry at Lib more than me. "They're self-contained, so they *could*. Never mind the blockade, never mind the havoc they'll wreak on the rest of the stead." He held out the scissors, trying to hold them on the edge of his hand. "They'll—they'll—" The scissors fell to his desk and he pounded his desk.

"Unbalance things?" Thor asked.

"*That*." He picked up the scissors again. "There's air chambers," he muttered. "Ballast. We can fix this. Someone can fix this. But I need to take care of this, first. Just a minute. Just a minute."

"We need your approval for something," I said, pulling up the contract with the ADs on my own gadget. "Just thumbprint this, okay?"

For a second, I thought he'd do it, but then he yanked his hand back and pounded his desk with his scissors. "You're trying to trick me!"

"No, of course not," I said, dodging away from him as he tried to grab my gadget. "But you know there's an aid ship trying to land, right? Do you know that?"

He was still furious, but focused again on the paper. "I might have heard something, but this is important. I need to deal with this, first."

"Yeah," I said. "We'll take care of the the aid ship for you, so you can focus on what you need to do." He glanced up at me, his eyes still smoldering. "Do you know if it's true the U.S. is going to bomb us?"

"Might be in my e-mail."

I edged back toward his desk. He made no sudden grab for me, and I looked at his gadget. There were messages about Lib threatening to unship. About the U.S. withdrawing the Director (he wasn't an "Ambassador," technically) from the American Institute. About the aid group—actually, some of these messages were *from* the aid group. I discreetly opened one. Maybe it had a phone number? *Yes.*

Paul was suddenly pounding his desk again. I jumped back. "*Leave it.*"

"I need this information!" I said.

"*Mine.*"

"Yeah, well, are you going to take the stupid vaccine and get back to your job instead of cutting paper? Sal created the problem, I'd think they'd be able to solve it!"

He leaped up, and I dodged out of the way, but he wasn't going for me—he was going for his own gadget. He hurled it across the room, shattering the screen. Then he sat back down, picked up his scissors, and resumed cutting.

Thor edged over to me. "Did you get what you needed?"

"A phone number." I rattled it off. "Help me remember?" He nodded. "How bad is it going to mess things up if Lib pulls out?"

"For us? I think we've got time, unless they're unshipping *now*."

"No, I mean, for the whole stead. If Uncle Paul is this out of it—who even knows what's going on with the person who usually deals with the air chambers and ballast—"

Thor chewed his lip, staring at Uncle Paul. "I think if we had one more person we could take him," he said, and flicked my pocket, where I had the jar of pills.

"Getting another person would be tricky."

"We could call the ADs."

"They already said they won't do anything without the authorization. Which only covers the action on the dock." I looked around the office, pondering, and my eye fell on a little refrigerator. "Uncle Paul?" I said. "Are you hungry?"

He looked up, calmer. "Ravenous. I can't remember the last time I ate."

I opened up the fridge. He had sandwich fixings, four apples, a six-pack of beer, and a tub of yogurt. "You know what?" I said, keeping my voice even. "There's yogurt in here. If you can tell me where to find a spoon, I could spoon it right into your mouth and you won't have to stop cutting."

"Perfect." I could hear eagerness and relief in his voice. "Right-hand top drawer, there are some utensils with the pens."

There was a sharp knife in the drawer, too, which made it easy to break open the capsule. I poured the powder into the spoon, then dug quickly into the yogurt. "Okay, Uncle Paul," I said. "Open up for some yogurt."

He opened his mouth and let me spoon-feed him like a baby.

"That's better, isn't it?" I said, as I scraped out the bottom of the yogurt. He nodded. "You'll be able to sleep, then, when you're done with some of this."

"Maybe," he said, his voice rough and a little bit desperate.

"Would you do me a favor?" I asked. "Since I helped you out with the food and all."

He nodded.

"I just need you to thumbprint something. You don't even have to put down your scissors."

"How much damage do you think he's going to cause when the hallucinations hit?" Thor asked.

"Well, he's already smashed his gadget," I said. "Besides, we don't know if it causes hallucinations if you've already been through the illness."

"We don't know if it *works* if you've already been through the illness."

"True enough." We gotten far enough away that I wasn't worried Paul would realize what we done and come running after us, so I leaned against the wall and took out my gadget, sending the contract off to the ADs. "I'm going to call the aid ship. Do you still remember the number?"

"Yeah," Thor said, and reeled it off. I dialed, wondering if they'd actually answer.

Two rings, and someone actually picked up. "You've reached the Mary Ellen Carter. Is this by any chance Paul Brynn?"

"No," I said. "Uncle—Paul Brynn—um, he's indisposed. But I've done what I can to make it possible for you to dock with us—not yet, but soon—and I have one pill left of the vaccine, because I'm hoping you can make copies of it."

There was a moment of silence, and then the voice said, "*Who is this?*"

"My name is Beck Garrison, but I'm not, like, an elected official or anything." Another pause. "Look," I said. "Things have been a little chaotic here, and I was one of the first to get the vaccine, so I went out to see if I could do anything useful and I found out about the dock. We really need some help, because there's the plague that gives people crazy compulsions, and there's also cholera, on Lib."

"Not crazy," Thor muttered. "Work-related."

"Anyway, are you still willing to land, once the Alpha Dogs take the dock? Paul Brynn will be more useful in a little while. I fed him some vaccine mixed into yogurt so maybe in about four hours, he'll be able to talk to you. Although he's really exhausted so it might be longer, I'm not sure."

"We're willing to land," the voice said. "Let us know when you think it's safe. In the meantime, we all be a bit more comfortable if you yourself would retreat to the safest location you can think of."

Thor and I decided that the safest place we could think of was the *Stead Life* studio. My apartment had my father, his apartment had his father, and we didn't really want to run into either of them. Leah was done with her hallucinations; the studio was a complete shambles, though, and she was slowly putting things away when she let us in.

"Did you get any good footage for me?" she asked.

"I want to re-watch the bits we got of Uncle Paul," Thor said. "Can you show me how to do that?"

Leah showed him how to pull up the feed from the two cameras on her computer's editing program.

"*Motherfuckers on Sal,*" I watched Uncle Paul say, slamming his scissors down. From the angle of my camera, I could see deep red lines in his hands from where the scissors were rubbing against the skin. "*We can solve everything*, they said. *Those bondworkers will line up like children and roll up their sleeves*, they said. It wasn't supposed to be *contagious.*" He picked the scissors back up and cut feverishly as we tried to get more out of him. "They said they had a solution to the union problem. I never liked the idea. Old solutions are always the way to go. I was right, too. *Motherfuckers.*"

"The plague was planned," Thor said. "I mean, they didn't expect *this*. They screwed it up. But the *plague itself* was something Sal engineered on purpose." He pointed at Paul, frozen on the screen with his scissors. "They were trying to solve the union problem by engineering something that would make the bondworkers focus on their jobs. That would make them *happy* slaves instead of cranky, discontented slaves. Only they screwed it up. It was contagious, it affected everybody, and it didn't work the way they'd wanted it to."

"When he said they'd roll up their sleeves—" I realized that I was shaking. "The health benefits they were offering. That was probably to give them cover. Holy *shit.*"

We looked at Leah.

"I'll air it if you want me to," she said. "But you might want to give your father a heads up, because people might kick in his door, and throw his burning corpse over the side of the stead." She chewed on her lip. "I could hold it for a while, first. There's plenty else to talk about right now, like the cholera epidemic, and the aid ship."

"Hold off," I said. "Please. At least for now."

"Are you going to let her air it?"

Leah was doing a broadcast. Thor and I had shut ourselves into the lavatory so that we had a sound-insulated door between us and the studio and could have a conversation. I was sitting on the toilet (with my pants *up*. I was basically just using it as a chair) and Thor was leaning against the sink.

"I can't stop her, can I?"

"She made it pretty clear she won't air it unless you say it's OK with you."

"I guess."

"You can call your dad and warn him. You don't even have to tell him that it's up to you if it gets aired."

"I know."

"Or you could call your dad and check on him. He might be on Sal now, not Min, you know?"

"That's true." I pulled out my phone and checked to see if he had called me, and I'd missed it. He hadn't. I called my dad. No answer. I sent him a text: *Need to talk. Call me!*

We sat in silence for a few minutes.

"You think I need to let her air it," I said.

"It's not just your dad," Thor said. "The people who did this shouldn't get away with it. If it means new leadership for the Stead, that's a good thing."

"Maybe," I said. "Or maybe it'll be people who are even worse."

"You can't let that fear stop you from doing anything."

"It's easy for *you* to say," I snapped. "*Your* father doesn't work for Sal. *Your* father isn't in any danger of getting murdered by furious vigilantes."

"No," Thor said, quietly. "But he is in some danger of winding up a bond-worker, you know."

My cheeks burned. I stood up. "It's your turn to sit down for a while," I said, and jerked my head at the toilet. Thor started to protest, then went ahead and sat.

"I'm sorry," he said.

"Well, you're right," I said. "It's true. My dad is the Mad Scientist who Unleashed the Omega Plague. Maybe he *should* get murdered by vigilantes."

"No," Thor said. "I am a fan of the American approach of charging people with war crimes and giving them proper lawyers and all that. I do think he should be charged with crimes, just like my father ought to be. My dad ought to be in jail right now, serving ten to fifteen years."

"Ten to fifteen?"

"Yeah, I looked it up. I mean, I looked up the sentencing guidelines for the precise crime they probably would've let him plead down to, accounting for stuff like his lack of prior convictions and the fact that he would've had a good lawyer." Thor pulled something out of his pocket. "Sandwich?"

"Where on earth did you get that?" I said, realizing looking at it that I was *ravenous*. When had we last eaten? I couldn't remember.

"I raided Uncle Paul's fridge while you were feeding him yogurt. It's soy-based bologna and the cheese is the sort that you peel off the plastic."

"At this point I'd probably eat liverwurst with limburger." He made a sandwich for each of us, and then stuffed them into his sweatshirt pocket.

We were finishing the sandwiches when Leah knocked on the door. "We're on a Plant Break and I need you two to vacate the lavatory on account of I need to pee."

I was feeling restless and antsy and couldn't imagine staying in that studio much longer. "Why don't we go to the dock?" I said. "We could get some footage of the ADs, maybe. And the aid ship landing."

"Didn't they ask us to stay somewhere safe?" Thor asked.

"Yeah," I said. "I bet my dad would've liked that, too."

We left while Leah was still in the bathroom.

There was actually a deck that overlooked the dock, so that you could watch big ships come in, and no one was checking passes today (although someone was scrubbing the floor) so we just went in.

We arrived just in time to see the ADs invade. They came via a speedboat, blasted the dock with a tear gas grenade, and then shouted through a megaphone that they were the Alpha Dogs, and if the people on the dock knew what was good for them, they'd throw down their guns and surrender.

Which they *did*, although in part I think that was because they thought the ADs were their allies in protecting the stead from a real invasion. "We're on your side, bro," I could hear the leader say as Zach put him in plastic cuffs and patted him down for more weapons. "All you needed to do was tell us who you were, we weren't going to fire on our own kind!"

"Uh huh," Zach said, and the rest of the ADs hauled off the dock defenders. They checked it over thoroughly, established guards at each entrance, and then Zach took out his gadget. My phone rang. "Ms. Garrison?" Zach said. "The dock is secure. I assume you know how to reach the aid ship?"

"I do," I said. "I'll let them know it's safe to land."

I called the *Mary Ellen Carter*. "This is Beck Garrison," I said. "The Alpha Dogs have taken the dock so that you can land. Do you need any assistance from our end?"

"No, so long as no one's shooting at us."

"Yeah, I *think* that's been taken care of."

Thor jabbed me, alarmed. "What if they don't come?" he hissed.

"I'm *pretty sure*," I corrected myself. "The ADs are really good at what they do."

"Do you want to go down and meet them?" Thor asked when I'd hung up.

"Yeah," I said. "I mean, we know where the cholera is, we have the vaccine pill, and you know, I think Uncle Paul's probably still having hallucinations. They're pretty much going to *need* us, don't you think?"

The *Mary Ellen Carter* was a former whaling ship, flying a U.S. flag and then a white flag with a red heart on it. I filmed it coming in, hoping I was holding the camera steady, and Evgeni the AD helped them tie up and lower a gangplank.

The woman at the top was wearing a white coat with a patch that had an embroidered red heart. "I'm Captain Stephanie Drake," she said. "I'm guessing that you're Beck Garrison. Do you have the vaccine with you? Come on up."

Thor and I went up the gangplank. I handed over the plastic pill bottle, the last capsule still rattling around the bottom. "I had three extras," I said. "I gave one to Leah, who's the woman who runs the TV station. I sort of force-fed the other to Uncle Paul, who's the one who SHOULD have been taking care of things like securing the dock so you could land."

"We like to examine you, as well, if you don't mind," she said to me and Thor. "To get a sense of what this does in your bodies. My guess is that both the illness and the vaccine are nanotech-related."

We followed her down a steep set of stairs into the hold, where there was a well-equipped medical lab. "Is that—" someone asked, her eyes filled with shock.

"Yes, it's startling to see how *young* our contact is, isn't it?" Captain Drake said, riding through whatever the woman was starting to say.

"Are you a doctor?" I asked her.

"Nurse Practitioner, actually. We have a mix on the ship. Do you mind?" She held up a needle. "I'd like to draw some of your blood."

I let her draw my blood, and Thor let her draw some of his, and she slid the samples into a machine that displayed both on a screen. "Yeah," she said, chewing on her lip. "Definitely a nano-tech vax. Which makes things much more complicated, but we did bring facilities . . ."

One of the other doctors or nurses or whatever had come over. "I think we probably want to start by treating with the vaccine. We have good facilities for replication. We can do decon on a small scale, but people will just get infected again. If we can fully vaccinate the population, we can decontaminate late . . ."

"What do you think the odds are that we'll be able to fully vaccinate the population? Unless we engineer contagion, which of course will defeat the later attempts at decon."

"We have to vaccinate to whatever extent we can. Maybe the Feds will send in a large-scale decon operation later. Or do it with an EMP."

"We're hoping to *avoid* an EMP."

Thor was watching them argue and looked alarmed. "Is the U.S. going to *nuke* us?"

"No," Captain Drake said. "There's talk of using a targeted electromagnetic pulse—just the pulse, not an actual nuke—to disable all nanotech. The problem, of course, is that it would permanently disable all electronic devices on the seastead."

I thought about just how many things would stop working. "That won't do anything good for the cholera outbreak," I said.

"Your water purification is probably largely mechanical . . ."

"Yeah, the people on Lib who *aren't* sick are boiling water. Would an EMP knock out our electricity? Because it seems like probably."

The women mulled it over.

"Would people be more accepting of a vaccine if it came from the scientists on Sal?"

"No," I said. "It's better coming from you."

"Well, we'll do what we can," Captain Drake said. "And now, if you don't mind, I'm going to have to see you to one of our state-rooms."

"What?"

"Thor, you're free to go."

He stared at them, alarmed. "What the hell? Why are you making Beck stay here?"

"Because her mother's on this ship," Captain Drake said. "And Beck is a minor, and she doesn't have her mother's permission to leave."

I probably could have taken her, or at least made a hell of a mess of their medical lab, but what would *that* do to their ability to get medical care to the stead? I opted to go peacefully, fuming, to a small, tidy room that was labeled 'Captain's Quarters.'

The door swung open, and—there she was, waiting, and I actually recognized her, though more from the photo she'd sent than my memories. My heart leapt. "*Becky,*" she choked out through what sounded like a sob, and pulled me into a hug.

Her hug was not like my father's hugs: he hugged me sometimes, but was always stiff when he did it, even when I was little. My mother held me so tight it almost hurt, like she was afraid someone would come and rip me away from her.

"It's Beck now," I mumbled, awkwardly.

"Of course, Beck, I'm sorry," she said. "I'll try to remember."

I pulled back, finally. "What are you doing here?" I asked.

"I'm a nurse," she said. "And I have some expertise on seast-ead culture, so when I called to volunteer . . ."

"Then you'll understand that you can't *keep me prisoner* here." "What? You're not a prisoner!"

"Captain Drake said I couldn't leave this ship *without your permission.*"

"I thought—" her voice caught. "Honey, I want you to come home with me."

"You could have *asked*."

"Your *father* never asked."

We stared at each other for a second, breathing hard. My mother's eyes had teared up when she saw me, but now I could see some steel in them. She didn't want me to hate her—but she was convinced that if she could just get me back to California, I'd come around.

But they're going to be here for weeks! I wanted to scream. The idea of being kept prisoner for *that long* in a tiny room—when there was so much work to be done!—made me feel sick.

"You can't keep me here," I said.

"From what I understand, your father kept you in your apartment for an entire month."

"*I'm needed right now.* And even my father let me out to go for tutoring. Do you realize—do you know—"

We were interrupted by shouting, and someone pounded on the door. "Open up, Lenore!"

My mother's lips tightened and she opened the door. Captain Drake jerked her head at me. "Up on deck. Now."

I followed her back up the stairs, my mother tagging behind me. Down on the dock, Thor was standing next to Zach. "Look," Captain Drake shouted down. "She's FINE, do you see? FINE."

"Beck," Thor called, "Are you okay?"

"Would you at least call off your count?"

"I'm okay," I said. "But they don't want to let me leave."

"Can we talk about this?" Captain Drake called down.

Zach checked his wrist. "You have two minutes and fifty-seven seconds," he said. "So you'd probably better talk fast."

Captain Drake turned to my mother. "I'm sorry, Lenore. They gave us five minutes to have her back on the dock or they're storming the ship to get her."

"Who?" my mother said, blankly.

"The *guys with the guns*," Captain Drake said.

"I guess I' better be going, then," I said. "Bye! It was good to see you!"

"Rebecca—"

"Look." I turned back to my mother. "You can call me. You can come find me. But don't expect me to come onto this ship again, because the ADs don't work cheap."

Back on the ground, Zach offered me a fist-bump. "How much did that cost you?" I asked Thor.

"*Cost* him?" Zach said. "We don't leave our own behind, kid."

My father's apartment opened when I punched in my code. "Dad?" I asked hesitantly, coming inside.

No reply.

"It's Beck. Are you here?"

It's a small apartment—two curtained alcoves for our beds, a living area, a tiny bathroom, and my father's study. He wasn't in his own bed, or in mine, or on the couch. The bathroom stood open. The study door was closed, but when I banged on the door and got no answer, I opened the door. It wasn't locked.

His computer was gone. The painting of the girls and the piano was gone. And he certainly wasn't there. But there was a note on the desk, in an envelope, addressed to me. I tore it open.

> Beck,
>
>   It's tempting to leave a long explanation of how much I was able to predict—I was certain that Mr. Lundquist would refuse the vaccine, leaving you spare vaccine to take to someone who could replicate it. Someone other than the research labs of

Sal—which aren't trusted by anyone, at this point. Even me.

I was certain that left to your own devices, you'd find something useful to do with that pill.

I was also quite certain that you'd eventually learn just how much of a hand I had in this. And while I appreciate that you bought me some time—and the fact that that the pitchfork-and-torches brigade is at present rather occupied with doorknob hygiene—I thought it best that I absent myself as promptly as possible. For I might be able to trust your discretion, but I surely can't trust Leah's for long. Or Uncle Paul's.

I know your mother would like to see you; perhaps you might go visit her in California? If you'd like to make the seastead your permanent home—now or in the future—you'll find gold boullion in the lower left-hand drawer in sufficient quantity for you to buy yourself a stake. Perhaps you would think of me more fondly if I left you enough to buy yourself a comfortable apartment, as well—but all in all, I think it's best when children make their own way in the world.

I remain,
Fondly,
Your father

I sat in the fading light of his office for a long time, watching the sun set through his window.

Looking out at the sky, I made my decision: I would go back to California with my mother.

PART FIVE
JUBILEE

CHAPTER ELEVEN

It took ten years to build the seastead. Obviously, at the end of that first decade, it was pretty small. But it was functional—the colonists had ships and platforms anchored into place, a stable population, desalination plants and power generators, and a cooperation agreement between Min, Rosa, Lib, Pete, and Amsterdarn. (Sal came later.)

The seastead is forty-nine years old now. There's actually a big Golden Jubilee celebration planned for next year. Or at least, there *was* a big Golden Jubilee celebration planned.

Two plagues, a blockade, a bunch of atheistic do-gooders, organizational gridlock, and an *enormous mess*: there might be someone out there who considered that a terrific party, but not me.

Thor and I laid out a card game on the living room table. "Morning status reports," I heard Captain Drake say wearily from the other room. The Humanists for Humanity leadership team had taken over my father's office as a meeting room. Since my mother wanted me staying in the apartment unless I absolutely had to leave, I wasn't eavesdropping; I just happened to be stuck in a spot where I could hear every word they were saying at their meeting.

The Humanists at the meeting delivered a series of increasingly grim-sounding reports. Overnight death count, and counts of newly infected patients. They confirmed that the disease on Lib was cholera. Since cholera is water-borne and all our water comes out of desalinators, Captain Drake thought this one ought to be easy to solve, but the water expert hadn't even managed to figure out where on Lib the water treatment plant was located. Also, Lib was terrifying, and she didn't want to go back without an escort.

"Sensible," I muttered, putting down a card. *I* wouldn't go to Lib without an escort. And I'd have told them so, if they'd have listened.

They moved on to the other disease. People had started calling it the worker bee flu, even though it was not even remotely related to influenza. For one thing, influenza could be deadly. The worker bee flu didn't kill people directly, though reports were flooding in about people who'd died from falls or drowning or exhaustion. This seemed like a specious distinction to me, but the Humanists considered it key.

On Rosa and Min, half the citizens were ready to riot to get to the vaccine against the worker bee flu; the other half said they'd shoot anyone who tried to force it on them. Amsterdarn had gotten a late start on the nanotech disease, but was suffering from some interesting civil disorder. Sal was apparently locked down and non-responsive. One of the Humanists had taken a speedboat over and shouted through a megaphone, with no results.

Thor won the hand, and I picked up the cards to re-deal. In the meeting room, people's voices were rising in frustration. Normally, when they arrived somewhere to help after a disaster, they worked with the people in charge. That was how things were *done*—aid groups like the HfH cooperated with the government and existing NGOs. That did not work *at all* on Lib, which had no government. On Min, they had Uncle Paul, but the Uncle Paul equivalents on Pete, Rosa, and Amsterdarn were nowhere to be found. Uncle Paul had given my mother a list of the twenty people on the Seastead Governing Council. She managed to find exactly two of them, and one of those was Uncle Paul.

"Are the rest dead?" asked Captain Drake. "Or just missing?"

"Does it matter?" I heard my mother say. "Either way, they're not helping."

"If they're around somewhere but infected with the worker bee flu, we could get them treatment and *then* they might be helpful."

"I'm still not convinced we need any of these people," said a different voice. "Can't we just hire those guys with the guns who cleared the dock for us?"

"No," Captain Drake said, shortly.

"I did *try* to explain the situation before we came," my mother said, drily.

"Yes, Lenore. We know."

The meeting broke up and everyone headed out except my mother. "Mind if I have some of your coffee?" she asked me.

"Help yourself," I said. She poured a cup and I sat back against the couch, letting my cards dangle. Thor had beaten me again, anyway.

"I got the reading list from the high school where I'll be enrolling you when we get back to Pasadena," my mother said, brightly. "I sent it on to you, did you see?"

I blinked at her, disbelieving. Of all the things to bring up . . .

"You know that list of twenty people," I said. "There are only about six with any real power. If you're going to look for any, you should focus on those."

"Don't you think those six probably took off, same as your father did?" she said.

"Yeah. But you really don't need to worry about the rest."

She shook her head. "Not true. People will sometimes rally around leaders who have no real power, just the symbolic kind."

"In that case you don't want people on the governing council," I said. "You want people like Debbie. Union leaders."

My mother's phone went off and she pulled it out to look at

it. "Sorry," she said, "I'm going to have to go. We can discuss this another time."

"Whatever it is you need to go do," I said, "you'd be more likely to get it done if you *let me help you*."

"I really appreciate that you want to help, sweetie," my mother said. "We'll talk about it tonight."

The door slid shut behind her. "I'm not *four* anymore," I said to the closed door, and threw my cards down on the table.

Thor gathered them up and shuffled them. "On the plus side—for me, anyway—you're not leaving until things are more stable, right?"

"Yeah," I said. "There's that."

"Are you looking forward to going to California?"

"I don't know," I said. "I want to see California. I want to get to know my mom. But this is my home. And I want to know that I have a home to come back to."

Speaking of homes to go back to (or not), Thor had been sleeping over in my apartment because his father had locked him out completely. Mr. Lunquist was still refusing the vaccine, and had shouted through the door that he didn't trust us not to sneak it to him somehow. I'd demanded that he return the MREs from my father and he'd yelled "no refunds!" and refused to answer any more questions.

Fortunately, with my own father gone, there was a spare bed as well as the couch. Thor had my father's bed, my mother had the couch, and two of the other Humanists had been sleeping on rolled-out mats on the floor.

"If you think of a way to get the vaccine-refusers to be more cooperative, *I'd* like to hear it, even if the Humanists don't think you have any good ideas," Thor said as I started a fresh pot of coffee.

"Put the vaccine in the drinking water," I said.

"Oh, that's good. Why aren't they doing that?"

"It's risky, since the vaccine causes some side effects. They don't want people taking it without knowing what they're getting into. Also, someone thought it wasn't ethical."

My gadget pinged and I checked it to find a message from my mother. She promised to bring us lunch, since she didn't want us going out, but she'd been delayed. She get it to us soon, she promised.

"I'm starving," Thor said. "She won't mind if I go out, right? I can bring food back for both of us."

"Screw that," I said, and stuck my gadget in my pocket. "If she didn't want me going out, she should've sent food. Let's go."

The corridors were quiet and I noticed that quite a few were sort of dim—lightbulbs had worn out or broken and the people who usually replaced them were sick, hiding, gone, or dead. Or maybe just not coming to work, because they didn't think they were going to get paid. Or maybe we were running out of supplies, with the blockade.

We passed Gibbon's, but I hadn't really expected they'd be open, and I was right. "Let's try Primrose," Thor said. "I heard they were handing out boxed meals during the worst of it."

Primrose's doors were open and I could smell food cooking from halfway down the hall. Inside, employees were washing the wall of windows and mopping the tile floor, and as we came in, I spotted a steam tray of food in the back.

"Hi, Thor," the lady with the food said as we walked up. "Oh, and Beck. Are you two hungry?"

"Yes!" I said. "What are you serving?"

"Nothing fancy. Unfortunately, our vat tech disappeared, and everything in the vats . . . well, we think it's non-toxic but it definitely doesn't smell good. We're serving vegan split pea stew today."

"I'll take it," I said. "Um, I don't have a subscription . . ."

"No worries," she said, and handed us each a bowl of light yellow mush. Thor and I sat down by the window and tucked in.

Split pea soup is not my favorite, but I was hungry, and whoever had made it had put in plenty of spices.

"Bus your own bowls, please," the woman called to us as we finished, so we carried them back into the dish room and stacked them in a rack to go into the dishwasher. I went back over to the woman who'd been serving.

"Who's been running stuff?" I asked. "Is the owner around, or . . .?"

"Toshiro's not here right now because I sent him home to sleep. During the plague, Toshiro said we try quarantining the dining room, and any of us who wanted to stay here could stay. We shut down the dining room, handed out grab-and-go boxes for our customers, and just sort of camped out. It was great until people started getting sick anyway."

"So your vat tech didn't take him up on the offer?" Thor said.

"No, we haven't seen him. Some of us tried to keep the vats working, but the plague made us pretty stupid." She sighed. "On the plus side, all the coffee cups are now *completely free of all stains*."

"Has everyone been treated now?"

"Oh, yeah. Toshiro insisted on taking care of that before he went home to rest. We've all had the treatment or the vaccine."

I pondered that, along with the fact that as far as I knew, none of the other cafeterias had re-opened yet.

"What if you opened up to anyone," I said, "just temporarily, if you served food to anyone on the stead who came. If the Humanists set up a vaccination station here, and in order to get served, people had to get the vaccine, or else show proof they'd had it. Do you think Toshiro would go for that?"

The woman set her ladle down. "Let me call him."

"I don't want to wake him up," I protested.

"No, this is a good idea," she said. "He'll want to get up for this. Don't go anywhere."

*

Between Rosa, Min, and Pete, there were probably 50 or 60 cafeterias, although some were really small or super-specialized, like Edna's, which did nothing but breakfast, or Rabbit's, which was vegetarian. (True vegetarian, I mean. I know plenty of people who won't eat meat that used to be an animal, but Rabbit's doesn't serve vat-grown meat, either.)

Thor and I walked through the steads, trying to find cafeteria owners (or managers, if the owners were missing or dead.) Rabbit's door was open, but it was going to be a while before he'd be serving food; the worker bee flu had convinced him he needed to start an organic farm in the eating area of the cafeteria, and he'd covered the floor with a thick layer of compost. But it wasn't a wasted trip, because Rabbit could speak Russian, and offered to pitch our idea to the cafeterias on Pete.

I knocked on the Gibbon's door, and just kept banging until the assistant manager opened it. Gibbon was one of the ones who'd disappeared; he'd left his assistant manager in charge. The assistant manager was jumpy and indecisive, and I wondered if he was a bond worker. At least he'd stayed healthy, huddling behind the locked door all alone, and I pointed out that he was in much better shape to re-open than some of the cafeterias.

"I sent messages to all the other employees this morning," he said. "About half checked in. But the vat tech wasn't one of them. It'll take at least a week to have any meat going anyway, and without a tech . . ."

"Bean soup," I said. "That's what Primrose is serving."

"*Primrose* re-opened?" he said, dismayed, and I could see him calculating how many customers would cancel their contracts and move, if he didn't open up too. "I wish Mr. Gibbon would call. I don't know how I'm supposed to know what to do next. He said he'd be in touch, but he hasn't been. I don't know why he hasn't called."

He was probably wanted for bioterrorism, like my father. Or

maybe the worker bee flu had struck when he was miles out in open water. "He's not coming back," I said.

"How would you even know that?"

I didn't answer and instead pitched my idea about encouraging vaccination. The assistant manager was hesitant and jumpy and indecisive a bit longer, and then said that he didn't want the Humanists in the cafeteria without permission from Mr. Gibbon, but he could have someone at the door checking everyone's vaccination status.

"This isn't going to get my father out of the apartment," Thor said as we walked down to Clark's. "But you know what would?"

"A small explosive charge?"

"No. Well, that probably would too but it seems unnecessarily risky considering Erik and Serena. No, I mean, a *job*. A job would get him out of there."

"What did he do? In that job where he got arrested?"

"He was a Development Project Manager at a Bioengineering firm. That's pretty useless, but back when he was in college, he worked in food service at the college dining hall. *As a vat tech.*"

"Send him up to Primrose," I said. "By the time you talk him out of the apartment, I bet they'll be set up to give vaccines."

When the 5 p.m. meeting was held in the Humanist's ad hoc board room, Thor wasn't there; he was down in his own apartment, babysitting for Serena and Erik while his father re-started the Primrose vats. I lay on my bed, pretending to read a book while I listened in. When one of the Humanists noted that they'd found an unexpected ally in the cafeteria owners, who'd united to deny entry to the people refusing the vaccine, I called, "You're welcome."

There was a long pause.

A Black woman with a head scarf came to the doorway of my father's office. "You're Rebecca, right?"

"Yeah." At least she hadn't said, *You're Lenore's kid, right?* "I go by Beck."

"Beck. I'm Faduma Adawe. Come sit down with us for a minute."

I ignored my mother's scowl, just as I'd gotten used to ignoring what my father wanted me to do, and pulled up a chair at their conference table. "Tell us exactly what you did," Faduma said.

I explained that I'd been at Primrose, and I'd had the idea, and I'd thought the Primrose staff would go along with it. And while all the cafeterias operate independently, Primrose sets a lot of standards, and I knew exactly which ones would follow suit. The smallest ones would all go along with it because the last thing anyone wanted was to be the go-to place for people *refusing* vaccinations.

Faduma looked across the table at Captain Drake.

"This?" she said, pointing at me. "*This* is what I need when I go to Lib."

"You are *not* taking my daughter, my *minor child*, to Lib," my mother said.

"I wouldn't go to Lib without someone to watch my back," I said.

"The Alpha Dogs haven't wanted to work with us. We've tried. Do you think they'll work with you?"

"Yes," I said.

Faduma shot a look at Captain Drake.

"The answer is no," my mother said. She turned to try to fix me with an authoritative stare, but I ignored her.

Captain Drake turned away from my mother and leaned forward onto one elbow, looking at me with sudden interest. "Beck," she said. "Assuming the Alpha Dogs are willing to provide an escort, are you willing to go to Lib and assist Faduma?"

"Yeah, of course," I said. "I saw just a little bit of what cholera was doing on Lib. I want to stop it as much as you do. Maybe more, since the stead is my home."

Captain Drake nodded and then shot my mother a look. She

didn't even have to say anything; my mother looked down at the table, fuming and silent.

"Can you and someone from the ADs meet me tomorrow morning at eight a.m.?" Faduma asked me.

"I'll need a budget to hire them."

Faduma pulled a wad of U.S. hundreds out of her pocket and slapped it onto the table.

"Where do you want to meet?" I asked.

CHAPTER TWELVE

THE WHOLE SEASTEAD WAS A MESS. BUT LIB WAS A *CESS-pool*. Cholera, in case you're not familiar with it—and if you live somewhere with a reliable safe water supply, you probably aren't—causes massive diarrhea.

It would be bad enough to come down with cholera when you lived in a full-sized apartment with its own bathroom. (What you should do if you ever get cholera, by the way, is drink rehydration fluid: 1 liter of clean water + 1/2 teaspoon of salt + six teaspoons of sugar. Since you can lose *ten to twenty liters of water a day* with cholera diarrhea you'll need a *lot* of rehydration fluid, but as long as you keep drinking, you'll probably survive.) But a lot of people on the seastead don't have full-sized apartments. Bond workers in Lib's skin farms live in tightly packed dormitories and share a handful of bathrooms that are definitely not set up to cope with a cholera epidemic.

Also, Lib's water was contaminated; that's where the cholera was coming from. Drinking it was making people worse.

If we could fix the water supply, the outbreak would end.

Zach met me and Faduma at the bridge over from Pete. The encampment of desperate dying people had been relocated and the floor here scrubbed clean. I introduced Zach and Faduma.

"I thought the Humanists were all atheists," Zach said, looking Faduma over. "Isn't that head scarf a religious thing?"

"HoH has a non-discrimination policy, and it's called a hijab," Faduma said, and hoisted up a backpack to her shoulders. "Shall we go?"

Lib is built into an old Russian cargo ship, and even at its best, it's not especially pleasant. The desalination plant is below the waterline, but most of the above-waterline parts of the ship don't have windows either. It's full of skin farms and drug production operations that produce really foul smells and other things that nobody on the other steads would tolerate as a neighbor. Plus a few eccentrics who actually prefer to live there, just because. The floors are always filthy.

We reached a steep staircase. "Wait a second," Faduma said, and produced three pairs of disposable gloves from a pocket of her backpack. "You're going to want to hang onto the railing, I'm sure," she said. "Probably best if you can strip these off later. We may not find good facilities for hand washing until we leave."

"You don't say," Zach muttered. I wiggled my hands into the gloves and we started down. "What do you think is going to happen?" he asked me.

"If we can get the water fixed, Captain Drake said people will stop getting sick."

"I'm not thinking about just the water," Zach said. "How are we going to clean up this mess? And it's not just Lib. It's everything. Did you know that a quarter of the above-waterline apartments on Lib are completely empty? You go up to the highest deck and it's more like half. Anyone who could leave, did."

"Huh," I said. "Just sitting empty? So people could just…. move in?"

"Well, *I'm* not going to complain," Zach said. "The owners might, if they come back."

The floors had probably once been marked by numbers, but were marked now with grimy, faded murals painted on the landing and the door. We passed a mural with a cartoonish sun and flowers, and a peeling mural of sunflowers. Now we reached a floor with a picture of giant bugs, including a grinning ladybug and a praying mantis the same height as me. At least, I was pretty sure that's what it was. We don't have praying mantises on the stead, or ladybugs, but I've seen pictures.

"The bug floor has the desalination plant," Zach said, and led the way down the hallway.

"What's the guy's name?" I asked, belatedly. "The owner, I mean."

"Everyone calls him Vodka Mike."

"Does he drink heavily?" Faduma asked.

"No. The word 'vodka' comes from the Slavic word for 'water.' Maybe you have to live on Lib to find it funny."

"What's he like?" I asked. "I mean, would he poison people on purpose?"

"I doubt it," Zach said. "It's bad for business."

"Well then how did the cholera even get in there?" I asked.

"The bacteria thrives in warm ocean water," Faduma said. "It could be in the water all around you. Normally, however, any process that takes out the salt would take care of the cholera."

This level was quiet and dimly lit. There were a lot of rust stains on the walls and doors. One door had a big blue water droplet painted on it, and Zach banged on that one. "Vodka?" he yelled. "Open up."

No response.

He banged again. "This is Zach from the ADs. You've got ten seconds before I kick the door in."

Faduma tried the knob; it turned easily. A moment later we all fell back a step, gagging on the smell of decomposing corpse.

Vodka Mike wasn't going to give us any trouble.

*

In addition to disposable gloves, Faduma had filter masks in her backpack, and she gave one to each of us, saying they might make us more comfortable. I looped the elastics behind my head and squeezed the nose clip around my nose; the filter blunted the stench but didn't actually eliminate it. I'd thought Faduma might check the body over to see if he'd died from cholera or something else but she just stepped over it and went to check the equipment in the next room.

I stared at the body. I'd never seen anything like this before. It had been sitting for days at room temperature; one of the insects we have here are flies. The body was *oozing*. I thought about following Faduma, but the thought of stepping over all that made me imagine losing my balance and stepping *on* it. I glanced at Zach and was reassured to see that he also looked completely grossed out.

Faduma was back pretty quickly anyway. "That looks like it was jury-rigged by a crate of marauding raccoons. Did this guy have an assistant?"

"No," Zach said.

"Wife? Kids? Anything?"

"Nope."

"I figured it was a filtration-based system but it's distillation-based. It's obviously still taking out the salt or people would have quit drinking it, but normally, a distillation-based system involves heating the water enough that the cholera bacteria wouldn't survive. It must be getting contaminated somewhere else in there but seriously, come and look at this." She waved me and Zach into the room with the system.

So now I *had* to step over the body, but Zach did it without flinching so I braced myself, held my breath, and did it, too. In the room with the system, I tried to focus. "I don't know a lot about water purification," I said, looking around at the massive tangle of hoses snaking their way around the room, the collection of enormous vats, and the machinery—pumps? I really wasn't sure. "I wouldn't know what's wrong."

"What I need is an expert," Faduma said.

"I thought you *were* an expert."

"I'm a water quality expert," Faduma said. "Not a system hacking expert."

"Beck is an expert at finding people," Zach said. "And even more an expert at talking them into shit that was not on their to-do list that day."

Given that Faduma had insisted on bringing me along, I probably shouldn't have been surprised that she tilted her head toward me and said, "Right. Any ideas?"

I was already thinking about people who might be able to help with this—the owners of the water purification plants on Rosa, Min, and Pete, for instance. But which of those people would still be here, and who'd have left—well, it was going to be a lot more challenging to find a water plant expert now than it would have been last week. Also . . . "Can someone get the body out of here, at least?"

"Oh," Faduma said, and looked down at it, like she forgotten it was there. "Yeah. Definitely."

"In the meantime, I think people have a right to know their water isn't safe," Zach said.

"I have printed notices," Faduma said. "I was going to ask where the best places were to put them up."

Zach shook his head. "There are an *awful* lot of residents on Lib who don't get out much." He glanced at me, knowing I would know what he meant—bondworkers in skin farms who weren't allowed to leave. "But it's fine," he added. "I know where we can get some people to deliver them."

Outsiders find it hard to get their heads around the fact that there are *no laws on Lib*, and Faduma was no exception. Though in Faduma's case, what baffled her was not how Lib managed to continue functioning, but why anyone would *choose* to live there. "My grandparents immigrated from Somalia to the U.S. in the 1990s," she said. "Lawlessness was what they were trying to get *away* from. They moved from the equator to *Minnesota* so they could have exactly what these people—" she waved her hand "— decided they wanted to live without."

"Yeah, well," I said. "It's a lot less exciting on Lib than people tend to imagine."

"So what if Vodka Mike *had* poisoned everyone on purpose? What sort of recourse would anyone have had? If he'd been alive when we got there, I mean."

"Oh, trust me," Zach said. "He have *wished* we merely had the *legal* sort of recourse."

Zach's idea for handing out pamphlets was really straightforward. He grabbed two of the ADs—Evgeni the chipper Russian guy with a boyfriend on every other stead, and a very quiet, very big guy named Butch. Then he asked me if there were any businesses on Lib I had a particular grudge against.

"Butterfield," I said. "He isn't a client these days, is he?"

"Nope," Zach said.

"Are you thinking we'll just raid Butterfield's skin farm for people to walk around putting up notices about the water?"

"Yeah," Zach said. "Think they'll go for it?"

"If they're not all dead," I said. "It beats the hell out of being chained to a bench next to dangerous chemicals."

Faduma stared in alarm at Zach, and then at me, and then clearly decided not to ask any questions.

The door to the Butterfield skin farm labs had been blank and unremarkable on my prior visit, but now bore a small plaque saying, *Protected by the Tigers*. Zach rang the buzzer. "I'm here from the ADs," he said. "You want to open the door for me or should I bust it down?"

There was a pause and then a voice said, through the inter-com, "I have already put in a call to our Security force."

"Yeah," Zach said. "I checked on the Tigers the other day. Half of them are stuck on other steads and the others have cholera. No one's coming. And you are not paid anywhere near enough to risk pissing me off."

The lock clicked and Zach nudged the door open. He was still wearing his mask and disposable gloves.

Inside the factory, things were quiet. The reek was what I remembered—stomach-turning and eye-watering, but it was neither the stench of human waste nor the stench of human rot. Zach strode over to the office and opened the door. "You the guy I was talking to just now?"

A nervous, balding man nodded.

"You're not actually Butterfield, are you?"

He shook his head.

"Is Butterfield here?"

The guy swallowed hard. "He had a yacht," he said. "I think he left the stead. He said he'll be back, but I haven't heard from him."

"Who else is here?"

"Well, there's me. And the bond-workers."

"Is anyone sick?"

The overseer glanced past us, nervously, like he thought Vodka Mike might be eavesdropping, and then said, "We had one person who got sick early but one of the other bondies said it was probably from the water. We've been boiling all the drinking wa-ter since. That was the last order Butterfield gave before he took off, 'boil all the water.'"

"Right." Zach gestured to Faduma, and when she looked at him quizzically, said, "Give me one of your notices." She silently handed it over. "You were right about the water. We're going to borrow your staff."

"The skin's going to rot if it's not tended."

"Not my problem. And not yours, either."

"Like hell it's not my problem," the overseer said. "He'll flay me alive. I'll never work anywhere again."

"First of all, he's not coming back," Zach said.

"You don't know that."

"Second of all, there's going to be no buyer for that skin for months. It's all going to die anyway. And third of all, I'm Zach from the ADs, and you're not paid enough to argue with me."

The overseer shrugged. "Do whatever you want. I guess you will in any case."

Zach glanced at me. "I was going to ask him for keys, but he makes an excellent point. I think I'd rather break shit."

The overseer irritably threw a ring of keys across the desk. "Don't exert yourself or anything."

Zach tossed me the keys. "Let's get everyone out of the labs, to start with."

When we come to rescue Lynn, I had noticed the stench, the dim lights, the fact that Lynn had been chained to her work-bench, and the unpleasantness of the work. I'd worked very hard to avoid noticing the other twenty or so people in her lab, because although I was pretty sure that I could get Lynn out and off of Lib to the American Institute, I knew that trying for even one more would be pushing my luck.

This time, I looked at all the workers. They weren't all women—a third of the workers here were men. About half of them were white; the other half were Asian or Hispanic. I tried a couple of keys before I found the one that fit the shackles, and I set to work unlocking people.

"Who are you, and what are you doing here?" one of the women asked.

"I'm Beck Garrison," I said. "And we need some healthy people who can hand out fliers. I thought you'd probably consider that better work than what you're currently doing."

There was a murmur of agreement.

"Did you buy our bonds?" someone asked.

"Not exactly," I said. "But no one's going to try to stop you from walking out."

Faduma met me as I came out. "Let me get this straight," she said. "We're stealing slaves. Are we making them *our* slaves? Because I am morally not okay with that. I'm fine with freeing them. Not with re-enslaving them."

I looked around at the bond-workers who were milling around in the hallway outside the labs in their blue smocks. "We've gotten them out of their chains," I said. "They don't *have* to do anything we tell them."

"Do *they* know that?"

Zach and I exchanged a look. "You're dead set on making this harder, aren't you?" he said to Faduma.

"If by 'harder' you mean 'in accordance with international law and basic morality,' yes."

Zach caught my eye. "*This* is why I didn't want to work with them until you got involved," he said.

"Okay," I said. "Fine. I'll make it clear we're asking for volunteers."

Zach kicked a bench out into the hallway so I had something to stand on, and he bellowed, "hey, LISTEN UP!" to get everyone to quiet down and listen to me.

I cleared my throat, considered asking what they knew already, and decided that would be a recipe for confused babble, not clarity. "I'm not sure what you've been told," I said. "But in the last few weeks, a lot's gone wrong on the stead. Lib had a cholera outbreak—" that got a hum of excited whispering "—and the rest of the stead had a virus break out that caused hallucinations and then strange behavior. A relief organization arrived a few days ago. Faduma Adawe is one of their representatives." I gestured, and reluctantly, Faduma waved.

"I don't think I can tell you just *how much of a mess* things are outside your doors. There are people dying in the corridors of Lib. There are corners heaped with bodies and running with shit. Of the powerful and rich of the stead, many—possibly most—have fled. We came here because we need healthy people to help." I glanced at Faduma. "We're asking for volunteers. We didn't buy your contracts. You don't have to help us unless you want to."

"If you didn't buy our contracts, are you going to at least rent our labor and pay some of our debt off?" asked one of the women.

Someone else asked, "Is the American Institute still giving rides off this shitty boat?"

I answered that question first. "The American Institute evacuated their people, and there's currently a U.S. Navy blockade to try to keep people from leaving."

"What about our contracts?" the first woman asked again.

I didn't know how to answer this without going back and explaining again what a mess everything was. There were people who cared a great deal about enforcing the contracts, but how many were even still on the stead? Butterfield, for sure, had gone. And this was Lib, where there weren't actually any laws, which was why the bond-workers tended to be kept in literal chains. The closest thing to an authority here right now was Zach.

No, wait. Actually, that wasn't true.

The closest thing to an authority here was *me*.

"All your contracts are void," I said. "For the work we want you to do . . . what is your current hourly wage here?"

Someone called out a depressingly low number.

"Double that. Track your hours. Traditionally people buy in, gain citizenship, with cash. You want in, you can buy in with labor. If you don't, well, eventually I expect there'll be rides off the boat again."

People were shifting around, looking suddenly interested.

"What do you want us to do?" the woman asked.

Faduma had printed paper notices to distribute throughout Lib, warning people to boil their water or haul it over from the other steads. But there was more to this project than just taping notices up to doors, she explained. She was hoping that if people answered the doors, we could determine whether anyone inside was ill. If no one answered their doors, she had a vapor detector to hold up to the cracks around the door that would hopefully tell us if someone inside was dead.

"If they are dead," one of the workers asked, "should we break in to remove the bodies?"

I could tell from the look on Faduma's face that she hadn't been planning to ask them to do that. "We're paying pretty well," I said, in an undertone.

"We're paying in IOUs," Faduma said back, and then raised her voice slightly. "If you're willing to handle bodies, let me know. Those will be specialized teams. We'll assign you a bodyguard—no one should be breaking into apartments without one—and I'll give you some forms to fill out, so we have numbers and information on exactly who's dead. We'll outfit you with body bags. I think it'll be easiest to bring them up to the top deck."

"What, no cart?" Zach muttered. "'Bring out'cha dead . . .'"

"Oh, and that reminds me," Faduma said, "We'll need you to notify us about anyone who's seriously ill. Getting help for them, even if they're on the brink of death, is your top priority. I've seen people make a full recovery after an infusion of fluids. We're not writing anyone off."

"What about bond-workers?" someone asked.

"Why would that even make a difference? *Especially* bond-workers."

"What if we find other healthy bond-workers who want to help with cleanup?" asked a short woman in the front row. She was looking steadily at me, not at Faduma.

"If their bond-holders are not present to enforce the contract," I said, "they're all void."

*

I didn't know the names of the people who owned the desalination plants on Min, Rosa, and Pete, but I did at least know where the plants were. Rosa's was being competently run by an employee, but Faduma quickly determined he wouldn't be expert enough to unravel the jury-rigging on Lib. On Min, the guy who'd stayed behind to keep things operating had clearly fallen victim to the worker bee flu and was now *utterly obsessed* with ensuring everything in the Min desalination plant continued running. So their water was fine. But he needed treatment, not a new project.

Pete's desalination plant had a small cadre of workers who'd been camping out, trying to avoid both the cholera and the worker bee flu; apparently they'd been successful. Faduma glanced around at the setup as the men eyed us suspiciously. "Do any of you speak English?" she asked. They didn't answer, which might have meant that they didn't, or might have just demonstrated their general suspicion toward anything we might want from them. She tried French, Spanish, and a language I didn't recognize, then pulled out her gadget to do machine translation. Staring at the guys on the other side of the desk I realized that I recognized one of them.

When my father threw me out, and I spent some time sleeping in the below-waterline maze of ballast stacks and power plant machinery, I'd run into a group that was sleeping down there regularly. This one had been the one in charge of the water—Leo, the water boy. Water boy *of the day*. So maybe he didn't actually have any particular expertise—but he also worked at a desalinator. "Leo," I said, and his head snapped up. "Quit pretending you don't speak English. You are *exactly* what we're looking for."

The body was gone, and the floor had been scrubbed clean, although there were still flies buzzing around in the corners of Vodka Mike's office. In the system room, Leo surveyed the mess of pipes, and then turned and gave me a silent, incredulous look.

"Down in the encampment on the utility level, weren't you the one putting together the water and toilet every night?"

". . . maybe."

"Then I'm sure that with you for the jury-rigging and Faduma for the water systems expertise, you can get it working properly."

"This is way out of my league," he said, not moving.

Announcing that I was cancelling all the bonds had been exhilarating—I could see why my father quite liked power—but I didn't have enough authority to *make* anyone do something they didn't want to do. Being listened to was delightful. Having to actually figure out solutions to problems: less so. But at least I could see an option here.

"Let me put it this way," I said. "The owner of this catastrophic mess was found dead on the floor earlier today. And Lib has no estate law. You fix this? It's yours."

Leo turned back and looked at it for a long moment. "The weird thing," he said, "is that if the desalination process weren't working, people wouldn't be drinking it, because you can taste salt. And you can filter out cholera with clean *fabric*. It is *way* harder to get rid of salt."

"This system is distillation based," Faduma said.

"What, *seriously?* That's *even weirder.*" Leo took out a pen and started tracing back some of the pipes that ran through the office. "Let's number everything. See if we can figure out what's leading where."

It took two hours of patient untangling of pipes, but Leo and Faduma figured it out: Vodka Mike had been recycling the graywater—from the sinks and baths—without sanitizing it properly. There was a graywater collection unit—and Mike had been just letting it settle, and then putting it back in the system.

"So someone was *shitting in the sinks?*" Zach said, horrified.

"I wonder how much he saved on filters?" Leo said. "It's a good thing the toilets on Lib all run on seawater . . ."

We disconnected the graywater collection from the rest of the system. Once it was flushed out, the water would be safe to drink again.

Faduma had a few other errands on Lib. She set up food and water delivery to the big makeshift infirmary, which had moved into one of Lib's two large cafeterias. The Humanists had moved in and set up pallets on the floor for people to lie on, with IVs for the most desperate cases. They pushed all the tables to the side, but caregivers and the sick-but-mobile were clustered around them, drinking tea or oral rehydration packs, depending on their health status. My mother was working here: I saw her checking an IV line as we came in. As Faduma checked in with one of the other nurses, I spotted someone else I knew.

"Debbie?" I said.

Debbie was drinking tea, which was good to see. She looked like she hadn't eaten a proper meal, slept, or showered since the plague had hit. "Beck," she said, trying to summon up a smile. "Come sit with me."

"You look like you should go home and take a nap," I said.

"That's what the Humanists said. I told them I don't have a home at present and they didn't know quite what do with me."

"There are a zillion empty apartments right now. Find one that doesn't smell like someone died in it, and move in."

"That's a great idea," Debbie said. "Only problem is, I'd have to go find one, and that would require standing up!"

"Let me check with Faduma," I said. "She might know where some of them are." I turned to wave at Faduma, but instead my mother came over and sat down.

"You're Debbie, aren't you?" Mom said. "I remember you from the documentary."

"And you're this hell-child's mother!" Debbie grinned at her and offered her a handshake. "Are you planning to take her back to California? Good luck. You'll need it."

"We fixed the water," I said to my mother, brightly. "I mean, it still has to be flushed, but the cholera should quit spreading really soon."

"Good," she said, and then grudgingly added, "Nice work."

"Hey," Debbie said. "Is it true that the entire Seastead Governing Council jumped ship?"

"No," I said. "Uncle Paul's still around. And I heard there was one other."

My mother shook her head. "The other guy died today."

"I *also* heard," Debbie added, "that all the bond workers on Lib were broken out, with the promise that if they work on clean up they'll get citizenship."

"Yeah, well," I said. "It seemed like a good idea."

"So the way I see it, it's not just the empty apartments right now, you know? If we sweep this place up and glue it all back together, it's ours. Like you-break-it, you-bought-it, only not exactly. You fix it, you own it. You pulled it off the curb on garbage day . . ."

"What's a garbage day?" I asked.

Neither answered. My mother was laughing, incredulously. "You want to own the worst mess in the Western Hemisphere?"

"It won't be a mess forever," Debbie said. "There's a vaccine for the worker bee flu, and with the water treated, the cholera should stop."

My mother leaned back in her chair and started ticking things off. "Half the population has gone missing, including most of the experts in things that kept your economy running. There's civil disorder on Amsterdarn. We're not even sure if anyone's alive on Sal. You're still under quarantine and you're running out of food. Frankly, I think your best bet is to just turn yourselves over to the U.S. and ask the government there for help; they think of this as their territory, anyway."

Debbie and I exchanged looks. She leaned in and in a stage

whisper said, "Your mom. Is she *always* this cheery?"

"I have no idea," I said. "We only met a couple of days ago."

"Look, at the very least," my mother said, adopting a more conciliatory tone, "I should let you know that after the documentary aired there were a half-dozen groups that offered to hire you a lawyer. If you want to come home, you could probably negotiate probation for that drug charge you skipped out on."

Debbie gave my mother a pitying look.

"This might be a falling-down house," Debbie said. "But it is *our* falling-down house. We'll figure it out."

She gave me a fist-bump and drank the last of her tea.

"Now," she said, turning to me. "About those empty apartments. Do you know of any with full kitchens? If I'm going to squat, I might as well squat in style."

PART SIX
BEHIND THE SILICON CURTAIN

CHAPTER THIRTEEN

AT THE NEXT AID WORKER STATUS MEETING, I HAD A SEAT at the table. I felt mostly decorative—Faduma was the one who delivered the report on the resolution of Lib's water purification problems, not me. But she gave me credit for my contributions, especially finding a tech who could solve the problem. "Good work," Captain Drake said to both of us, and moved on to the report on the vaccination project.

I looked over at my mother, who was drawing a cartoon picture of an animal on the last page of her memo pad. She brought an actual paper memo pad with her to every meeting, but apparently just to draw on; her important notes went straight into her gadget. She glanced up and gave me a quick, wry smile before delivering a report on the status of the cholera infirmaries. Even with the water purification finally working properly again, it would take time for all the cholera patients to recover.

After the meeting broke up, I poked through my father's desk drawers, something I'd never been allowed to do before he disappeared. I was looking for paper for my mom. There was a jumble of lanyards and plastic key cards. One of the lanyards was the one I'd made for him out of knotted hemp cord when I was eleven; it had been a Father's Day gift. He worn it daily until it wore out.

He tried to tie it, where it broke, but the threads had gotten too weak to hold. He must have kept it out of sentiment, even though it took up space in the drawer.

Under all that, there was a printed report on the plans for the seastead's fifty-year celebration. It was printed on only one side. I flipped through it. Fireworks? Dignitaries? A visiting brass band? . . . yeah, this was definitely scrap paper now.

I pried out the staple and brought the paper out to the living room, looking for Mom. She was in the kitchenette, rummaging through the cabinets. "You have no food," she said.

"There was snack food, but Thor and I ate it," I said. "But it's okay, because Primrose has re-opened, and probably Gibbon's too, by now. You know everyone here eats in cafeterias, right?"

"Primrose is all the way over on Rosa. That sounds exhausting," she said. In the back of the cabinet she found a box of pancake mix. I couldn't even remember why we had that—I think maybe I'd had a school assignment two years earlier that involved learning to use a stove.

"More exhausting than cooking?" I said.

"Cooking's easy." She turned on the stove. "I'll make us pancakes, okay?"

"There isn't anything to put on them."

"Yes there is. You've got strawberry jam in the mini-fridge."

"Oh, I suppose." We run out of peanut butter and bread, but there was a little jam. I came over and poked through the cabinet myself, coming up with a jar of cinnamon-sugar and some shelf-stable imitation butter. My mother pulled out the frying pan, the sauce pan, and the two plates. She shook pancake mix into the saucepan, ran in some water, stirred it up with a fork. I thought about pushing again for a trip to Primrose, but whatever. Pancakes were fine, if Mom was set on cooking.

"I found you some paper to draw on," I said. Mom looked up, surprised. "I noticed that you always draw during meetings. And you've almost finished your memo pad."

"It's just doodling," Mom said, sounding embarrassed.

I left the packet of paper on the living room table. Mom brought in two plates of pancakes and we settled in on the couch. I put butter and cinnamon sugar on my pancakes. Mom put jam on hers. They weren't as good as the Saturday morning pancakes at Gibbon's, but they were okay. We ate silently for a minute or two.

"Do you want to see some pictures?" she asked, abruptly. "Photos, I mean. I brought a picture of the house. *Our* house."

I nodded. She pulled out her gadget and brought up the photo album. "There's you and me," she said, pointing to a much younger version of herself holding a baby. I pretended to look, but found myself weirdly riveted by the photo next to it—toddler me, grinning, upside-down, my fingertips and pigtails brushing the ground. My father was the one holding my ankles, grinning broadly at the camera. He looked young. He looked charming.

"Where you guys meet, anyway?" I asked.

"College," Mom said. I wanted to ask her more—what was he like, back then? Did they talk about living on the seastead? But I could tell she didn't really want to talk about him. Her hand hovered over the edge of the screen uncomfortably. After a minute, I let her flip to the next screen.

It was definitely a house, with sage green paint, a red door, a striped awning over the big window in front. The yard wasn't grass, but chipped tan rocks and clusters of big sprawling plants. I tried to imagine walking up the brick steps and through the door. "What's it like inside?"

Mom flipped to the next screen, showing me pictures of the living room, the dining room, the kitchen. She taken these for me, I realized; they were clearly very recent, unlike that picture of me with pigtails. Her kitchen was *enormous*, with a four-burner stove and a refrigerator big enough to hold food for a dozen people. Though if you had to cook all your own food, you'd need more space. And a nice stove. I scaled down my estimation of the kitchen. Still. Never mind whipping up pancakes for two—you could lay out a dozen plates on that counter. Full-sized plates, like you'd eat a meal off of, not snack-sized plates like my father kept around.

Then another screen flip and there was a picture of a room with turquoise walls and filmy white curtains.

"That's your room," my mother said. "I painted the walls blue, when I first moved in, because that was your favorite color when you were little. We can repaint, if you want, when we get back, it's easy enough to do. What color do you like now?"

"Still blue," I said.

"We can get you a less childish bedspread. I was thinking of four-year-old Becky when I decorated."

"You didn't seriously keep an empty room in your house this whole time?" I said.

My mother looked slightly embarrassed. "I used it as a guest room when friends came to stay," she said. "Keeping it like a shrine seemed silly."

Oh, well, if she was taking guests, that was reasonable. Then she showed me some pictures of her garden, which was apparently on a plot of land behind the house and filled with flowers. She wanted to tell me the names of everything back there (and which were "succulents" and which were "cacti") and how she did the water management. After a few minutes she glanced at me and said, "I'm sorry. None of this means anything to you, does it?"

"The flowers are really pretty," I offered.

We paged through some more photos—of the neighborhood, the high school, the parks nearby. I'd seen hundreds of movies set in the U.S.—in fact, most of them had probably been filmed in California—so it wasn't as if I didn't know what a high school looked like, or a house, or a back yard. (Well, okay, the back yards in movies almost never looked like my mother's garden, but whatever.) Seeing these things because I was preparing to *go there*, though, was different. It felt like I was planning to move to Mars.

As I got quieter and quieter, my mother put her gadget aside and took my plate away to wash it in the sink. "Look," she said. "I

know this is hard. And I know we got off on the wrong foot. I'm
sorry I didn't bring you into the meetings right away; we're doing
a lot better with you than we were without you, I see that now."

"Thanks," I mumbled. Was she *apologizing* to me? It sounded
like it.

"I won't make that mistake again. You're the expert here, and
I would have to be stupid not to value your opinion." She dried
the dishes and put them back in the cabinet. "In turn, do you
think you can . . . keep me in the loop? *Tell* me about your crazy—
I mean, your highly creative ideas. Rather than just charging in."

"Yeah, okay," I said. "I think I can do that."

"Good." She turned and gave me a shy smile. "I think we're
going to do okay, Beck. I do. I think you'll like California. I think
this is going to work out fine."

I slept in the next morning and woke up to find a half-dozen
pumpkin muffins sitting on the counter along with a note from
my mother telling me that she'd eaten the other half-dozen and
I should have as many as I wanted. She drawn a little picture of
a pumpkin on the note, with twining vines around the edges. I
folded the note up and put it in my pocket, wondering where
she'd gotten the muffins from.

Thor turned up while I was eating. His mother had come back
from wherever she'd been, and taken over caring for his siblings;
things were actually getting back to normal for him, or as normal
as they ever were. We ate muffins and drank coffee and watched
news bulletins from Leah on the stead network.

"My father got wind of the vacant apartments on Lib," Thor
said. "So his latest brilliant idea is that we should go squat in one,
instead of paying rent in Rosa."

"There are way cheaper apartments than the one you're in," I
said, "But *I* wouldn't want to live in Lib."

"Neither would Mom," Thor said. "And neither would I. I told him that we spend all the money we saved, paying someone like the ADs to keep us safe. But once my dad gets an idea into his head . . . Anyway, they were arguing when I left." He stood up and went into my father's office, staring out the little window over the water. "Maybe *I'll* go squat in Lib and let them stay in Rosa. At least I wouldn't have to listen to them fight."

"Have they always been like that?"

"No," Thor said. "Back in the States they got along fine. It helped we had a lot more space so they could get away from each other. Also more money. We had a nanny to take care of Erik and Serena. Stuff like that."

"Has your mom ever at least talked to a lawyer? To find out how much trouble she'd be in, if she took the three of you and went back?"

"I don't know." Thor glanced up with a flicker of ironic humor. "Less trouble than your dad."

"Well, my father is wanted for bioterrorism, I heard. All your father did was steal."

"Don't forget about the tax fraud."

"That's not actually considered more serious than bioterrorism, is it?"

"No, of course not." Thor looked at my father's desk, wrinkling his brow hesitantly. "Did your father leave anything behind? He did work on Sal, didn't he?"

"He hardly ever went over there, but he was one of the partners." Thor looked confused, and I said, "You know Sal's not like the rest of the stead, right?"

Thor opened his mouth, closed it. "All I really know about Sal is, they're the ones who made the worker bee flu. And we can't walk across a bridge to get there."

"Well, it's owned by a partnership."

"Aren't all the steads owned by a partnership? I mean, on Min, when you 'buy a stake,' you're buying a share of the property, basically. That's what Mrs. Rodriguez said."

"I guess it's kind of a difference in scale," I said. "There are thousands of people on Min who have stakes. Sal only has twenty or thirty partners, and they own everything."

"They can't possibly run the whole stead!"

"No, of course not. They also have Associates, who are basically normal employees who live over there. Most of the actual biotech researchers are Associates. And they've got bond workers, like everyone else. There are almost a thousand Associates and bond workers."

"Have you ever been to Sal?" Thor asked.

"No," I said. "It's hard to get to, you know? Sal only lets you in if you've got business over there, and I've never had a reason to go."

"I thought the reason it wasn't connected was because people were afraid they'd get exposed to something creepy from the research. But it turns out the water doesn't really keep us safe."

"Yeah, I'd say the real reason it isn't connected is to keep people out. To protect them, not us."

"Could *you* get in?"

"My father left behind some key cards," I said, and dug them out of the desk drawer where I'd seen them this morning. I poked through, not really sure what they were for. Probably not Sal, now that I thought about it.

Thor picked up the cards and rifled through them. "Would any of these work, do you think?"

"Is there a reason you want to go there?" I asked.

He looked alarmed. "No! Why would I want to? I mean—" He put the cards down again, hastily. "I was just wondering."

"They probably do a biometric scan against a database of authorized people," I said. "The cards might get you around once you're inside, maybe, because they're not going to want to re-scan your retinas or your DNA or whatever every time you go through a door or up an elevator. But to get in through the gangway, there's got to be some kind of scan."

"So your father could've gotten in."

"Well, obviously. He probably still can. And, it's possible I could, too. He scanned my retinas and all the rest back when I was nine or ten and said it was 'just in case.' He never told me just in *what sort of* case, exactly." I started lining up the plastic cards, trying to figure out what sort they were. One was just a nametag. One was completely blank and I thought it probably had something inside to trigger doors as you got close, or . . . who knows. "Maybe I should tell the Humanists I could possibly get them inside. But, if he's got a scan to let me in, he probably also set a scan to keep my mother out, so if she insisted on going along . . ."

Thor chewed his lip, silently.

"*What*," I said.

"I got a message from Tyrone," he said.

The American Institute had closed when the worker bee flu first started, and the staff had been evacuated. "Is Tyrone still on the stead? I thought he'd left."

"He did leave." Thor went silent again for an agonizingly endless minute or so and then said, "He sent me a message saying that if I could get something from Sal, he'd arrange full amnesty for both my parents. We could go back to California."

"Well, it might work if I went with you."

"No, Beck, I'm not asking you—"

"I know, I know, but . . ." If Thor could come back to California, maybe I wouldn't be so alone living there with my mother. "Look, you've helped me a lot. You've gone to *way* more dangerous places with me than Sal. People on Sal aren't even allowed to have guns! Anyway, there's a good chance we won't be able to get in." I bit my thumbnail, thinking this over. "I mean, I do know it's a biometric scan at the entrance. If it's set to let me in, we'll be able to get in. If it's not, that'll be it, right? What is it you're supposed to get?"

Thor sighed heavily. "It's a set of computer files and a box of samples. Tyrone gave me instructions; he told me what the code name for the project was, what the file names would be, and where to find the samples."

There was literally no reason that this should make me more nervous than going to Lib. Sal was *safe*. I mean, aside from the fact that they do biotech research that could turn us all into compulsive doorknob-scrubbers. But the real threat here was my father. He hadn't been happy about my first trip to Lib. To put it mildly. He wasn't at all happy about my involvement in the unionization effort. But if there was one thing that would make his brain *explode* it would be me going over to Sal to steal information in order to pass it along to the U.S. government.

I stuck the key cards in my pocket. "I'm in," I said.

To get to Sal, you need a speed boat, and there are only two entrances. The big front door requires someone inside to operate the lifts for you. But there's also a small gangway a little above the waterline; you can tie up your boat and go up a flight of metal stairs to the scanners.

We rented a speed boat from an automated kiosk; it's only about a five-minute trip. We buckled on PFDs, I fired up the motor, and we started zipping over. When we were about halfway across, it occurred to me that maybe I should have left a note for my mother, just to let her know where I was going. Turning back at this point would have meant paying another minimum rental fee to get the boat back out, though . . . well, this probably wouldn't even work, and I'd be back before she knew I was gone. I never would have told my *father* what I was up to, not in a million years, but I also wouldn't have been concerned about *worrying* him. Mom was more trustworthy and more likely to worry.

I tied up the boat at the small gangway; we left our PFDs in the boat and climbed the stairs, which clanked under our feet. Fortunately, the ocean was really calm that day, so we weren't soaked in spray just climbing out. I opened the door to the vestibule.

There was a rumor, which I hadn't told Thor because I was 99.9% sure the story was bullshit, that an industrial spy had once tried to slip onto Sal, but they figured out he was coming, and when he ran his credentials in the vestibule, the door locked and they gassed him to death and threw his body in the ocean. I thought this sounded far-fetched on just about every possible level, including the idea that Sal kept poison gas spigots in the vestibule of their back door, and that an industrial spy's approach would be to sneak in through the back door rather than sending in a resume and trying to get hired. Nonetheless, I'd brought tape to keep the latch open and a little wedge of plastic to keep the door slightly propped.

I'd also brought my father's cards, but there wasn't anywhere to insert anything. Instead, there was a little cubby with a pane of glass on the bottom. "Please rest your hand on the scanner," a pleasant-sounding, synthetic female voice instructed.

I put the palm of my hand on the scanner; there was a faint whir as something scanned it, and then a swab tickled the back of my wrist. "You may remove your hand," the voice said. "Next person, please rest your hand on the scanner."

Thor wiped his hand on his jeans and hesitantly stuck his hand in. Another whir.

There was a long pause. I wondered what the pause was for, whether it actually was taking this long to ID us or if it was purely to make us nervous.

Then a click, and the box spit out two plastic tokens, round like poker chips, with our pictures on them. "Welcome, Rebecca Garrison and Guest of Rebecca Garrison," the synthetic voice said. "Please keep your badges on your person as you move about the complex. Note that Guest of Rebecca Garrison must stay with Rebecca Garrison at all times. Have a pleasant day." Another click, and the door out of the vestibule and into the ship unlocked.

"Well," I said. Thor was staring at the door dubiously, like he was already regretting this expedition. "Let's go."

CHAPTER FOURTEEN

THE CORRIDOR INSIDE WAS CARPETED, WALL TO WALL, with a thin carpet in a pattern of mauve and beige. Thor didn't seem impressed by this. I wondered if they'd be annoyed at the moisture and salt and who-knows-what I was tracking in. Floors in the rest of the stead are tile everywhere but inside someone's private apartment. There is a really nice rug in our apartment, but we also take off our shoes when we come inside. The floors in Min tend to be dirty; there are people whose job is to mop them—there have to be, or the tracked-in salt would corrode too many things away—but there aren't that many, and it's way more efficient to mop a tile floor than vacuum carpet. Wall-to-wall carpet was impressive. It was probably intended to impress. To say, "welcome to Sal, where we make so much money we can buy bond workers to do nothing but *vacuum and steam-clean carpet all day.*"

The walls were painted a uniform yellow-beige and were also spotless. And identical along every corridor we passed. "I should've brought a ball of string," I said. "To get us back out when we're done. What is it you need to find?"

"The code name for the project is 'rubicon,'" Thor said.

"That's ominous," I said. *Crossing the Rubicon* was supposed to be an expression for taking a drastic action you couldn't undo. "Okay. I guess we need to get to the lab. Maybe there'll be a map by the elevators, if we can find the elevators."

There were elevators a bit further down the hall, and an interactive map that cooperatively showed me that the Project Rubicon development lab was down two levels and past the security area.

We got on the elevator. We still hadn't seen a single actual person.

That changed when the elevator doors opened.

"Don't let the door close! Don't let the door close!" someone shouted as the doors started sliding open. Thor blanched and stepped in front of me, like he was afraid I'd get trampled in an incoming stampede. People didn't stampede, though; they grabbed us by the arms and dragged us out. Someone else put a concrete block in the elevator doorway, so the doors wouldn't shut.

We were in another corridor, but this one was jammed with people. We got pulled away from the elevator and firmly into a corridor cul-de-sac, our backs against a set of closed doors. The people around us were dressed in lab coats and blue scrubs, each with a lanyard holding a photo disk like the one the entrance machine had spit out. The walls and floor were nearly as spotless as the entry area, but a close, humid smell hung in the air, like people had been stuck in this spot for too long.

"Who is it?" I heard someone shouting from the back of the crowd.

"Well, it's definitely not Ron," someone else said.

A tall woman with curly blond hair elbowed her way from the elevator over to us, and frowned at us both suspiciously. I wondered if telling her I was Beck Garrison would get me into less trouble, or more trouble.

"How you get down here?" she asked.

"I pushed the button on the elevator," I said.

She raised her voice slightly. "Ida, identify the newcomers."

The computer's synthetic female voice said, "I'm sorry, but you do not have clearance for that information."

On impulse I said, "Ida? Who am I talking to?"

The computer responded instantly. "This is Gloria Bienkowski, Operations Manager of Silicon Waters."

There was a somewhat daunted hush and Gloria took a step back. At least she was backing off, rather than stuffing a sock in my mouth. I probably should have thought that one through before I tried it.

"Wait," said a voice from the back. "Let me up. Let me see her. I think I know who that is."

The crowd shuffled out of the way. The woman who stepped forward looked familiar, but in the uniform worn by maintenance bond workers on Sal, her hair cut short and covered, it took a minute.

"Lynn?" I said, dumbfounded. I'd half figured she was dead.

"This is Beck Garrison," she said. "Paul Garrison's daughter. I don't know who the boy is."

"I'm 'Guest of Rebecca Garrison,'" he muttered. "Beck? I can't remember, does she like you, or hate you?"

"I'm not sure," I said.

Lynn gave me a long, uncertain look and then said to Gloria, "She's probably on our side."

Gloria Bienkowski, Operations Manager was now staring at me like she thought I was an entire squad of Alpha Dogs, here on an assignment to save her ass. "You can operate the locks," she said. "You can get us *out* of here."

"Well, I can open doors," I said, cautiously. "But I didn't bring a very big boat. How many of you are there? Also, do you mind if we run an errand in the lab before we start breaking people out? Also—why do you need to be broken out? If you're the Operations Manager . . ."

"There are eight hundred and fifty-six people still here," Gloria said. "And although I'm the Ops Manager, Ron Kankol is the Security Manager and he's put a Level Four lockdown into place. Maybe you can call him off . . ." She looked me over, thoughtfully. "You're *Paul Garrison's daughter* . . ."

"She's fifteen," Lynn said, derisively.

"Sixteen," I corrected.

"It doesn't matter. Ron's going to see a kid."

"Will he see a kid, or will he see *Paul Garrison's daughter?*" Gloria said.

"So . . ." Thor said. "Ron's locked you all in?"

"Yes. The whole stead," Gloria said. "We're out of food, at least in this section. He's not letting anyone on or off."

"Was this door locked?" I asked, and pushed on the door I'd been backed up against. It swung open without hesitation and with a noisy sound of approval as about half the crowd drained into the next section. I had no idea what they were after—food? Showers? A change of clothes?—but that took the population of our part of the corridor down to me, Thor, Lynn, Gloria, and four people who appeared to be trying to disassemble the elevator control panel.

"Look," I said. "I want to help you get out of here. But there's something we need from the Project Rubicon development lab. You help me get that stuff, and I will do whatever I need to do to foil Ron and fling the doors open. Deal?"

Gloria silently held out her hand, and we shook on it.

The Silicon Waters staff had been pretty much entirely out of the loop for the last few weeks. The interior is deliberately impenetrable to cell and satellite signals (to foil industrial espionage, Gloria explained matter-of-factly) and when Level Four security went into effect, their network was cut off from the outside world. They been trying for the last week to get someone onto a deck (to use a phone) or even just to a window (to signal with a light) but since Ron controlled the doors . . .

"So Ron doesn't report to you?"

"No," Gloria said. "We're on the same level in the reporting line, plus we report to different partners. That was never an issue before, but now . . ."

"Does he have a private stash of food? I mean, isn't he also worried about running out?"

"Who knows?" Gloria said, disgustedly. "It doesn't matter. All he cares about is the instructions he got before the partners left."

The lab doors unlocked. Thor retrieved the samples and—on Lynn's advice—stashed them in an insulated case with a chilling pack. "What about the data?" I asked.

Thor explained to Gloria what he needed. She raised an eyebrow and escorted him to a workstation. "There's another layer of biometric identification," she said.

The workstation had a keyboard, a set of monitors, and a biometric reader. I hit a key and brought up the lock screen, then put my palm on the reader to let it scan it. This would work, or it wouldn't, right?

It unlocked. Or at least it partially unlocked. I found the files Thor wanted, tried to transfer them to my gadget, and wasn't able to.

"You need an encrypted drive," Gloria said.

Thor started digging through the desk drawers and came up with something pretty quickly. I plugged it in, and started the files copying. "What is Project Rubicon, anyway?" I asked.

"It's a bioweapon," Gloria said. "Designed to be tuneable in some very specific ways—you can tune it to go after someone with a specific genetic code, if you want to use it for assassination. Or you could kill everyone in the world with blue eyes, if for some reason you wanted to."

Thor recoiled, looking down at his cooler. "Why did Tyrone want *samples* of *this*?" he said, aghast.

"Who's Tyrone?" Gloria said, sounding a bit surprised. "I assumed you were here on Paul Garrison's behalf."

"No," I said. "Tyrone is the U.S. Ambassador."

"Oh, well." Gloria shrugged. "They're the client, though we're not supposed to know that."

"The . . ."

"They hired us to make this."

Thor shot me a look of guarded horror.

I felt a surge of horror, too. Horror and puzzlement. Why had Tyrone sent us in to get this, if the U.S. was the client? If they'd paid for it, they didn't need to steal it! Even with the partners missing, once the mess had been sorted out, Gloria would have delivered the product. Maybe a little delayed, but . . .

Unless.

Unless their plan was to destroy Sal, and they'd sent us in to salvage their research so as not to tip anybody off.

"Gloria," I said. "How long would it take to evacuate Sal?"

"At the moment? I'm not even sure. With the lockdown, you are the only person who can open anything. We have some water taxis, but not very many. Probably a few days."

"Don't you have life boats?"

"Of course we have life boats," Gloria said, sounding a little exasperated. "But those are as locked down as anything else. You could get them out, one at a time, but I think it might be faster to run the water taxis."

"That's going to take too long," I muttered. "Right. It's Ron the Security guy who locked everything down, right?"

"Right."

"I want to talk to him."

Gloria walked Thor and me to Ron's office. It was down a series of hallways and up to the top deck on the elevator. Gloria gave me a side-long look with each set of doors, like she was wondering, *will she* really *be able to do this one?* But each new lock clicked open when I arrived at it.

We found Ron alone in a cramped office that smelled like feet, mildew, and stale potato chips. Clearly he'd locked himself down as faithfully as anyone else, though he'd provisioned himself with more food. He whirled around, shocked, when he heard the door open. "What are you doing here?" he shouted at Gloria. "How did you get the door open?"

"Looks like a partner turned up, finally," Gloria said, and jerked her chin at me.

Ron's face twisted in contempt. "That's a *kid*," he said.
I straightened up and tipped my head back slightly, like I was looking down my nose at him. Time to bluff. Except, was this even a bluff? Maybe I *was* a partner. I sure had all the access of one.

"I'm Rebecca Garrison," I said. "Paul Garrison's daughter."

Ron's eyes went wide, and then a little narrow. "I see," he said. His eyes flicked nervously around the office, like he was seeing what I was seeing: his bare feet, the overflowing trash bin, the grime. Then his eyes went back to me and Thor. He straightened up, looking less disreputable, even without shoes. "Welcome to Silicon Waters, ma'am. In the absence of an authority, I locked down Silicon Waters. I've been receiving regular status reports from staff, which you can . . ."

I heard an angry huff of breath from Gloria.

". . . read at your convenience, and—"

I held up my hand and he paused.

"I'm giving the order to evacuate," I said.

"Oh? . . . which sections, roles, offices . . .?"

"I want every person currently on Silicon Waters to be evacuated to the rest of the stead, and I want all data and all samples in the labs to be destroyed."

This was an *insane order*. For the first time, Ron and Gloria exchanged looks like, *oh, wait, we* are *on the same side. The not-crazy side. Unlike her.* Which was an opening of a sort, actually; if they were on the same side, they could cooperate, make a reasonable plan, get people off here before the U.S. sent a ship to take Sal in tow.

But *no*. No. Screw it. Their research was terrifying. Their research was dangerous. Their research was illegal everywhere else, which is why the U.S. government was contracting with the labs here. I fought my instinct to swallow hard, lower my eyes, give any sign of weakness.

I am in charge here, I thought. *My father was in charge. He's gone. So it's up to me.*

"Ida," I said, "What is Ron Kankol's job title?"

"Ron Kankol is Security Manager of Silicon Waters," replied the AI's even voice.

I took a deep breath. This would either work, or it wouldn't.

"Ron is fired," I said. "Replace him with Gloria Bienkowski."

"Acknowledged," the AI said. "Gloria Bienkowski is now Security Manager of Silicon Waters."

Ron and Gloria stared at me, shocked speechless.

"Gloria," I said. "Evacuate everyone on Sal, and destroy all samples and data."

"Yes, ma'am," she said, and sounded the mustering signal.

That must have cancelled the lockdown automatically: every door on the ship unlocked. I hoped Sal was better than Min about actually drilling evacuation procedures occasionally—we had a mustering signal, but the joke I always heard was that it was so that any uncommitted atheists would have time to find faith and say a few prayers, not because we actually be able to abandon the stead. (We did drill partial evacuations, like if something went wrong with a piece of the stead, but if the whole stead had to be abandoned, that was definitely "make peace with your god, if you've got one" territory.)

I told Gloria to let the Humanists know they were about to get eight hundred new arrivals. Captain Drake would undoubtedly be *thrilled*. I decided that wasn't my problem.

The full evacuation took only an hour. Thor spent most of the hour carrying around the cold pack of samples. I pretended not to notice. I could give orders on Sal, but I wasn't going to give orders to Thor.

We were on our way down to the lifeboat when Thor caught my hand.

"I'm sorry," he said.

"For what?" I asked.

"For letting them use me. For letting them use *you*. You're the reason Tyrone contacted me—he knew I could get to you, and you were the only person who could get in."

I shrugged, uncomfortable. I knew he was right. "Well, it's probably a good thing you did," I said. "Because everyone's getting off safely."

Thor's grin briefly lit up his face. "Yeah, see, that was their mistake," he said. "Involving you was not going to go well for them." He dropped the samples and disk on the table. "These should be destroyed with everything else," he said. "I'm not taking them."

I looked at the insulated bag. "Are we worried they'll get on and find them?"

"Oh, maybe." There was a microwave oven in the break room that we used to ensure that nothing in the bag was salvageable. The US might be able to get onto Sal, and might be able to retrieve some or all of what they wanted, but we didn't have to make it *easy* for them.

Thor and I walked back down to where I'd left our boat.

"Goodbye, Rebecca Garrison," the computer said as I passed through the door. "Please, come again to Silicon Waters."

We climbed down the staircase and put out for Min.

The Humanists met us when we were about halfway back. We were informed that we were going into quarantine, which seemed patently ridiculous (were they quarantining all eight hundred of the Sal refugees? Surely not.)

I should have known—I should have *refused*—when they moved me onto one yacht, and Thor onto another. One of the Humanist doctors ran a series of tests and declared me free from novel diseases, and then my mother came over and met the yacht with a large duffel. "You should take a look," she said, as she dropped it on the deck. "If anything's missing, we'll have the HfH bring it when they come home in a few months."

"If anything's . . ."

"We're going to California. You and me. Right now."

I went hot and cold, dizzy with shock and fury. "What?"

"We had an agreement," she said. "Between the two of us. I would treat you more like an adult. And you would *keep me in the loop*. Do you have *any idea* how much danger you were in on there?"

"Do you have any idea how much danger the eight *hundred* people on Sal were in if I *hadn't* gone there?"

"If you'd discussed this with me, I could have let you know that the U.S. Navy has been in touch with the Humanists to warn them that they were planning to tow the ship containing Silicon Waters further from the populated areas of the stead, then sink it."

"So you were fine with them potentially killing *eight hundred people*, as long as I stayed safe?"

"The plan included evacuation."

"In which case I'd have been *fine*."

"That doesn't mean there have been no casualties; they probably would have needed explosives to get in. Both of you could easily have wound up dead. So. Since you're clearly incapable of sitting on the sidelines here, we're going back to California, where I have at least some *shadow* of a chance of keeping you out of trouble."

"*I didn't even get to say goodbye to Thor.*"

"Maybe you should have thought of that *before* you went on yet another unauthorized adventure, Rebecca."

It takes twelve hours by yacht to get from stead to shore. (Twelve silent, furious, fuming hours.) Just before we arrived, I got a message from Thor on my gadget.

It's okay, Beck, he had written. *Goodbyes suck, anyway.*

And we'll see each other again.

Just not as soon as I'd hoped.

I stared out over the ocean at the dark line on the horizon: California.

California.

"Welcome home, Beck," my mother said, putting her hand on mine.

That's not home, I thought. *That will never be home.* But I was going to have to live with her; I was going to have to make the best of this. I tried to say something like "can't wait," but my throat closed up. I nodded, and then pulled away and went to the stern of our yacht to look back out at the open ocean.

PART SEVEN
CALIFORNIA DREAMING

CHAPTER FIFTEEN

MY MOTHER PUT ME IN A WHEELCHAIR TO TAKE ME OFF the boat. I thought she was being melodramatic until I tried to stand up to get in the car and the world tilted sideways and took me with it.

When the nausea hit, I thought I was carsick. But the nausea didn't go away when we got to her house; it got worse. Mom assured me that this was just my body adjusting to land, but I didn't believe her. The second day was even worse, and she gave me pills, telling me it was my inner ear and everything would be better soon.

I didn't believe her, but the third day I felt a little better, and by the fourth day I could walk again.

Mom's house was enormous. There were two bedrooms, and Mom's bedroom was huge. Just her bed was bigger than Thor's entire bedroom *and* she had two dressers in there. My own bedroom had space for a bed, a dresser, a desk with a chair, a bookcase.

And I still wasn't over the enormous kitchen. I knew people *normally* had full kitchens here, but in addition to the four-burner stove, hers had an oven big enough to cook one of those whole plucked turkeys you saw in old timey pictures. You could have *bathed* in her sink.

And let's not even get into the closets. Statesiders have *so much stuff*.

The bookcase in my room had a shelf full of odd little items that were left over from my early childhood: a snow globe with a leaping unicorn, a doll in a historical costume, a pink teddy bear, a plaster handprint glazed turquoise blue with BECKY etched into the plaster along the bottom. I held my hand over the tiny handprint, feeling like I *should* feel a connection here, even though I didn't. I didn't remember owning the doll or the snow globe. I didn't remember making the handprint.

I left it all where it was, because it made the enormous room a little less empty.

Once my stomach had settled and I'd learned how to walk again, Mom took me shopping, to an enormous store with long aisles full of stuff and a large crowd of people. I was initially excited by the idea of choosing from so many things, but quickly got overwhelmed and started feeling ill again and we wound up going home with one package of socks. Mom said she'd order the rest of my clothes delivered.

"I don't *need* any more clothes," I said. "I have plenty."

"We have to do our own laundry here," Mom said, patiently. "I only run laundry once a week."

"No problem," I said. "I'll wash my own clothes. You have a washer and dryer, right? I'm sure it's not *that* complicated."

"But you'll need new clothes," Mom said. "Or at least, you'll want some new clothes for school, won't you? School starts in two weeks."

School?

"Um," I said. "I guess so."

*

"There must be things you don't hate," Thor said. I was lying on my bed, on a pile of pillows, my gadget in my lap, and hearing him say that immediately made me feel guilty. It's not that I wanted to trade places with him—I wanted to go back to the seastead, but I wanted him there with me, and of course he really wanted to be in California.

"Fruit, all the time, as much as I want," I said. "I had kiwi fruit today. They have this weird brown fuzz—I guess you probably knew that."

"Yeah, I really like them. We got them on the stead sometimes, at least in Primrose. They keep well, so they're a good fruit to ship in."

"I've had them," I said. "I hadn't ever seen them in their skins, though. Mom said to cut it in half and scoop it out with a spoon."

"What's your mom like?" Thor said. "What's she like at *home,* I mean. I met her a few times when she was at the stead but she was kind of aggressively on duty."

"She keeps calling me Becky and having to correct herself," I said.

"At least she's correcting herself," Thor said, with a little bit of a laugh.

"Yeah, I guess." I readjusted the pillows and flopped back down. "I think she's trying to give me space, because she feels guilty for dragging me back the way she did, but mostly what that means is, she doesn't talk to me much."

"Have you tried talking to her?"

"I don't know what I'd talk to her *about.*"

"Did you ever talk to your dad?"

"We used to watch *Stead Life* together."

"Maybe you could do that with your mom," Thor said. "Use it as a chance to tell her about your life?"

I tried to picture doing this. It was hard to imagine it going well, but . . . "Maybe," I said. "How are things on the stead?"

"It is weirdly so great with all the rich assholes gone. I mean, other than my dad, although I don't know if he counts, he's spent most of our money. At some point the fact that everything needs a lot of ongoing maintenance or we'll sink into the sea is going to catch up with us, but right now, it's like . . . everyone's pulling together and doing what needs to be done and we just let everyone move in to the empty apartments all the people with yachts left behind."

I felt a stab of longing.

"It's not right not having you here," Thor added. "I wish you could see it."

"Well, as long as it doesn't sink into the ocean in the next two years, I'll be able to come back."

"Did you take your gold with you?"

"Yeah. It's locked in some safe at a bank. Mom says it's safer there than under my bed."

"A safe deposit box?"

"Oh, you've heard of them?"

"Yeah, and she's right, it's a lot safer to keep things there than under your bed." Thor scratched his chin. He needed to shave. "Is there any news coverage of the stead in LA?"

"There was a news article yesterday with the headline, SEA-STEAD IN CHAOS and it said something like, this would-be utopia built by libertarians has been beset by every possible misfortune in the last week, other than rabid sharks."

"That's not *wrong*," Thor said. "But we're sorting things out."

"I wish I could be there to help."

"Here's the thing," Thor said. "You did. You are. Like, the stuff you put in motion, going around and telling people you'd cancelled their bonds and they could keep working to earn a stake? Telling people that if they take charge of running stuff, it'll be theirs? That's been working."

"Good," I said, though this didn't make me any less homesick.

"Have you heard anything from your father?"

"He's wanted for bioterrorism. I doubt they'll ever catch him. But no, I haven't heard from him since that note." I tried not to show Thor how much that bothered me.

That evening, Mom made us hamburgers on the stove and served them with a sliced fresh tomato. The tomato was kind of a revelation. We have fresh tomatoes on the stead sometimes but they don't taste like much. This one tasted sweet but also rich in a way that canned tomatoes and ketchup were sort of reaching for but not really hitting. Mom watched me eat it, and then she got another one from the basket on her counter, and sliced it up, dividing the slices between two small plates. She had a green leafy plant growing in a pot in the windowsill and she pinched a sprig of leaves off it, minced them up, and sprinkled them on top. She finished with a drizzle of olive oil. "Here," she said, presenting me with one of the plates. "Try it this way."

I felt a little dubious about the houseplant leaves, but the scent was enticing and I took a bite of tomato. "These are incredible," I said.

"Fresh tomatoes are really good," she said. "Well, *good* fresh tomatoes, the kind that stay on the plants until they're properly ripe. I grew up in Iowa and the tomatoes in my grocery store tasted like cardboard. We only got good ones when we grew them in our garden."

I finished the last slice. "What's the plant?"

"Fresh basil." She got up and opened a cabinet, taking out a plastic jar. "Same herb as this, but fresh. You've had this in spaghetti sauce and pizza and stuff like that." She unscrewed the top and gestured for me to sniff it. The dried herb smelled like spaghetti sauce, but the tomatoes, weirdly, hadn't.

I thought about asking if she wanted to watch *Stead Life* with me—they'd done episodes profiling each major cafeteria, the food served and who ate there—to see how I got food on the stead, and like I said to Thor, I didn't see that going well. But I did like it when she showed me stuff like this, so I tried, "Thank you."

"No problem." She put away the basil. "When you were little, you used to help me in the kitchen. Hand me things, stir, stuff like that. Do you remember that at all?"

I did not. My life before the stead was a handful of images. "Maybe," I said, because I didn't want to hurt her feelings. "I don't actually remember much."

"Sure," she said, like she was trying to reassure me that was okay.

"Here's one thing," I said. "I have this memory of a tree as big as a house. Like, maybe it just seemed that way because I was little? I'm not sure. But it's one of the things I remember from before the seastead, a tree as big as a house."

Mom looked over at me, surprised. "That's the Sequoias. We took you there—this would've been in the summer after you turned four. Right before—anyway, you're remembering correctly, the trees are as big as houses."

"Do you have any photos?"

"No. I mean, not of us. There are plenty of pictures around of the trees, if you want to see those?"

"I'll look them up later," I said. "How far away are they?"

"Three, four hours by car."

"So like half a day? Could we go there sometime?"

"Oh, definitely!" Mom said. "I mean, it's do-able as a day trip, but we could maybe take a whole week in the northern part of the state and see Yosemite—look up El Capitan, it's this amazing cliff face there—the Sierras, there's just a lot of beautiful stuff."

"Okay," I said.

Mom cleared away our plates—I jumped up belatedly to help her, although I'd given up trying to put them in the dishwasher because she always rearranged them when I tried. She got some ice cream out of the freezer and scooped it into two dishes, handing me one without asking and eating hers while leaning against the counter instead of sitting back down.

"Or," she said. "Or I could call in sick and we could just go tomorrow as a day trip. See the giant trees, and do the rest some other time. Would you like that?"

I thought that over. "Will you get in trouble for calling in sick if you're not actually sick?"

"No," she said. "I won't get in trouble."

"Then yeah," I said. "That would be really cool."

"Excellent," she said. "We'll want to leave really early, like maybe six a.m., if you think you can pry yourself off your pillow by then? And I know it's hot here, but bring a sweater and long pants because it's a lot cooler up in the mountains."

I don't usually like getting up early, but getting up early for a road trip turned out to be easy. Mom had made coffee, and handed me mine in a travel mug. I'd packed a sweater and jeans in the bag she'd given me. "You might want a book," she added. "It's going to be three or four hours in the car."

I had been a little bit disappointed when I realized Mom's car didn't have manual controls. Some of my favorite movies are about road trips—*McKanna*, *The Final Race*, *Lucifer's Canyon*. (That last one is kind of obscure: it involves the Devil, like from Christian mythology, turning up in New York City and trying to get to the Grand Canyon. It's a really underrated movie.) In road trip movies, people hardly *ever* let the car drive. In *The Final Race* the automatic mode quits working and they're forced to use the manual controls. In *McKanna* the protagonist is a complete control freak and doesn't like anyone else driving, either. In *Lucifer's Canyon* there's a dozen different drivers (Lucifer mostly sort of hitchhikes) and almost everyone just uses manual controls without any explanation. At one point you think someone's using an autopilot system but then it turns out to be an angel who's psychically controlling the car . . . anyway, I was surprised when I got to California and no one seemed to even *have* manual controls.

"It costs extra," Mom said when I asked. "And it's illegal in most California cities to operate a car manually even if you have the special operator's permit."

We got in and buckled up. Mom had a pillow, and she settled it against the window and took a nap as the car took us out of the carport and glided through Pasadena, which meant I couldn't bombard her with questions.

When I first arrived, everything about Pasadena was fascinating—the palm trees, the red tile roofs on some of the houses, the sidewalks with people walking their dogs. Over the weeks, the novelty of Pasadena itself had worn off. The unpopulated areas beyond Pasadena, though, were brand new to me, and within a few minutes, we were leaving the city streets and settling into the stream of cars on the highway like a drop of water sliding out of a faucet. I stared out the window as buildings and billboards gave way to hills.

I didn't really even know how you described this sort of landscape. Scrubby? Semi-arid? I watched the wind whip down the hill at one point, making all the brush and grass ripple and sway, and thought, *the forest is choppy*, even though obviously that's not what anyone actually says about trees, and also, it wasn't really trees, mostly it was bushes, but I didn't know what you called something that was lots of bushes and not a lot of trees.

An hour into the trip, the car pulled off the highway and into a little roadside area with a big neon sign saying SPEEDY SUPPLY. Mom plugged in the car and said, "if you need to pee, there's a bathroom here."

I was a little unsteady on my feet—being in motion made my inner ear think I was back at sea—and Mom grabbed my elbow as we went into the little shop. Inside we were met with a blast of air conditioning and crowded rows of snack food in bags. "Do you want anything?" she asked.

"I don't know," I said.

"I have a picnic lunch in the car for when we get to Sequoia. But it's a ways off still."

Mom was getting herself a bottled soda and a bag of chips, so I picked out a soda and something crunchy. I'd never even seen half the snacks here. We opened the bags as we settled back into the car. "Did you need a charge already?" I asked.

"No, but I wanted snacks and a bathroom," Mom said. "I figured we might as well charge up a little while we were there."

Back in the car, Mom put away her pillow and started pointing stuff out as we passed, helping me sort out some of what I was seeing. The flat greener expanses were mostly farms, she said— food crops that were being irrigated, which is why they were green instead of brown. We passed a vineyard, with weird twisted plants she said were grapevines for making wine.

Mountains are big, and I'd sort of assumed we be seeing them from a long way off, but I just saw brown foothills until the car was turning to head up a steep path and I realized we were almost there.

The blast of cold when we opened the car was *shocking*. We gotten into the car in summer and ridden 200 miles to *late fall*, or that was what it felt like, anyway. I immediately got back in the car to change into my long pants and put on my jacket. It was still a very sunny day. "You'll want some sunblock," Mom said, and handed me a little squeezable tube. I put on the sunblock and then she added, "also bug spray," and handed me a squirt bottle.

I looked around but didn't see any bugs, so I started to put it in my pocket. Mom laughed and said, "You need to put it *on*. Here." She took the bottle back and squirted *herself* with the spray, misting her arms and legs and the back of her neck. "You know what, just stand like this—" she demonstrated a wide stance, arms and legs out— "and close your eyes and hold your breath a minute." The bug spray was cold and sort of tickled, but I held still and she was done quickly.

The initial trees I saw were not the size of houses, but they were towering pine trees that looked like a proper forest out of a movie. The cold air smelled green and woody and the ground was covered with so many tiny brown straws that it felt like standing on a cushion. I realized after a second they were pine needles. Our car had pulled into a parking lot with chargers, and Mom parked under a bank of solar panels and plugged in the car before opening the back to grab a backpack full of food and water and her own jacket and hat.

We followed a short trail that took us to a wide path, paved, and this one had the *enormous trees* by it. The path formed a loop around a meadow, and after about ten minutes of walking, Mom pointed at a table sitting in the shade and said, "let's have lunch there."

I laughed out loud. "Why is there a *table?*"

"It's a picnic table," Mom said. "They're there for people to eat at when they come to the park."

She opened up her bag and took out some slightly squashed sandwiches and a bunch of grapes. Once I got close enough for a good look at the table I could see that it had been built to last, it wasn't something that had just been hauled up here and left behind. We ate our sandwiches and I alternated between staring at the trees and looking at the other people who'd come to see the trees.

"I had a picnic once at the seastead," I said. "When I was over at Thor's, because his family has a balcony, since his father has no sense and got them a really expensive apartment. Anyway, we had lunch out there. It was going to be just me and Thor, but then his little brother and sister decided they wanted to come too. Which was sort of cute but sort of annoying."

"I kind of wanted to ask but didn't really feel like I could," Mom said. "Why doesn't Thor's mom just leave with the kids? It doesn't sound like she's happy."

"I think she's worried about going to prison for the tax stuff," I said.

Mom was silent for a minute or two and then asked, "Does Thor's father abuse her?"

"I don't know," I said. "Thor hasn't mentioned it but he's . . . I don't know, kind of scary."

"Not all abuse is *punching*," she said.

"I don't know," I said again. "He was pretty awful when I was shut in with him but it was a stressful situation."

"She should really talk to a lawyer."

"I don't think she has the money she'd need for a lawyer."

"I'll give you a phone number you can pass along, I know a lawyer who'd probably take her case for free. Or at least let her pay in installments, later. Beats going to jail or being sold into debt slavery. Personally, I'd rather do a couple of years in minimum security prison than live the rest of my life on the seastead."

"I'll pass it along but I'm pretty sure if she was willing to leave, she'd have left."

"You never know."

"Thor's going to leave as soon as he turns eighteen. He said."

"Good," Mom said.

"I think I'm going back," I said. "Once I'm old enough to go."

Tightness flickered across Mom's face. "It'll be your choice," she said.

When we were done with the paved loop, Mom and I hopped on a shuttle that circulated to other spots around this section of the park, including a trail with a fallen Sequoia whose roots towered over my head, and a log cabin someone had made out of a fallen tree trunk about two hundred years ago, so "as big as a house" was pretty accurate. I wanted a good picture to send Thor, so Mom took my picture by the giant roots, inside a split in a trunk formed a thousand years ago, next to a tree called the General Sherman that was the biggest living thing, according to the sign, on earth.

"Do you want me to take a picture of you together?" a complete stranger asked as Mom was taking a picture of me in front of the General Sherman.

I was a little wary, but Mom handed him her gadget and came over to stand with me. "Can I put my arm around you?" she asked.

"Sure," I said, sort of surprised. Dad never asked, the times someone took our picture together—he'd pull me close, act the part of an affectionate parent. I remembered hating that when I was ten.

Mom slipped her arm around my shoulder and leaned in, hesitant, and I heard a whirr-click as the stranger took a couple of pictures. "Thank you," Mom said, going over to retrieve her gadget. She showed me one of the pictures, then looked up at the sky, blue with a few small puffy clouds. "Do you think you'd be up for a hike?" she asked. "Or really, I should ask, some stair climbing. The walk to the trail isn't bad, but the trail itself is stairs."

"How many stories up?"

"Huh." Mom had to think that over. "What was a set of stairs like on the stead? Was it like . . . a flight down, a landing, then another flight down angled the other way? Is that one story?"

"Yeah, I guess."

"Okay, that's probably like . . . twenty steps? Or thirty? Building stories are high. So like . . . twelve stories up. We can take breaks to rest."

I thought about my trip down into the bottom recesses of Min, and then back up again. Twelve stories didn't sound *that* bad. "Okay," I said.

Even the first 30 steps left me shockingly winded. "We can rest a minute," Mom said, with a worried glance up.

"I'll be fine," I said.

"What kinds of exercise did you get on the seastead?"

"Walking places, mainly." I pictured Thor bounding up the stairs, gripped the handrail, and said, "Let's keep going."

When we were halfway up, Mom told me to look back. We were up above the trees now—even above the Sequoias themselves. "We can go back, if you want," Mom said.

"What, turn around *now*? When we're halfway? Are *you* tired?"

"No," Mom said.

"Okay then," I said, and continued trudging upward.

I had to rest again when we were within sight of the summit. "It feels like there isn't enough air in the air," I said.

"*Oh,*" Mom said, like she'd just realized something. "You're not wrong. You've lived your whole life at sea level. We're at 2,000 meters above that. Of course you're getting winded easily."

"You live in—" I gestured, like I was pointing back at Pasadena.

Mom, unable to control herself, pointed behind me. "It's that way."

"Whatever. It's sea level. Ish."

"It is," Mom said. "But I go mountain hiking often enough my body's used to it. This is the first you've been up here since you were really little."

I nodded, then turned back to the top and climbed the last stretch of stairs.

The view from the top of Moro Rock was spectacular. I spent a long time staring at the mountains around us and down at the forest below. Mom took more pictures of me and this time I also took a picture of her. Finally it got late enough that I could see she was getting anxious, so we went back down the stairs and took the shuttle back to the car.

We got a quick dinner on a patio in a town outside the park, and then settled wearily back into the car. It was going to be very late when we got home. Mom didn't say anything like *this is why I thought it might be nice to do it as an overnight and not a day trip* but I thought she was probably thinking it.

"Thank you," I said. "That was a really nice trip."

"We can come back," she said. "See some of what we missed. Not tomorrow, though."

"Let's, what was it you said, take a whole week sometime?"

"Sounds good," she said.

Night had fallen, and with darkness beyond the car there wasn't much point in looking out the window. Mom had shared the pictures she'd taken so I sent a bunch to Thor along with some text about the trip, but it felt weird having a conversation with him while sitting next to my mom so I told him I couldn't talk tonight.

"Can we listen to some music?" I asked.

"Oh, sure," Mom said, and pointed at some buttons on the dashboard. "Use that one to turn the radio on, that one to change stations."

The radio came on with a burst of very loud static, but after some experimentation I found some music.

We rode in the dark for a long time, listening to the radio. Hours passed.

"Are you awake?" I asked, finally.

"Hmm? Yes, I'm awake," Mom said.

"There's something I've been wondering," I said. "For months, actually. Like, basically since I found out you were alive."

"Okay," Mom said.

"You left messages at the embassy for me. But for years I never got them because I wasn't allowed to go there, and I didn't have any reason to break my father's rule about that."

"Yes," Mom said.

"Why didn't you hire someone else to deliver it to me?"

Her breath caught, and I could hear her let it out very slowly.

"I did, one time," she said.

"And?"

A long silence. Then, "There's a couple of pieces to the story," she said. "First of all, when you were four and your father first took you to the stead, I tried hiring some of the mercenaries that work on the stead to get you back. That didn't work because your father had gotten to everyone first. In addition to having the Alpha Dogs on retainer for protection, he paid a little fee to all the other groups as well—just enough so they wouldn't agree to take any jobs from me. They just wouldn't answer my calls at all, and when I had a friend call them, it turned out none of them would take a job involving you or your father. So that route was closed—for getting you back, but later I figured it probably wouldn't work to get you a note, either, and if I tried, probably all that would happen was your father would be alerted to the fact that I was *trying* to communicate with you."

I nodded. That made sense.

"I started seriously thinking about how to make contact with you when you turned thirteen, because teenagers have more autonomy. Even if I'd gotten you a letter when you were eight, what could you have done with the information? Your father had you right there, he could tell you whatever lies he wanted. Once you got to be a teenager, I had this fantasy of convincing you to sneak away to the embassy and ask for their help getting home. I knew that going myself—" She cut herself off again, took a deep breath, let it out.

"It would've been really risky," I said.

"I haven't really gotten into the details of what happened when your father left," Mom said. "But he tried to kill me. Not in a 'grabbed a gun and started shooting' way, but he sabotaged my car—I had mechanical controls back then, we both did—and switched out some medication I was taking for something that would screw up my reflexes. It almost worked. I mean, I did crash the car, and he took you while I was in the hospital, recovering. But he was not someone I could trust . . . at all. I wanted you out, I wanted you *back,* but going somewhere with people your father could pay to murder me, that really wasn't a good idea, so I didn't ever come myself, until I came with the Humanists."

I thought about his story, that she'd died in a drunk driving accident.

"Okay," I said.

"But right, okay, when you were . . . I guess this would have been when you were fourteen. One of my old college friends was planning a trip to the seastead and I got in touch and asked her to carry a message to you. It was really short, not a full letter, just saying I was alive and you could communicate with me through the embassy. The problem was, I didn't actually know where you were, other than I was sure your father wouldn't be living on New Amsterdam, and I didn't know anything about your daily routine or how she might find you. She said she was up for trying to figure it out if I'd cover the cost of her water taxi off New Amsterdam. So I gave her the money and the note and waited."

She paused there for a long, long time and then said, "She sent me a message one morning that she was going over to Min and Rosa to see if she could track you down. And then I heard absolutely nothing from her for eighteen hours. She turned back up in the infirmary on New Amsterdam, with no memory after hailing the water taxi. We both assumed she was drugged. After that, I didn't . . . it didn't feel right, asking someone to literally risk their life. Unless I could send a message with someone your father couldn't touch, it was too dangerous. And I couldn't think of anyone your father couldn't touch."

We rode in silence in the dark for a long time, and I thought about it. At fourteen, I was usually eating lunch alone. Shara's mom had found out Shara and Maureen were excluding me and made Shara invite me along again, but I'd decided I didn't want to be there if they didn't want me, so I usually walked over to Gibbon's and ate lunch and read a book. I was out and about enough that someone *could* have approached me, although they'd have needed some good luck to even spot me.

What kind of luck had my father had, intercepting Mom's friend? He probably paid a bunch of people to just let him know if anyone ever turned up asking questions about me. I wondered if the friend had actually woken up in the hospital, or if my father had paid her a pile of money and told her what story to tell. Would Mom's friend have taken that sort of bribe? Without having ever met her, it was hard to know.

But fundamentally, Mom wasn't wrong to be worried, and she wasn't wrong to be afraid, I just didn't like the answer being, "she did the best she could under the circumstances." I wanted to be able to judge her for how she'd failed.

"The world is really big, Beck," she said. "So much bigger than the seastead, and there's so much you haven't seen. You can go back if you want, but maybe see a little more, first?"

I looked out the window of the car at the dark landscape dotted with occasional light—somewhere out in that darkness was the Pacific Ocean, and somewhere west of that, the seastead. I had a *place* there—it was a mess, but it was my mess, or at least, *our* mess. It was a place where I felt like I belonged. Who was I, away from the seastead? What did I have here?

Trees as big as houses, I thought. I had things to see. Things I hadn't gotten to see because I'd never been allowed off the seastead, not even for a trip to the Caymans. I had a mom, it turned out. I could get to know her, like Thor suggested. Today had been cool.

"Thanks again for taking me to see the giant trees," I said. "Can we go to the Grand Canyon on our next road trip?"

Mom laughed. "Sure," she said. "We can go wherever you want."

ABOUT THE AUTHOR

NAOMI KRITZER is a science fiction and fantasy writer living in St. Paul, Minnesota. Her fiction has won the Hugo Award, the Lodestar Award, the Edgar Award, the Locus Award, and the Minnesota Book Award. Her last book before this one was *Chaos on CatNet*, which was a sequel to *Catfishing on Cat-Net*. She also has a collection of short fiction called *Cat Pictures Please and Other Stories*. You can find Naomi online at naomikritzer.com.

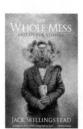
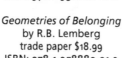
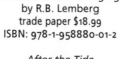

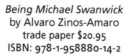
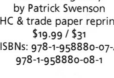

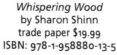

Printed in the USA
CPSIA information can be obtained
at www.ICGtesting.com
LVHW042020251023
762006LV00020B/108

9 781958 880166